# ANOTHER LITTLE CHRISTMAS MURDER

## LORNA NICHOLL MORGAN

# ANOTHER LITTLE CHRISTMAS MURDER

## LORNA NICHOLL MORGAN

SPHERE

First published in Great Britain in 1947 by Macdonald & Co Ltd as *Another Little Murder*
This reissue published in 2016 by Sphere

1 3 5 7 9 10 8 6 4 2

Copyright © Lorna Nicholl Morgan 1947

The moral right of the author has been asserted.

A CIP catalogue record for this book
is available from the British Library.

ISBN 978-0-7515-6770-0

Typeset in Spectrum by M Rules
Printed and bound in Great Britain by
Clays Ltd, St Ives plc

Papers used by Sphere are from well-managed forests
and other responsible sources.

MIX
Paper from
responsible sources
FSC® C104740

# ANOTHER LITTLE CHRISTMAS MURDER

LORNA NICHOLL
MORGAN

# Chapter I

As she drove, Dylis Hughes sang to herself, a habit of hers not confined to any special occasion. Which was as well, for her present circumstances, to the majority of those who knew her, would have appeared to warrant bewailing rather than singing. But then the majority of her acquaintances, Dylis reflected, were pessimists. Regarding all or any of her plans they seemed to take a morbid pleasure in telling her, 'You'll never do it, Dylis, or if you do, you'll be sorry.'

'Why don't you take my advice, and *wait*?'

Or, with a friendly but foreboding shake of the head, 'I can't think what you see in running round the country alone. Aren't you ever going to settle down?'

To the last question, Dylis had no answer. For the present, she was reasonably content to run round alone, in a little two-seater car, the age and deficiencies of which were the despair of garage hands wherever she called for mechanical aid in England, Scotland and Wales. Particularly Wales. With the loyalty of the true owner-driver, Dylis failed to see why they made so much fuss about the unreliability of her vehicle. In her opinion, all vehicles were unreliable, and therefore it was better to contend with the faults she knew, rather than procure a new one, and start getting to know it all over again. In her brief career as a commercial traveller, the car had served her well. It might break down many times on her tour of the roads but, as she frequently pointed out with quiet triumph, it always got her home. Neither had she ever experienced a serious accident.

It was, then, in her usual spirit of optimism that she had set out, one December afternoon, upon the road to Reeth from Richmond, in Yorkshire. She had completed a successful morning's business, capping it with an excellent lunch, and had planned, after a visit to a prospective customer in Reeth, to spend the night there. But then it had occurred to her that by pushing on the same day, she could probably reach her next objective, the little town of Raggden, before nightfall, and thus be all ready for another day, bright and early in the morning.

She had, of course, been warned about the roads. Winter had descended upon Yorkshire with startling coldness that year, bringing with it the threat of frozen pipes and farms and hamlets cut off from their neighbours, for a heavy fall of snow lay everywhere, burying the smaller hills and making the lonelier tracks impassable. But a little hard weather had no terrors for Dylis. She was warmly clad, her car had been overhauled in Richmond, and a spirit of exhilaration urged her on, despite or perhaps because of the awful predictions of the pessimists.

For this was her first adventure into the wilder parts of Yorkshire, and the impressive grandeur of the Swaledale country demanded exploration. But towards the close of the afternoon she was forced to admit that the pessimists were, for once, somewhat justified. The roads were not only bad, they were incredible. Her car, upon which she normally expected to do a comfortable forty miles per hour, between towns, gradually dropped speed

2

until it was behaving most uncomfortably at ten. Her feet, encased in soft leather boots lined with sheep-skin, had ceased to feel like feet, and seemed to have turned instead to lumps of stone. Nevertheless, her spirits still kept at an admirable level. The scenery was worth such minor inconveniences.

In its wildness, it became more breath-taking every mile of the road she travelled. She had passed stretches of gaunt, snow-covered moors, fascinating in their desolation, hills rising starkly above the frozen valley, farmhouses austere in their isolation, walled in by stone to protect them against the bitterness of the winter wind. She had glimpsed the snowy heights of mountains, bleakly defined against the background of the fading sky, bringing to her the desire to get acquainted with their stern loneliness, if only she had the time.

But in the gradually dying light the sky had become more and more overcast, the mountains and the nearer hills turned misty grey and finally disappeared from view beneath the darkness of night, and Dylis became aware that she was upon a very lonely road, the turns and twists of which were quite unknown to her, while it seemed to climb ever upward without arriving anywhere. But she went on singing. After all, if she did not reach Raggden that night, she could put up somewhere else. Her quarters might not be so comfortable, but it would be an experience. She would stop at the next hamlet and have tea, then if it appeared impracticable to drive farther, she was bound to find someone who would provide her with a bed, and breakfast in the morning.

Her headlights were working, that was something. Not infrequently, they gave up altogether when the going was rough. All things considered, the car was behaving remarkably well. But no sooner had the thought crossed her mind, when the road zigzagged with startling suddenness, and she was confronted with a road so steep that even her optimism was quenched at sight of it. But not for long. Smoothly she changed gear, and began to creep slowly up, the headlights playing on the glittering snow, the air getting keener every minute. The engine had developed noises that sounded ominous to her attentive ear, but as long as she reached the top . . . She did, to find that the road narrowed considerably and then forked right and left, with no indication as to which way she should take. Neither appeared to be much more than a track, and the car engine was now emitting noises so horrible that she dare not stop to consult her map.

She chose the left, but had not gone more than a mile or so before she bitterly regretted the impulse. For this road was even worse than the last. It climbed and dropped at irregular intervals, threw stones and boulders in her path, and generally spread itself to trip the unwary traveller. To add to her difficulties, snow had begun to fall: great flakes whipped against the windscreen by a wind so ferocious that the little car rocked beneath its fury. The windscreen-wiper worked but sluggishly, and with her hands seemingly frozen to the wheel, she strained her eyes to fathom what further horrors the night had to offer. At this rate, she would be lucky if she arrived anywhere before midnight.

Reaching a point where the road widened abruptly and seemed to bend back upon itself, she halted with stern resolution. She must, she decided, have taken the wrong road. She would go back and investigate the other. It certainly could be no worse than this one. At least, she hoped not. Her hands were so numb she had difficulty in reversing the vehicle, and when it did consent to move it behaved in a fashion quite unpredictable, running backwards up an incline in the bend of the road, there to repose, sunk deeply on one side into a bank of snow. The noise of the engine died down, and all was silent save for the shrieking of the wind.

Dylis sat for a while, thinking hard thoughts about mechanical contrivances. She pressed the self-starter several times, and nothing happened. Mustering all her philosophy, she buttoned her camel-hair coat, gathered up her torch and climbed cautiously out to where she hoped the road might be, to sink immediately up to her calves in snow. From a careful, all-round inspection, it was not easy to see how the car was to be extricated from its present position without help, and help, in this place of solitude, was not to be reasonably expected. The headlights revealed the land rising steeply on one side, and appearing to slope off into infinite space. At the back of the car the light from her torch showed nothing but a void filled with whirling snowflakes. They touched her face like icy fingers, and quickly covered the shoulders of her coat, and the hood she had pulled over her head. There was a sound of desperation in the moan of the wind as it hurled its way across the surrounding heights.

With resignation, she climbed back into the car, closed the door and fastened the window against the biting blast. She pulled off her gloves and rubbed her hands until the circulation improved. She was not without solace. Upon the passenger seat reposed a bag of apples and some sandwiches which she had picked up earlier in the day. There was also a slab of chocolate, and tucked away in the side pocket of the car was a half-bottle of brandy, supplied by her firm against emergency. She consulted with herself as to whether this could be called an emergency, and decided that it could. She withdrew the cork and poured herself a measure in the little metal cup packed for the purpose. She lit a cigarette and meditated.

More than ever she felt that this solitary stretch of road was unlikely to yield any kind of assistance. It had that look about it. On the other hand, she did not much relish the idea of abandoning the car and her belongings, and walking along the other road in the hope of finding habitation. Indeed, to judge by the blizzard that had now set in, walking anywhere would be a great mistake. Far more sensible to stay where she was until morning. She would miss her dinner, as she had already missed her tea, but the chocolate would prevent her from getting too hungry.

To prove her point, she ate a piece, followed by an apple and a sandwich. She felt much better. The brandy had warmed her, right down to her toes. Her feet were human again. The intense cold outside and the effect of the falling snow in the glare of the headlights made her drowsy. She closed her eyes.

Time had ceased to mean anything, but she guessed she must have been sitting there for a considerable while, for her body was stiff and cramped, when above the wind there came to her ears the unmistakable sound of a car coming steadily up the road along which she had driven. She saw the lights a few moments later, as they heralded the approach of the vehicle around the bend. And mingled with the combined noise of the wind and the engine, she heard a man's voice singing, 'She'll be coming round the mountain when she comes'.

So surprised was Dylis that she made no movement to attract attention. But the progress of this other car was slow, and as it rounded the corner its lights cut across hers, the driver drew in on the opposite side of the road, and called through the open window.

'Hallo, there! D'you want any help?'

It seemed impossible to Dylis that this was not a mirage, called up by the urgency of her imagination. If the car had gone right by, she would just have continued to sit there, unbelieving. But the voice was human enough, and with a swift return to the practical she clambered out, accepting with equanimity the coldness of the snow around her thinly-stockinged legs.

'I want a lot of help, please,' she shouted back. 'That is, if you're any good at digging cars out of snowdrifts.'

'I'm better than good, I'm wonderful. I've dug myself out twice today, already. This is a borrowed car, and I'm pledged to return it intact.'

He alighted as he spoke and tramped across towards her, and she saw that he was a large size in men, hatless and wearing a heavy overcoat, the collar turned up about his ears. His car did not appear to hold any other occupants. He paused, taking in her predicament, and rubbed his chin with a gloved hand.

'Where were you trying to get to?' he asked.

'Raggden. Well, that was my original idea. But I don't know this part of the country and ...'

'You're on the wrong road. You should have forked right a few miles back. But I doubt whether you'd get there tonight, anyway, with the roads as they are. It's miles beyond Cudge.'

'It doesn't matter particularly. I'd be glad to put up anywhere, if I could only get the car started again. Do you think you could help me move her?'

'Frankly, no. I wouldn't risk it on a night like this and without any rope. In daylight I could try giving her a tow ...'

He moved towards the rear of the car and she would have followed, but he waved her back.

'But you haven't even tried,' she said, impatience getting the better of politeness.

He was floundering about in the snow, apparently looking for something. He brought out and flashed on a torch to aid him.

'I'll tell you where you are,' he said. 'You've backed up with a few inches to spare on the edge of Harry's Hole.'

'Who's he?'

'I never knew him personally, but there's an ancient legend in these parts about a bloke named Harry who landed himself in a hole, and that's it. There's a sheer drop below of about three hundred feet, so I don't suppose he got out in a hurry. Neither would you, if you'd overshot the mark.'

Dylis thought about that for a while, and the more she thought, the less she liked it.

'I wish you hadn't told me,' she said at last. 'I could have gone on sitting there quite happily until morning. Now . . . '

'You'd better come with me. I'll just put a wedge against the wheels if I can find something large enough. Have you got anything you want to bring with you?'

'My case. It's in the back. And my handbag, and a few little things.' She opened the car door and began to gather her belongings, trying not to think too much about Harry and his hole. If this man would take her as far as the nearest village or hamlet, she could find lodging for the night, and work out the car's destiny tomorrow. She did not like the idea of leaving it, though. She hesitated as, his task accomplished, he came round with her suitcase in his hand. She was clutching the bag of apples and sandwiches, the chocolate, her handbag and case of samples. She said, 'I think perhaps I ought to stay. How do I know the car will be all right?'

'I shouldn't think there's much chance of anyone pinching it.' His tone suggested that he did not see in it any foundation for the mother-love of its owner. 'And I can't go off and leave you sitting on the edge of a precipice in the midst of a howling blizzard. It's not sense. Anything might happen.'

He took her arm, and reluctantly she slammed and locked the door and went with him across to his more sumptuous vehicle.

He helped her in, stowed her possessions upon the back seat, climbed in beside her, and they sat for a few moments, shaking the snow from their clothes and hair, and laughing with relief at having escaped from the driving elements. She began then:

'If you could put me down where I can get a room for the night . . . '

'I'm afraid there's nothing on this road,' he cut in. 'You can get to Raggden this way eventually, but it makes a detour through Deathleap Pass. It's a good job you didn't get as far as that, because it's dangerous, even if you know it.'

'Well, where are *you* going, then?'

'I was just going to tell you. I'm on my way to my uncle's place, Wintry Wold. It stands about half a mile off this road, before you get to Deathleap Scar, and the Pass is a bit higher up. Why not come along? My uncle and aunt will be glad to put you up.'

She thought it did not sound very cheerful, not much better than sitting on the edge of a precipice. And her independent nature shied at the prospect of forcing herself upon strangers. Still, she could hardly expect him to go out of his way to find her more orthodox accommodation, especially on such a night. He went on:

'As a matter of fact, I had a letter from the old man, asking me to drop in and to bring a friend. I don't quite know what he meant by that. Probably thought I might find it tedious on my own. Or they may be having a party, I really don't know. It's years since I've seen him, and I've never met his wife. But if I bowl in with you it will be perfectly all right.'

This airy dismissal of formalities did nothing to reassure her, but she said:

'Well, I'll be glad to come if you're sure they won't mind. But your uncle probably meant a man friend. What made you come alone?'

'I haven't so many friends in England.' He had already started the car, which was a powerful one, designed to stand more wear and tear than her own sorrowful specimen. Even so, in comparison to the speed it should have commanded, their pace up the hill was negligible. 'My people live in Switzerland. They've an hotel there, which I help them to run, not far from Geneva. My mother's health isn't too good, and the climate suits her. I came to London recently, on business for my father. I've a few friends there, but none of them were keen to face Yorkshire in winter. One of them was decent enough to lend me a car, though.'

'What's wrong with Yorkshire in winter?' Dylis asked. 'I think it's grand country. I was getting a big kick out of it, until I fell foul of Harry and his wretched hole.'

'I agree. I spent a lot of time here with my uncle when I was a youngster. But everyone doesn't think the same. I suppose some people feel the cold more than others. I love snow. Can't have too much of it. We have a wonderful time during the season. Ever done any climbing?'

'Only in and out of cars,' Dylis said. 'But I'd like to try.'

'Why don't you come out to Switzerland some time? We'll be glad to put you up. No charge to our friends.'

'Are we friends already?'

'Naturally. I look at it that if you meet someone in the middle of a blizzard and you get along all right, well, then you're friends. Don't you agree?'

'Perhaps. But I think I'd feel normally friendly towards anyone who rescued me out of a night like this.'

'Not necessarily. You might loathe the sight of them. How do you feel about me?'

'I don't feel capable of giving an unprejudiced opinion at the moment,' she said.

He laughed and resumed his singing, in a pleasant voice that sounded as if he used it quite a lot. The road was getting worse at every stage of their progress, and the car, buffeted by the wind and with everything weighted against it, seemed as if it were fighting a losing battle. But the driver was in no way concerned. Feeling grateful that she had not fallen in with a pessimist, and anxious to reciprocate, Dylis asked, 'Would you care for some chocolate? Or an apple or a sandwich? They're all on the back seat.'

He laughed again. 'No, thanks very much. I'm hoping we'll get dinner shortly. But if not, and we're marooned on the lonely highway, we'll demolish your stores piece by piece. What are you doing, careering about the country in that two-by-four contraption of yours?'

'I'm a commercial traveller,' Dylis said, with less warmth in her voice, resenting his description of her recent mode of conveyance. She had been about to offer him some brandy, but promptly decided that he was a strong man and in no need of it.

'No, really? I can't see much of you, but you're a bit out of character, aren't you? What do you find to sell in the Yorkshire Dales at this time of the year?'

'This happens to be the beginning of our best season. Ointments, rubbing oils, everything to cure rheumatism, stiff joints, coughs, colds, aches and pains. We're a firm of manufacturing chemists. Compton, Webber and Hughes. I'm Hughes.'

'Good Lord!' He indulged in a shout of laughter. 'Part of the firm, eh?'

'Sole representative. I've done some pretty smart business today. It may sound callous, but the winter setting in suddenly like this sends up our sales with a bound.'

'I bet Compton and Webber will be bucked. What are they, men or women?'

'Men,' she said. 'If you'd lived longer in England, you'd know more about our products. In a quiet way, we're famous.'

'Not so fast. I do know something. I sat for an hour on a station just lately, waiting for a train, and there was an advert, showing an old gentleman sitting in a bath, massaging himself with something or other, and a rhyme underneath that said something like, "Rub-a-dub-dub, one man in a tub . . . " I can't remember the rest of it, although I read it through about seventeen times.'

'That was my idea. Rubbitin ointment is wonderful for stiff joints, if applied while taking a hot bath . . . '

'All right, I believe you. So you're publicity manager as well? You've got a nice little job, Miss Hughes. And while we're getting acquainted, I'd better tell you that my name's Brown. Now it's your turn to laugh.'

'Why should I?'

'Because when I say "My name's Brown", everyone always does. It usually takes me quite a long time to convince them. I suppose, being such a general sort of name, they think I'm pulling their legs.'

'But someone's got to be called Brown. The Brown families can't stop having children just so that the name won't be too common.'

'That's what I like about you,' he said. 'You're so practical. Except in the matter of cars.'

They lapsed into silence then. Dylis, warm and comfortable now save for the wetness of her stockings, realised that she was hungry, and hoped that the Browns were people who indulged in hearty dinners. She glanced at her gold wrist-watch, given to her as a present from Compton, last Christmas. Its luminous hands pointed to 8.25. Her thoughts turned to Compton, who had not wanted her to undertake this journey. He was the cautious one of the firm, always looking for trouble and quite often finding it. She smiled a little at the recollection that he had once wanted to marry her. Webber was different. He was all for going ahead and getting things done, loud in his praise of her smallest success, sympathetic over the most minor of her misadventures. It was he who had introduced her and her modest capital into the realm of business. He would see nothing amiss in her spending the night with the family of a man whom she had met on a lonely road. Dear old Webber. Her smile deepened as she remembered that he, too, had wanted to marry her.

She had sunk into a reverie, and almost forgotten the man at her side, when he said:

'We're nearly there now,' and turned off the road and into an even narrower track that seemed as if it were going to plunge off the surface of the earth altogether. 'This road goes right past the house and along to Deathleap Scar, and joins up with the Pass on the other side.'

'It sounds intriguing,' she said, slightly yawning. 'But I think I'll put off further exploration until the spring.'

'You're right. It's wonderful then. By the way, have you got a Christian name?'

'Of course I have,' she said, and gave it.

'Good. I thought they might have called you something fancy like "The Intrepid". But my uncle is very much one of the older generation, and I didn't want to have to say to him, "Uncle, meet Hughes". I'm Inigo. You can laugh at that, too, if you like. Most people do.'

But Dylis no longer felt like laughing. She was suddenly very tired, and the thought of meeting two strange people and probably more was becoming increasingly distasteful. But it was too late now. And presently, when they turned in through open

13

gates set in a high stone wall, and ploughed their way along a driveway deeply embedded in snow, she made a conscious effort to get a grip upon her usually capable faculties. The drive wound along between thickets of trees and shrubs, heavily overgrown, sparkling as they caught the headlights. Inigo Brown, peering through the windscreen, said:

'It looks a bit neglected, doesn't it? This used to be quite a show place. But Uncle's getting on now, I suppose. Must be over sixty. What the hell's that?'

They had emerged from the drive and were cautiously approaching the house, and he jammed on his brakes just in time to avoid cannoning into the back of another vehicle blocking the way. At the same time he swung the wheel and they hurtled into a deep drift of snow collected at the edge of the clearing. The car stopped at a lop-sided angle, and he switched off the engine.

'That's that,' he said. 'I'm not doing any more digging out tonight. Let's go and see what idiot left that thing there.'

But when they alighted and moved off, heads bent against the still driving storm, there was nothing to be seen by the combined light of their torches but an enormous van standing slantwise to the broad frontage of the house. It bore no name, had no lights switched on, and appeared to have been there for some hours to judge by the snow that covered it.

'I suppose they're not moving out?' Dylis asked hopefully, still being possessed by a strong desire to avoid further strange company. She could not see much of the house, but a dim light etched drawn curtains in a window to the left of the porch they were approaching. It looked a large window, and appeared to be a large house. Her companion said, raising his voice to be heard above the wind:

'If you're still worrying about anything, put it out of your mind. If we were marauding strangers, they couldn't refuse to put us up on a night like this.'

He gripped her arm and hurried her up the broad steps and into the shelter of the porch. He flashed his torch round, disclosing a door of immense and solid proportions, located the old-fashioned bell, and used his strength upon it. Dylis stood just behind him, feeling the cold whistling around her legs, and not liking anything. They had not long to wait. Within the space of a few minutes there came the tapping sound of wooden heels upon a wooden floor, and the door was flung open. A woman's voice exclaimed:

'Come in! Come in, quickly!' And thus bidden, and with the force of the wind behind them, they did not pause to question the effusiveness of her welcome, and were literally blown into a small entrance hall, without illumination save for a soft light radiating through an open door on the left-hand side. The front door slammed behind them, and automatically they stepped through into a large, square-shaped entrance lounge, from the ceiling of which was suspended an old-world oil lamp, its soft rays diffused by a shade of delicate rose. The woman followed, and Dylis observed with interest that she was very small, young, and dressed in an exquisite rose velvet dinner gown. Furthermore, she was staring at them in sheer incredulity. Dylis looked from her to Inigo Brown, and was surprised to find that he was younger than she had thought, not much older than herself, probably. He was smiling as he said:

'Shocking night, isn't it? I'm Inigo, Mr Brown's nephew, and this lady is a friend of mine, Dylis Hughes. We've just dropped in to see my uncle.'

He paused there, obviously waiting for the girl who had admitted them to say something. But she went on looking from one

15

to the other, her small, beautifully kept hands playing with the rose chiffon handkerchief she carried. They must, Dylis thought, be giving a party, and this was one of the guests. But why should she open the door to visitors? Surely a house this size should have a butler, or someone of the kind. Then the girl's face brightened with a conventional smile. She said:

'Why, Inigo! Of course, your uncle has often spoken about you. This *is* a surprise! I'm his wife, your aunt Theresa.'

# Chapter II

Dylis gave up then. She just stood by, smiling feebly as the young woman who claimed to be Mrs Brown stood tip-toe on her little, high-heeled shoes and kissed her newly found nephew on either cheek. Inigo Brown had eyes so dark and thickly fringed it was impossible to fathom what he might be thinking. His smile was easy and tolerant. He took one of his hostess's hands and shook it warmly. He remarked:

'An unexpected pleasure, Aunt Theresa. Sorry to bust in on you like this. Are you having a party?'

'My dear, no.' Again she looked from him to Dylis, and hesitated before adding, 'Your uncle is too ill for that kind of thing. But you must be dead with cold and fatigue. Take off your things, both of you, and warm yourselves by the fire, and I'll call one of the servants.'

She walked quickly across the parquet flooring and disappeared through another door on the opposite side of the room, and her nephew turned to regard Dylis with close attention. He seemed satisfied, for he said:

'The last time I got to know a woman in the dark, I swore I'd never do it again. But you can't always be unlucky, as this occasion proves. Here, let me take your things.'

'As far as you're concerned, I'm still in the dark,' Dylis said, as he helped her out of her coat. 'Where did you find an aunt like that?'

'I didn't find her. I've never seen her before. We knew my uncle got married some time ago, because he wrote and said so. He told us he'd met a little woman who had made him the happiest man on earth. It sounded a bit far-fetched to me, but I begin to see what he means. She's a real slice of Hollywood, isn't she?'

'And then some,' Dylis said. She was wondering why a girl with Theresa Brown's looks should marry a man over sixty. He must be very wealthy. She sat down on a wide settle before the glowing log fire. It was a pleasant room, panelled in oak, with thick skin rugs upon the polished floor. Everything had an air of great antiquity, including the oil lamp. Inigo said, spreading his hands to the warmth:

'I've stepped up one. I bet Compton and Webber haven't an aunt like mine.'

Dylis refrained from replying, for the door had opened again, and Mrs Brown returned, followed by a man pushing a trolley loaded with wine and spirit decanters and an array of glasses. But though Dylis felt a quickening interest at the sight of such welcome refreshment, it was the man in charge of it who caught and held her attention. He was a tall, broad-shouldered man, with dark hair growing low on his forehead, a resolute face full of character of a rather doubtful kind, and an air of ferocious concentration. If this were the butler, his clothes were singularly out of keeping. He wore a black leather lumber jacket buttoned up to the chin, and corduroy breeches with gaiters after the style of a gamekeeper. With more force than elegance, he wheeled the trolley across the room, kicked into position one of the rugs he had displaced, favoured the two guests with a scowl, and withdrew. Mrs Brown said, with the charming smile of one woman to another:

'So difficult, the servant problem, isn't it? Out here we find it impossible to keep anyone but menservants, and they won't always stay. Women find it far too lonely. I can quite understand that, of course. Young single women want picture palaces and such things. There's nothing to interest them in the wilds of Yorkshire. Were it not for my husband, I might spend more time in town myself. But he loves this part of the country, and really I've come to love it, too. What will you drink, Miss Hughes? Whisky, sherry, a dry Martini, perhaps?'

'Sherry, please,' Dylis said, reflecting that the servant problem in these parts must indeed be acute, if butlers had kicked over the traces so far as to appear in breeches and gaiters. Or perhaps it was an old Yorkshire custom. Not knowing that country, she found it difficult to decide. Inigo, leaning against the carved oak mantel, his hair still wet with melted snow, said:

'Make mine a whisky, please, Auntie. Isn't Uncle Warner joining us?'

She had settled down upon a damask-covered pouffe, from where she dispensed the drinks with dainty gestures. Looking up as she handed him his glass, she said, with a sorrowful shake of her head:

'I'm afraid not, my dear. He's far too ill to leave his bed just now, poor darling. I expect you heard that he had pneumonia? I nursed him through that. The doctor advised me to send him to hospital, but how could I let him lie in a horrible bare ward, all alone? I'm sure he would never have recovered. Even the doctor had to admit I was right, when he saw how quickly Warner got better, under my care. But you know how obstinate he is. He would get up before his time, and then down he went again with a relapse, when this awful weather set in. I've hardly been near my bed for the last fortnight, and the danger is not over, by any means.'

'Is anyone with him now?' Inigo asked. 'I'd like to go up and see him. Might be able to cheer him on a bit.'

'My dear, I'm afraid it's impossible for you to see him tonight. He's far too ill to see anyone, except myself, of course, and Ledgrove, his valet. Ledgrove is with him now. We take it in turns by day and night to watch at his bedside.'

Somewhat uncharitably, Dylis thought that she did not look as if she had missed much sleep lately. Her young face was smooth and unlined, her eyes bright, the shadow on their lids due solely to artificial application. Neither did the role of nurse warrant such an elaborate toilet. She wore her hair parted on one side and hanging in ringlets rather childishly about her face. Her hands bore many rings beside the single gold band that denoted her married state, and all of them looked expensive. Perhaps she was arrayed thus to encourage Mr Warner Brown in his struggle for life. Dylis doubted it. There was something brittle and unsympathetic in Mrs Brown's personality, something which the pleasantness of her manner failed to hide. She smiled but rarely, and when she did, it was an expression designed to show her teeth to the best advantage.

Sipping her sherry, and listening only half-heartedly to the conversation, Dylis observed that about the room were many mirrors, and from the position she had taken, Mrs Brown was able to scrutinise herself from various angles, which she did, with many surreptitious turnings of her head, and sly glances appreciating her own reflection. Yet it was of her husband that she continued to speak.

'I don't know whether you will be able to see him in the morning, Inigo. I hope so. The doctor was here earlier today, and said that on no account must he be in any way excited. Rest and peace is what he needs. The doctor may be coming again tomorrow. He said he would, if he could possibly manage it. But, of course, transport is so difficult at the moment, and he has so many calls to make. Everyone in the district seems to be sick with something. I try to remember that my husband is not the only one.'

Inigo finished his drink and put the empty glass upon the mantel. He said:

'I don't want to do anything to upset him, naturally. I'm too fond of him for that. But I wish there were something I could do. Couldn't I sit up with him tonight, and give you a chance to get some sleep?'

Mrs Brown languorously closed her eyes and opened them again, as if the effort of thinking were almost too much for her weakened state.

'Seriously, I would not advise it. Although he is under my care, I dare not go against the doctor's orders. And you mustn't worry about me, my dear. Women are so much more cut out to bear with illness than men. Another sherry, Miss Hughes?'

'Thank you,' Dylis said. And partly from curiosity and partly from politeness, she added, 'Can I help in any way? I've had a little experience at nursing. I even took a course of massage at one time. It must be wearing for you, having so much responsibility.'

'It's very kind of you, my dear, and I do appreciate it. But really I'd rather manage things my own way. We all have our burdens to bear and this is mine, although I hope it is only a temporary one. And you must be tired after your journey. I've told one of the servants to prepare rooms for you and Inigo. Most of the house is shut up now, but we'll do our best to make you comfortable. You've not yet had dinner, I suppose?'

'No,' Inigo said. 'It's an awful time to descend upon you with an appetite, but don't trouble about us. Any old thing will do.'

Dylis added her voice to the statement, but Mrs Brown waved it aside with a graceful gesture, and rose to her little feet.

'As it happens, I've not dined, either. We were going to, just before you arrived. A friend of my husband, Mr Carpenter, is here, and we were playing cards to while away an hour or so, and the time just sped on. He's been a wonderful help to me during Warner's illness. Sometimes I don't know what I should have done without him.'

Mr Carpenter, Dylis decided, would be a tall, handsome man in the prime of life, the friend of the family, the silent admirer of the child-bride. Or perhaps not so silent. Intrigue, she felt, was weaving its way within the portals of Wintry Wold. Mrs Brown went on:

'If you're ready, I'll show you to your rooms. You'll want to wash and tidy up before dinner. I'm glad to say that we've plenty of hot water laid on, although our lighting arrangements are a little behind the times. But Warner would not have them changed, and really I think he is right, in a way. Oil lamps have great charm, don't you think, Miss Hughes?'

'Call her Dylis,' Inigo cut in. 'That's all right, isn't it, Dyl?'

'Perfectly, Nig,' Dylis said, with an unaccustomed touch of malice. 'I've come through too much tonight to mind what anyone calls me.'

'I can see you two are wonderful friends,' Mrs Brown remarked, taking Inigo's arm with a small sigh as of one whose youth had long since flown. He patted her hand sympathetically. He said:

'I'd better nip out and bring in our cases from the car. Is it all right to leave it in the middle of a flower bed? I don't feel like coping with any more tonight.'

'Of course. You can run it into one of the garages tomorrow.'

'Oh, by the way.' He had flung his coat round his shoulders, and paused, halfway to the door. 'What's that pantechnicon doing out there? Never seen such a thing in my life. I nearly buckled my lights on it.'

Mrs Brown had now transferred her hand to Dylis's arm, and was leading her away. She said over her shoulder:

'How very careless of them to leave it there. I told them to draw in to the side. Two vanmen came along about teatime. They were having some kind of trouble with it, and wanted to know if they could telephone to a garage. Imagine trying to phone from here! I told them the best thing they could do was to go to Cudge, but they said they couldn't get it any farther. So one of them stayed here, while the other went off for help. He should be back any time now. Shall I tell the other one to move it? He's in the kitchen quarters somewhere. We gave them tea. It was the least we could do.'

'Don't bother him,' Inigo said. 'He'll have enough trouble when the garage people turn up. In fact, if this blizzard continues, they'll be in the devil of a mess. Shan't be a minute.'

He went out, and, shivering delicately from the draught that swept in as he closed the door, Mrs Brown conducted Dylis out of the entrance lounge and into a corridor beyond. From a wall-bracket, she lifted down a three-armed candlestick, and by the light of the tall green candles therein they went up a staircase that began broad at the bottom and gradually narrowed as it wound up to the next floor. The first storey of Wintry Wold was so complicated in its design and structure that Dylis felt she would never be able to find her way about in fifty years. Corridors twisted this way and that and doubled back on themselves, and everywhere were odd steps up and steps down, causing her each time to stumble, with Mrs Brown pausing beside her to murmur profuse apologies.

'Parts of it are so very old,' she said. 'Some of the rooms are not fit for use any longer, the walls and ceilings are simply rotting away. It's a great pity, but it would cost a fortune to have it all restored. And the trouble is that the unusable rooms are dotted all over the place, so that we can't shut up any particular part of it. But it has a certain charm, don't you think?'

Dylis, tripping over a worn place in the corridor carpet, agreed that it had plenty of charm. Mentally, she was wishing that she, too, had a large and derelict house, to which she could invite all the more pessimistic of her friends, and leave them to work out their own salvation. They would certainly have the advantage of her, if they could see her now.

They paused at length upon the threshold of a large and lofty room, where Mrs Brown cordially invited her to enter and take possession.

'You'll find clean towels and things,' she said. 'And the bathrooms are just round the bend of the corridor. There are two on this floor and another above, next to my husband's room. The first one is the second door on the right, on the other side of the staircase. I'll just light the candles for you, and then you'll be able to look after yourself, won't you? I'm so sorry we've no maids, but there it is.'

Dylis thanked her, and observed with wonder her graceful exit, looking like a little doll in the flickering candlelight. She turned then to a careful inspection of her abode. She saw a large bed, complete with silk-covered eiderdown, a wardrobe, a tall chest of drawers, an antique stool before the dressing-table, heavy

24

curtains pulled across the window, a rather worn, close-fitting carpet of some indistinguishable shade. The grate was empty, and the temperature felt somewhere below freezing point. But a stranded traveller could not afford to be too circumspect, and she hung up her coat in the wardrobe, pausing for a moment to regard the half bottle of brandy she had stowed away in one of the capacious pockets. She asked herself whether this could be regarded as another emergency, but decided that it could not. She put the brandy away in the top of the wardrobe.

She had some difficulty in finding the bathrooms, but located the first one after trying many doors on the way, all of which were locked. The hot water system was all that Mrs Brown had claimed, and presently she returned to the room allotted to her, feeling refreshed, and somewhat surprised to find that her sample and dressing cases had mysteriously appeared. She smiled when she recalled that Inigo was accustomed to supplying hotel service. She removed her snow boots in favour of a pair of high-heeled slippers, for she had no intention of allowing Mrs Brown to hold the monopoly of feminine atmosphere. She surveyed herself in the wardrobe mirror as well as she could by candlelight, and decided that she could not be bothered to change from the suit she was wearing into something more spectacular. She powdered her face and brushed her hair, and finding that her fingers were fast stiffening with the cold, hurriedly abandoned the icy room and descended to the ground floor, where she was attracted by the sound of voices coming from a room on the right-hand side of the staircase, the door of which was open.

Upon the threshold, she hesitated. It was obviously the drawing-room, spacious and handsome, if somewhat faded in its furnishings, with a pedestal oil lamp in one corner radiating a gentle glow. Before the cheerful fire, Inigo sprawled in the depths of an armchair, while Mrs Brown crouched upon a low stool at his side, her dress spread out around her, her delicate hands shielding her face from the flames. In that position she looked so small it was ridiculous. In an armchair on the farther side of the hearthrug sat another man, whom Dylis guessed to be Mr Carpenter. But he was not handsome, nor was he in the prime of life, nor did he appear to take any interest in Mrs Brown whatsoever. His face was furrowed and weary, he had glassy eyes, a bulbous red nose, blue-veined hands and an air of abandoned dissipation. He slumped in his chair within easy reach of the whisky decanter standing on a side table, and only looked up when Theresa said:

'Here is Dylis. Do come in, my dear, and allow me to present Mr Carpenter . . . Miss Hughes.'

The man rose, or rather stumbled to his feet, shook Dylis gingerly by the hand, and fell back as if the effort had taken his last remaining strength. Inigo, too, had risen, and pulled forward a chair for her. He said:

'I took your cases up. Did you find everything you wanted?'

'Thank you, yes.'

She sat down, and Mr Carpenter, without asking her wishes, poured her a glass of sherry and handed it across, apparently taking it for granted that she could not exist another moment without it. He remarked:

'Nasty night, Miss Hughes. Better in than out.'

His voice was rough, and his manners even more so. He tossed back the remainder of his whisky, wiped his mouth with the back of his hand, and immediately refilled the glass, omitting to add even the slightest splash of soda from the siphon.

'Mr Carpenter was just saying,' Mrs Brown interposed, 'that the situation will be really serious soon, if the snow continues.

26

We're likely to be marooned here for weeks, without any commu-
nication from the outside world. Fortunately, we've a large stock
of food to fall back upon, although it will mean making do with
tinned meat and milk and things like that.'

'It suits me,' Inigo said. 'How about you, Dyl?'

'I can't afford to be marooned anywhere for weeks,' she said
decidedly. 'I shall certainly have to do something about the transport question tomorrow.'

'You didn't intend to stay any time, then?' Mrs Brown asked.
'I thought that perhaps you and Inigo . . . '

'We ran into each other by accident,' Inigo said. 'And there
being a dearth of hotels on the road, I brought her along for the
night.'

'And I'm really very grateful to you for putting me up,' Dylis
added. 'But I'm a commercial traveller, and travel I must and will.'

'Oh, how interesting.' Mrs Brown leaned forward with as much
intentness as if she were hearing the adventures of the Pilgrim
Fathers. 'It must be wonderful to have a career like that. But then
I'm afraid I should be too fragile for anything of the kind. What is
your business, if it is not too personal a question?'

They were interrupted by the sound of the front door bell
ringing, and momentarily abandoning her poise, Mrs Brown
sprang to her feet. Seeing her making for the door, Inigo rose,
too, and asked:

'Is there a strike on in the kitchen, that you always answer the
door yourself?'

'We've only two servants,' she said. 'Vauxhall and Ridley.
They've enough to do as it is, poor things.'

'Then I'll go. You'll catch cold if you keep dashing out there.'

'No, *please*, Inigo. Do sit down, there's a dear. It's probably the
doctor. I rather hoped it was when you rang earlier.'

She went out, and he returned to his chair and offered Dylis a cigarette. Mr Carpenter already had one dangling from his underlip, as he lay back in his chair with closed eyes, looking as if he did not care who lived or who died. Inigo said:

'So you're determined to push off tomorrow. What a resolute little soul you are!'

Dylis said, laughing, 'If I allowed myself to be held up by things like snow and ice I shouldn't be travelling at all. I'm due back in London in another couple of days.'

He was about to say something, when Mrs Brown returned, a frown of agitation upon her smooth forehead.

'It wasn't the doctor,' she said. 'There are some people stuck in the snow just up the road, and one of them has come along to know if we can give them any help . . . '

'That's me,' a voice said, and a man followed her into the room, smiling round at the company with the ease of one who finds himself at home in any circumstances. He was a sturdy young man with bright eyes and a glowing pink face, his coat saturated with moisture, a wet hat in his hand. 'I'm sorry to come barging in like this, but I'm travelling with Mr Humphrey Howe, you may have heard of him, he's got a place somewhere up in the mountains, Westmorland way. All the car needs is a bit of a heave to get her out of the drift, and then we'll be on our way again. I thought if there happened to be a couple of good strong men and true . . . '

'Don't look at me,' Inigo said. 'I'm not feeling strong and I've been driving since dawn this morning. Can't we put them up for the night, Auntie? You've got plenty of rooms where you can stow them away, and then we can sort it all out in the morning.'

'But it's so difficult,' she said, 'with sickness in the house. I think we should do what we can to help poor travellers in this

28

terrible weather, but this gentleman would prefer to get along without any delay. Isn't that so?' She turned with one of her rare smiles to the stranger, and he expanded visibly beneath its influence.

'That's right, Madam. Personally, I don't care one way or the other, but Mr Howe is anxious to get home.'

'I'll call Vauxhall and Ridley,' she said. 'And I'm sure you don't really mind giving a hand, Inigo. That will be four of you, five with the other gentleman, and Mr Carpenter, I think you might go, too. You should certainly be able to put matters right between you.'

She departed, leaving the door open, and an unpleasant draught issuing round it, and the stranger said, as Inigo rose to his feet, still grumbling:

'I'm awfully sorry to put you to so much trouble, but you know how it is.'

'Only too well,' Inigo said.

Mr Carpenter was still lying back in his chair, letting life pass him by. Inigo went out, and with a bow to Dylis, so did the stranger. There followed a confused sound of tramping feet and men's voices, and Mrs Brown put her head round the door to say, with quiet emphasis:

'*Mr Carpenter!*' And when he sat up and opened his eyes, she added, 'You *are* coming to help them, aren't you?'

He muttered something that sounded like, 'Blast all cars to hell!' He got to his feet, blinked his eyes several times, and shambled obediently out of the room. Never had Dylis seen a woman so anxious to help her fellow beings in distress. It was positively uncanny. She walked across to shut the door, and could not resist peering out. Gathered in the corridor were Mrs Brown, Mr Carpenter struggling into an old raincoat, the butler and, presumably, his fellow servant, who was a man smaller than the other but no less picturesque in appearance. Both wore overcoats buttoned up to their chins, and trilby hats pulled down at a rakish angle. The stranger was standing a little to one side, still apologising profusely for causing so much commotion. Inigo came running down the stairs, fastening his coat the while. A man wearing a shiny black mackintosh and a driver's peaked cap came from the direction of the kitchen quarters. He asked:

'Anythin' I can do to 'elp, Ma'am?'

'No,' Mrs Brown said, more sharply than the occasion seemed to warrant. 'No thank you. We've got all the help we need. You had better wait around until your friend arrives. He ought to be here soon, I should think, and you might miss him. And I don't want that van outside my house any longer than is necessary.'

'That's right, Ma'am. Must wait for me mate,' the man agreed, touched his cap and went back to his vigil.

Mrs Brown accompanied the rest of them to the door, with strict instructions to do everything in their power to aid the unfortunate Mr Howe and his friend. By the time she returned to the drawing-room, Dylis was again seated by the fire, thoughtfully staring into the flames. With a sigh, Mrs Brown resumed her former position, looking up at Dylis with a pathetic droop to her mouth.

'I'm so sorry for all these poor people,' she said. 'But what can one do? Normally, I should be the first to offer them dinner, a roof over their heads, a bed for the night. But with my husband so ill and myself half out of my mind with worry, I can't possibly cope with it all. As things are, my two servants are thoroughly overworked. At one time, if anyone had told me that I should have to manage a big house like this with only two servants, I should have laughed.' Slowly she shook her head from side to side, indicative that laughter had left her lips for ever. 'I do most of the cooking myself, but Ridley is a great help about the kitchen, while Vauxhall manages almost everything else, acts as butler, chauffeur and *valet de chambre*. I often tell him he is a real maid-of-all-work. Naturally I have to allow them a certain amount of freedom. One cannot expect them to act like really well-trained servants, when one is so dependent upon their goodwill.'

Dylis failed to see that the wearing of breeches and gaiters could be any help to Vauxhall in his maintenance of personal freedom, but assumed that he had some latent inhibition which was at last being allowed full sway. She said, with an attempt at sympathy:

'I'll be glad to do anything I can, Mrs Brown, between now and tomorrow. I'm not much good at butling, but I can make beds, and people have eaten my cooking without finishing their days in hospital.'

'So sweet of you, my dear. Perhaps if you wouldn't *mind* just tidying up your room a little tomorrow. It all helps. And do call me Theresa. I can't possibly keep up this ridiculous relationship of being an aunt to a grown man like Inigo. He's such a big fellow, isn't he? He even makes *you* look small, and I'm sure I look like a child beside him. But then I've always been such a little person. At school they called me Teenie-Weenie.'

She looked down with some complacency at her feet, resting upon the hearthrug. Dylis had to admit that her own feet, even in slippers, looked like those of an elephant beside them. The fact was not lost upon Theresa, for she added:

'There are times when I wish I were not quite so tiny. All this responsibility is really too much for my strength. The doctor said that it is only my will that keeps me going. Such a strong will in such a delicate body, he said. It would be better for me if I were more of your build, with a tough, workmanlike frame and sturdy legs.'

Dylis, who had an unusually symmetrical figure and beautiful legs, looked down at her person in some astonishment. Described thus, she did not sound very attractive. Yet there were many who had thought otherwise, if their vows of undying devotion were to be believed. She said blandly:

'My dear Theresa, some women would give the third finger of their left hand to look like you. Of course, it's generally considered that to show off clothes really well, one should have height and a certain breadth of shoulder, not to mention a good bust and hips. And I do think in a bathing costume one needs a little flesh about the legs if one isn't going to cause roars of laughter. But otherwise I don't see that you've anything to worry about.'

Theresa got up slowly from her stool and made towards the door.

'I think,' she said, 'I had better go and see how the dinner is getting on. Otherwise it may be spoilt.'

'I'll come, too. I can't just sit idle, while you work your little fingers to the bone.'

The kitchen proved to be a long, draughty room, with a cold stone floor and high curtained windows, but it boasted a large size in ranges which offered tremendous heat upon near approach. There was also a boiler for heating the water, emitting a strong smell of burning coke, a white scrubbed table, several wooden chairs, a china cabinet and rows of shelves holding cooking utensils.

Upon one of the chairs in front of the table sat the man in the shiny mackintosh, with a newspaper, a bottle of beer, and a glass at his disposal. To judge by the pile of cigarette-ends in a nearby ashtray, he had been sitting there for a very long time. He looked up as they entered, remarked:

''Ope I'm not in the way, Ma'am,' and went on reading. He had a broad, friendly face, and gave the impression that he did not much care whether he were in the way or not. Theresa said:

'It's perfectly all right,' and having tied a dainty lace apron around her dinner dress, she picked up an oven cloth and made towards the stove. Dylis said:

'Let me do that, I've nothing to spoil,' and took the cloth out of her hand and opened the oven door. A smell of good roast lamb ascended to her nostrils, causing her inside to contract with longing.

'The last of the fresh meat,' Theresa said sadly. 'If the trades-people can't get here tomorrow, we shall have to start on the tinned foods.'

'Eat, drink and be merry, for tomorrow we die,' Dylis quoted. Some instinct made her glance up then, only to look away again, for the other woman was regarding her with a very strange expression. She closed the oven door and peered into the pots containing vegetables. They all looked overdone. She asked, 'I suppose your husband has to have something special?'

'He takes nothing, practically nothing,' Theresa said. 'Just little sips of brandy, and . . . '

She turned as the kitchen door opened, and a man thrust in his head. He was middle-aged, with grey hair and a pallid face infinitely weary in its expression. Dylis did not recall having seen him before. He glanced quickly round the room and remarked, addressing Theresa:

'The Master wants to see you. He says he's hungry, and he's being neglected. He wants to know . . . '

'All right, Ledgrove, I'll come at once,' she cut in quickly, and ran across and almost pushed him out into the passage, closing the door behind them. Dylis stared at the closed door, her thoughts perplexed. The man at the table went on sitting there, as if unaware that he were not alone. The front door bell rang, and dropping the oven cloth, Dylis went with some speed to open it. The vagaries of this household were beginning to tell upon her usually stoical nerves.

# Chapter III

It seemed to Dylis, as she opened the front door, that a positive regiment of masculinity flowed past her into the entrance lounge. There were Inigo and the stranger who had called for assistance, Vauxhall and Ridley, Mr Carpenter, and two others new to the party. Intercepting the servants as they were about to move off to their own quarters, Dylis said:

'Mrs Brown and I have been keeping watch on the dinner. I hope it's not entirely ruined.'

The one called Ridley stared indifferently from eyes set very close to the bridge of a prominent nose. He remarked:

'Thank you, Miss,' and he and his colleague departed, with much stamping of feet and rubbing of hands indicative of a recent tough fight against overwhelming odds. Without a word to anyone, Mr Carpenter slid past her and out into the corridor, trailing a dripping raincoat. He looked blue with cold. Inigo said cheerfully, taking her arm:

'It was a waste of time. We couldn't do anything useful. Their car seems to have everything wrong with it, but we can't tell exactly what until the morning. So I've invited these gentlemen to put up here for the night.'

He introduced them. The obvious head of the party, Mr Humphrey Howe, was tall and aesthetic looking, and might have been any age between fifty and sixty. His skin had a translucent appearance, and the hand which he extended with a regal gesture was white and well manicured. He wore his brown hair rather long, and Dylis had a shrewd suspicion that it was dyed. The other new arrival was his secretary, Mr William Raddle, who, lacking his employer's age, height and general air of command, yet managed to identify himself with the other by standing close at his side, watching his face and unconsciously imitating his mannerisms. The one who had descended upon the house in the first place proved to be Charlie Best, free-lance journalist, as he himself insisted upon mentioning.

'I expect you could do with a drink,' Inigo said. 'If you'll give me your wet things I'll take them out to the kitchen to dry. Will you show them into the drawing-room, Dylis? Where's my aunt, by the way?'

'Upstairs, with your uncle,' Dylis said. 'He sent for her.' She was not over enthusiastic about playing hostess to three strange men in someone else's house. It was all very well for Inigo to take so much for granted, but she had an uncomfortable feeling that Theresa was going to look down her childish nose upon this fresh invasion. But there was no alternative. The men had already divested themselves of their outer garments, which Inigo was bearing away with the smiling assurance of the accomplished hotel proprietor. She said:

'The drawing-room is through here,' and conducted them into its welcome warmth. Mr Carpenter had already ensconced himself in his former position, with a glass of whisky at his elbow. His feet were thrust out to the fire, and his eyes were closed. Neither did he show any sign of life when Dylis said to her enforced protégés:

'Will you make yourselves at home? Mrs Brown will be down presently, I expect.'

They might, or might not know who was Mrs Brown. She did not trouble to explain further. They murmured conventional phrases, and took seats within the circle surrounding the fireplace. Mr Howe said:

'This is a beautiful old house, Miss Hughes. But stuffy.'

His secretary murmured, 'Quite.'

'On the contrary,' Dylis said, 'it seems pretty draughty to me.'

She did not approve of this open criticism of a house whose doors had been opened, well, if not hospitably, at least opened. Especially a criticism so unjustified. For apart from those portions of it which were heated, it was quite the coldest house she had ever known. Charlie Best was eyeing her with veiled amusement. She was vastly relieved when Inigo came in, and began to dispense drinks all round. He said to her:

'I suppose there's no word from those garage people yet? About the van, I mean?'

'Not as far as I know. The driver is still waiting in the kitchen.'

'A pity. I was thinking if they did turn up they might do something to help our friends here, or at least arrange to send over a breakdown gang in the morning. But I expect they've closed down for the night. The roads are getting worse all the time. I wonder what's happened to that other bloke who was supposed to be doing something about his van?'

Dylis shrugged her shoulders, and looked with some disfavour upon the glass of sherry she had automatically accepted. It was exceptionally fine sherry, but she had no desire for anything further to drink. She wanted to eat. But no one else seemed to be of the same mind, and while they were drinking she felt she could not just sit and twiddle her thumbs. She remarked:

'He's probably packed up and taken a room somewhere for the night. And in weather like this, who can blame him?'

'Well, if nothing happens by tomorrow,' Inigo said, 'one of us will have to get over to Cudge and see what we can do. I take it you're in no desperate hurry, Mr Howe?'

The latter, sitting bolt upright in his chair, one thin hand toying with a very small glass of sherry, took some pains to reassure him.

'Mr Brown,' he said. 'I am never desperate, and I am never in a hurry. What I do, I do with method and precision. When I sent Mr Best to enquire of your good selves whether you could assist us out of our dilemma, it was not because I had any special urgency to reach my home, nor because I feared that a night spent upon the open road would do me any material harm. It was solely due to the fact that Mr Best is a man with a living to earn, and I felt it incumbent upon me not to waste his time. At my invitation, he is accompanying me to my home, Higher Uplands, in the mountain district of Westmorland, where he is to study my mode of living and to report, in the form of an article, to such of his readers who are interested. I had a call to make at York, hence this somewhat circuitous route. My mode of living, Mr Brown,' he continued with some emphasis, for Inigo looked as if he might interrupt at any moment, 'is unique and, I may say, outstandingly beneficial to the health. Fresh air is the keynote and the mainstay of my existence. I've no doubt you have read at least one of my many books on the subject. I can strongly recommend *Fresh Air Diet*, *Let Nature Do It* and *Whither the Worried World?*'

Inigo, drawing comfortably on a cigarette, agreed that fresh air was wonderful. Dylis and Best were also smoking, but neither Mr Howe nor his secretary were addicted to the habit. The secretary Dylis found particularly irritating. He was about forty, and had a puffy pink face, rather feminine in contour, childish blue eyes that stared roundly at anyone who spoke, and a habit of interjecting such remarks as, 'Quite', and 'An excellent point, that', into his employer's discourse. He might have saved himself the trouble, for Mr Howe took no more notice of him than if he had been a statue.

Charlie Best was not uninteresting. He, too, listened to Mr Howe with apparent respect, but there was a twinkle in his eyes and a slightly cynical twist to his mouth, suggestive that his thoughts were his own. Musing, Dylis came to the conclusion that his name was vaguely familiar. She might have seen it in a journal of some kind. She could not be sure.

'Dried grass,' Mr Howe was saying, 'carefully stewed and eaten three times a day, is excellent for the heart and nerves. The heads of fish, particularly that of the cod, broiled in milk with a little salt and pepper, are stimulating to the brain. But it is to the nettle that we have to turn for some of our greatest benefits. I refer, of course, to the Great or Common Nettle, also the Small Nettle . . . '

It appeared appropriate to Dylis that Mrs Brown should choose that moment to enter the room. She had added to her ensemble a tiny jacket of soft black marabout, that gave her the air of a cat about to seek the most comfortable place in which to sleep. Neither did she seem put out to find that the best places were already taken. She advanced quietly upon them as the men rose, all except Mr Carpenter, who was snoring with some abandon. Inigo made the necessary introductions, and she said, smiling:

'Welcome to Wintry Wold, gentlemen. Vauxhall told me of your predicament, and of course I am only too glad to give you shelter for the night. But I'm afraid our hospitality will be a little rough. I was explaining to Miss Hughes earlier that the best part of the house is shut up now, as we have only two servants, and I expect my nephew has told you about my husband being so ill?'

She was putting up a pretty good show, Dylis thought, and watched with a certain amusement as Mr Howe and his satellite assured her that they were accustomed to the simple life, and Charlie Best remarked that anywhere a dog could sleep, so could he.

'Well, if you don't *mind* roughing it a little,' she said, 'I'll give Vauxhall instructions. He's laying the table for dinner now.' She walked daintily round the circle and slid back a folding door which hitherto had escaped Dylis's attention, being partly screened by Mr Carpenter's chair. It communicated with a small room beyond, in which the versatile butler could be seen laying a long dining-table. She went on to explain, 'We usually dine in here now. So much more convenient and cosy than the real dining-hall, unless one is doing entertaining on a large scale. Vauxhall, you need not lay a place for me. I shall take something on a tray up in the Master's room.'

Here she was interrupted by expressions of hope from her uninvited guests that they were not putting her out too much.

'Oh, *no*,' she said, returning amongst them. 'You mustn't think that. I don't want anything to spoil the little hospitality I can offer. And I hope you won't think it rude of me not to join you. But my husband is in such a weak state, you understand, and he can't bear me to be out of his sight for long. He sent down a message just before you arrived begging me to go up to him.' She glanced at Inigo, and her voice was unusually sweet as she added, 'Of course, it *was* rather impulsive of my nephew to ask you to stay without consulting me, but he's used to hotel life, where people come and go at all hours of the day and night. I can't compete there, but I do hope you'll make yourselves completely at home.'

She smiled thinly upon them, and made what Dylis considered to be her best exit so far. A little while after, Mr Howe rose and said:

'If I may make a point, Mr Brown, your ideas on ventilation in this house are far behind the times.'

'Which times?' Inigo asked. 'These times, Victorian times, the Tudor period or the time of the Early Britons?'

Mr Howe regarded him dubiously and walked over to the window. But it was shut and bolted, with a bolt that had long since rusted into immovable position. Momentarily defeated in his search for fresh air, he investigated the inner room, and discovered french windows behind the heavy velour curtains. In triumph he withdrew the bolt and flung one of them wide. Immediately a tornado of wind hurtled itself through the aperture, sweeping the curtains aside, flapping the corners of the white damask tablecloth and setting the pendant lamp in that room swinging to and fro, throwing grotesque shadows about the walls and ceiling.

Inigo and Dylis stared at each other incredulously, Mr Raddle smiled and nodded. Charlie Best muttered, 'Silly old fool!' caught Dylis's glance, and laughed. Vauxhall, putting finishing touches to the table, looked up from his task to say:

'We'll have that closed, if you don't mind.'

'I do mind,' Mr Howe asserted. 'Lack of fresh air is the basis of all civilised troubles.'

'I've got troubles enough, without fresh air added to 'em,' Vauxhall said. 'We'll have it closed.'

He stamped across and reached out into the night, and it required all his strength to get the window shut and bolted again, having achieved which he stood with his back to it, glaring at Mr Howe an unmistakable challenge. Dylis's feelings warmed towards him. Here was a man of sense and some strength of mind, even if he were a little eccentric. Recognising, perhaps, that a man-to-man struggle with a butler was far beneath his dignity, Mr Howe returned to the drawing-room and directed an accusing glance towards Inigo.

'Your butler,' he observed, 'has the manners of a pig.'

'Possibly,' Inigo admitted. 'But in these difficult times it's a bold man who dare argue with a butler. Perhaps you're not bothered with any servant problem, Mr Howe, but I assure you that my aunt would be grateful even for the services of a pig, if she could find one sufficiently domesticated.'

They heard Vauxhall stamp out and bang the door of the other room leading onto the corridor, and Mr Howe said:

'In my home, Mr Brown, we have no servant problem. My secretary, my sister and I share the housework between us. We have bare floors strewn with rushes, no glass in the windows to obstruct the air and collect dust, our beds and our chairs are of wood, easily kept clean. We eat three simple meals a day from wooden bowls which require little scouring. From which you will see that our advantages are many.'

'Not the least of them being that you're unlikely to be troubled with many visitors. If ever I find I've had enough of the hotel business, Mr Howe, I shall certainly follow your example. Another glass of sherry?'

'Thank you, no. One glass of wine does a man no harm. Two glasses weaken his moral fibre, and three spell his ultimate ruin.'

There followed an awkward pause. Dylis was trying not to laugh, and suspected that Inigo laboured under the same difficulty. Charlie Best threw his smoking cigarette-end into the fire, and William Raddle sat moving his lips in soundless repetition of his employer's last words. Vauxhall made another heavy-footed entrance, and appeared at the communicating door to announce,

'If you people want any grub, it's ready.'

'And if you need any translation of that,' Charlie Best said, in a whispered aside to Dylis as they went towards the dining-room, 'he means dinner is served.'

'I for one, am glad to get it,' she whispered back. 'But I don't see any stewed grass for your two boy friends.'

'They'll survive,' he said, and moved quickly to pull out a chair for her at the head of the table. She felt rather as if she were attending a committee meeting as she sat down, but when Vauxhall, who evidently scorned serving at table, slammed down the dishes and plates in front of her, she decided it was more like being the matron of a boys' school. Inigo sat on her right and Best on her left, with Mr Howe and his secretary opposite each other farther down the table. As if by tacit agreement, they had left Mr Carpenter sleeping.

The meal proved better than she had hoped. It was all somewhat overdone, but none the less edible, and privately she complimented Ridley on his ability, for she could not imagine Mrs Brown performing culinary operations in her dinner dress. There was a good Bordeaux to accompany it, which Mr Howe and his secretary declined. Indeed, true to their cult they ate but frugally of vegetables, deploring the fact that they were not only cooked, but overcooked. Nevertheless, conversation might have flourished amiably, had not Mr Howe, in a dissertation upon the ills of mankind, scornfully dismissed as harmful all so-called cures such as medicines and other antidotes. Here Dylis felt bound to call attention to the fact that any relief for sickness was good, although advertised brands were better, and those manufactured by Messrs Compton, Webber and Hughes were undoubtedly the best of the lot.

'Do you mean to tell me, young lady,' Mr Howe expostulated, 'that you seriously believe these oils and ointments and such rubbish as you sell can *cure* a body sick from the folly of its own wrong way of life?'

'I do,' Dylis said. 'If you suffer from stiff joints, a little Rubbitin well massaged around the places affected while taking a hot bath will cure it overnight. On the other hand, Quickease, a scientific blending of curative oils, will take away lumbago in three days instead of the usual five. For sciatica, there is Si-rub, and for coughs, sore throats, and general chest troubles a little Baydrop does wonders. The common cold can be instantly relieved by inhaling a few drops of Nasalo in hot water, and Necktar oil is unrivalled for stiff necks. Also . . . '

'Miss Hughes,' her victim said, with undisguised annoyance, 'let me make it clear, before you try any further to interest me in your wares, that I have never suffered from any of these maladies, and having regard to my meticulous habits, I am not likely to suffer from them in the future. And I give you my solemn word that I shall leave no stone unturned to spread the gospel of my own way of life, and thus to cut the ground from under the feet of you purveyors of false hope and quackery.'

'No sale, Dylis,' Inigo said. 'Too bad you can't wire back to Compton and Webber that you've landed a whale of an order. But don't worry. I'll let you practise on me if you're a good girl.'

'I wasn't trying to get an order,' Dylis said, with some heat. 'I was simply trying to explain, for the benefit of Mr Howe's limited intelligence, that everyone is not in a position to live in a mountain retreat and eat out of wooden bowls. Most people are forced

44

to lead unnatural lives, and when they get sick, they've got to have a quick cure.'

'Well, let's go and be thoroughly unnatural in the drawing-room and have cigarettes and coffee,' he said soothingly, and picked up the tray which Vauxhall had deposited upon the side-board, and made a rapid departure. Dylis followed slowly. She did not know whether it was customary at Wintry Wold for the ladies to retire first, but evidently this was one occasion when they did not. Mr Howe and his secretary followed more slowly still, and the former said:

'I think, Raddle, we might devote the next hour to a little useful work, and see what progress we can make with Chapter 7 of *Give me the Air*.'

'You're not taking coffee?' queried Inigo, who was busy dispensing that beverage from a low table by the fire. Mr Carpenter still slept.

'No, thank you, Mr Brown. We need no stimulants of any kind. On rising in the morning, we take a draught of pure well water, and the same with our meals, and before we retire.'

'There, at least, we can accommodate you,' Inigo said. 'We've plenty of good well water laid on in the bathroom, as pure and icy as anyone could wish. Sugar, Dyl?'

'No, thanks,' she said, and accepted a cup of black coffee and a cigarette from the box he offered. Charlie Best, having finished the remainder of the Bordeaux, joined them then and announced that be would take his coffee with a lot of milk and two lumps of sugar. Mr Howe and his secretary retired to the corner where stood the pedestal lamp, and settling themselves upon stiff upholstered chairs, proceeded to ignore the rest of the company. Mr Raddle brought out notebook and pencil from an inside pocket, and his employer began to dictate in a voice of irritating monotony.

The group by the fire was silent until there came from the inner room the sound of Vauxhall clearing the table, when Inigo rose, and excusing himself, went inside to speak to the butler. Charlie Best moved to sit on the arm of Dylis's chair, and asked in a confidential undertone:

'What is all this Auntie business? Mrs Brown isn't really his aunt, is she?'

'By marriage, yes.'

'Strike me lucky! Some people get it all, don't they? What does his uncle look like, Julius Caesar?'

'I really don't know. I haven't seen him.'

'Oh, you haven't seen him. He's the one who's sick, isn't he?'

'So I understand.'

'It's a queer sort of household, this. Have you ever been here before?'

'Is this an official enquiry?' Dylis asked. 'Or just unofficial curiosity?'

'Sorry,' he laughed. 'But I like to get to the bottom of things. It's part of my profession. You'd be surprised the amount of material I get just by asking questions.'

Inigo returned, closing the communicating door, and ignoring a scathing look from Mr Howe as he did so. The latter remarked to the room in general:

'All apertures now being closed, we can expect shortly to sink into a state bordering upon coma.'

Dylis, warmed by good food, wine and coffee, was already approaching some such state. Inigo and Best did nothing to help matters by smoking one cigarette after another until the atmosphere of the room could have vied with the density of a London fog. They seemed, without having conferred upon the subject, to have entered into a subversive pact against Mr Howe and his views, for as fast as Inigo finished a cigarette, Best would tender his case, and vice versa, while they chatted amiably on this and that. Dylis, though approving their tactics, declined to participate on the grounds that she had already smoked more than was her custom. At length, when she had been forced to close her eyes from sheer weariness, Mr Carpenter came suddenly to life, looked at his wrist-watch, and remarked:

'I don't know if you people mean to sit up all night, but I'm turning in.'

Whereupon he rose and left them, without attempting to wish them the conventional good night.

'A nice, easy fellow to cater for,' Best said. 'Just a shot or two of Scotch and a seat by the fire. Who is he?'

'A friend of my uncle.' Inigo yawned, and glanced up as Theresa came in. She looked fresh and bright and her voice was brisk as she asked:

'Did you have a good dinner?'

'Fine, thanks, Mrs Brown,' Best said. 'We're just having a comfortable chat . . . '

'I've arranged your rooms,' she interrupted. 'So if you would care to accompany me, I'll show you the way.'

Mr Howe rose with alacrity and said, with a bow in her direction:

'Thank you, Madam. I may say that I shall be very grateful to find myself in quarters where the atmosphere is less injurious to the lungs.' And with his secretary obediently following, he strode out into the corridor. Inigo said:

'Just a few more minutes, Auntie, and Dylis and I will be up. We know the way.'

'As you please. But don't stay up too late, Inigo. You must be very tired. Are you coming, Mr Best?'

'You bet.' Reluctantly he got to his feet, and as she went out, he said in an undertone, 'How about swapping your aunt for one of mine, old man? I've got a splendid one living at Knightsbridge who'd just suit you.'

'You can lose that idea,' Inigo said. 'You may not have noticed it, but my aunt doesn't take kindly to strangers.'

'She's uncommonly keen on tucking us up early, though. Cheerio, folks, see you tomorrow.' He left them, and Inigo immediately flung wide the communicating door, went into the dining-room and returned with a bottle of Cointreau. He left the door open.

'Sorry to have turned the place into a smoking den,' he said. 'But I thought we might shift that old devil earlier. May his toes freeze. Did you ever hear such a lot of high-falutin' nonsense in your life?'

'I suppose he's entitled to his own opinion,' Dylis remarked sleepily. 'But I do draw the line when he tries to force it on everyone else. What's that for?'

'You! It's the privilege of a good host to keep the best drink for an honoured guest. Howe and his fellow sufferer wouldn't have touched it, anyway, and it's far too good for Charlie. He's got a swallow like a thirsty fish.'

'I don't really want any,' Dylis said. 'I've had enough to drink.' But she accepted a small glass, conscious that upstairs awaited her a very cold bed in a very cold room. She asked suddenly, as he poured himself a liqueur and took the chair Mr Carpenter had vacated, 'Is your uncle very wealthy?'

'Good heavens, no! I don't suppose he ever had an income of more than a thousand a year, and most of that goes in taxes. He's got another property in Cumberland, which is let to someone or other, but he can't get much out of it. Why do you ask?'

48

'I was curious. It's no business of mine, I know, but it seems so strange for a girl like Theresa to marry someone years older than herself, and to live miles from anywhere in this wild country.'

'You underrate the charm of my family. I haven't seen him for years, but my uncle used to be a decent-looking bloke, nice manners, easy to get on with. Why shouldn't she marry him? If I were still unmarried at his age, *I* should try and find a beautiful, devoted young woman to wait on me.'

'But she doesn't strike one as being the devoted type.'

'It would take another woman to see it, then.'

'Probably. To me there are two kinds of women, those who crouch, and those who don't. Your aunt crouches. What's more, she never makes a movement that hasn't been carefully studied in a mirror.'

Inigo laughed. 'I shall begin to think you don't like her in a moment. But likes and dislikes apart, whatever she married my uncle for, it wasn't his money. Anyone can see they haven't much of an income. Look at the state of this house. It used to be a beautiful old place, but nothing has been done to it for years. Even the furniture is falling to pieces.'

'Yet Theresa seems to have plenty of money to spend on clothes and jewellery. Where did your uncle meet her?'

'The Riviera, I believe.'

Dylis thought about that. She could imagine Theresa on the Riviera, beautifully dressed, mixing with the fashionable crowd. There she would pass without comment. It was only at Wintry Wold that she seemed out of place.

'It's all very odd,' she said. 'In fact, everything about this place seems odd to me.'

'What, for instance?'

'Well, when we first arrived she seemed to be expecting somebody else.'

'So she was . . . the doctor.'

'So she said. Then for some reason she doesn't want you to see your uncle.'

'I thought she explained that, too.'

'Perhaps. She was very annoyed with you for asking those people to stay the night.'

'You can't really blame her for that. As she said, I'm used to putting people up at a moment's notice, but she isn't, and hasn't the means to cater for them.'

'There's another thing,' Dylis went on. 'When we were in the kitchen, she was just telling me that your uncle isn't strong enough to take anything solid, when his valet came bursting in and said that the old man wanted to see her, and that he was hungry, and thought he was being neglected.'

'That's perfectly natural. Invalids always demand food when it's bad for them. I remember another uncle of mine who insisted on eating steak and chips with a temperature of a hundred and four. He died not long after.'

'But that's just the point. It's all very plausible, and yet somehow . . . This Mr Carpenter. He's a most extraordinary person. Your aunt says he's been a wonderful help, yet all he does is to sit around and drink and take no notice of anyone.'

'You're not being very tolerant,' Inigo said. 'Perhaps he's had so many late nights he can't bear the sight of people. He looks rather like that. Vauxhall is feeling much about the same. When I bribed him to produce the Cointreau, he said in so many words that he loathes all men, and women give him a pain.'

'There you are! There's another extraordinary one. You can't argue him away. Theresa says she has to allow the servants to do

50

more or less as they please, otherwise they wouldn't stay. But she's the very woman I would have backed to do the heavy mistress and keep everyone's nose to the grindstone.'

'Wintry Wold has certainly gone down a bit since my time,' Inigo mused. 'Now if a butler wants to wear anything he fancies, from gumboots to a hat like a Pope, you've just got to put up with it, or do without. It's the new age of freedom. Personally, I like it. I used to be scared stiff of butlers, but this one . . . why, you can treat him like a brother.'

'But apart from his clothes, he doesn't *look* like a butler.'

'That's nothing to go by. You don't look like a commercial traveller. Shall I tell you what you do look like?'

'I don't want to know,' Dylis said, annoyed at being drawn away from the subject. She finished her liqueur, replaced the glass upon the table and relaxed for a few minutes with her eyes closed. She heard no sound, was unaware that he had moved, until he leaned over with a hand on either side of the chair and kissed her.

'I'm sorry,' he said, as she opened startled eyes. 'I shouldn't have done that. You're tired aren't you? But you looked so sweet I couldn't resist it.'

She looked thoughtfully up into the strange darkness of his eyes for a moment or two, and said:

'You're a peculiar person. And this is a peculiar house. I think I'll go to bed.'

'Good idea.' He put out a hand and helped her to her feet. She waited while he returned the Cointreau to the dining-room, and as they went out into the corridor together, he asked, 'You're not annoyed with me?'

'Not particularly.' She could not imagine anyone being annoyed with him for long, but refrained from saying so. He took a small oil lamp from one of the tables in the passage, and they started up the stairs. At the top of the first flight they met Theresa descending, carrying a candle in yet another ornate holder. She said:

'I was just coming to see where you were. Are you turning in now?'

'Right now,' Inigo said. 'What about you?'

'I shall just go and see that everything's locked up, and then I'll try and snatch an hour or so.' They renewed their offers of help, but she refused with gentle insistence. 'No, thank you just the same. My husband is sleeping now, and Ledgrove is with him. If he doesn't call for me before then, I shall take my turn in the early hours. That's the most dangerous time for a sick person. Good night. I do hope you sleep well.'

They reciprocated her wishes and continued up to the first floor. The way she had turned and walked slowly downstairs was calculated to make anyone feel large, clumsy and incompetent. Dylis shrugged away the feeling as they negotiated the interminable corridors, with Inigo holding the oil lamp as sole illumination. She thought it would be infinitely more convenient were they to have such things placed at strategic points all over the house. The ground floor was adequately lighted, but above an inky darkness was everywhere, and the shadows cast by the light of a single lamp were not inspiring. She was glad of Inigo's company as far as her room, where he entered and lighted the candles for her. He asked then, faintly smiling:

'Sure you've got everything you want? Or shall I open the windows and let in a little fresh air?'

'Don't you dare!' she said. 'There's enough cold air in this room to kill a regiment. It's pouring down the chimney and through that ventilator, and I'm turning to ice as I stand.'

'Well, you'll soon be nice and warm whoever else freezes. I

52

asked Vauxhall to put a hot water bottle in the bed. And I'll send you up a bowl of stewed grass in the morning. Cheerio!'

She walked across to the window when he had gone, pulled back the curtains and peered out. But it was too dark to see anything. Snow was still falling heavily, to judge by the flakes that whirled against the window-pane, and the wind howled dismally.

# Chapter IV

The hot water bottle, Dylis found, was a nice idea, sole comfort in an otherwise pitilessly cold bed. But the length and breadth of her travels had accustomed her to cold beds in out-of-the-way places, and to offset such drawbacks she was in the habit of wearing warm pyjamas. So that it was not very long, as Inigo had predicted, before she was both warm and comfortable. The windows and door of her apartment rattled abominably, and it occurred to her that she might have had the foresight to wedge them. But once beneath a mound of blankets crowned by the sumptuous eiderdown, it seemed hardly worth while to crawl out again into the icy atmosphere, and gradually her mind accepted the symphony of sounds within and without, and she drifted into a pleasant sleep.

Yet as the night wore on, other and more unaccountable noises seemed to twine themselves into her subconscious, causing her to move restlessly. She woke at last, spent some minutes trying to remember what part of the country she was in, settled the point to her satisfaction, and was about to return to slumber, when her ears caught an unmistakable shuffling sound in the corridor. Slowly it came nearer, shuffle, shuffle, shuffle, like tired feet in slippers upon a bare floor. Someone, she supposed, on their way to the bathroom, or Mr Howe going down to get some fresh air. The idea amused her, and she smiled sleepily.

Then she stopped smiling, and sat bolt upright. For the shuffling, which should have continued down the corridor until out of hearing, had stopped exactly outside her door. She sat and waited. In a moment, of course, whoever it was would move on. But she wanted to make sure that they did. Gusts of wind came down the chimney and round the edges of the windows, causing her to shiver. She sat and waited for what seemed a very long time, but still there was no further sound from outside. Resolutely, then, she climbed out of her nest of bedclothes, felt for and found her slippers and dressing-gown. People might shuffle to and from anywhere they liked, but she would not have them pausing outside her door for indefinite intervals, particularly as the door had no key, a fact which she had observed earlier without interest.

In the inky darkness that surrounded her she could see nothing, neither could she remember where she had put her torch. Cautiously she began to feel her way towards the mantelpiece, where stood the candlestick and matches. The door was rattling even more violently, almost as if someone were trying to get in. But that was a ridiculous idea, because if they wanted to get in they could do it without rattling. More likely they would enter and close the door quietly. Perhaps this mysterious shuffler had already done so, and was even now creeping across the room through the darkness.

As she was struggling against this unpleasant thought, she reached the mantel, located the matches and hastily lit the candles. To her relief, the room was empty, and she stood for a moment, straining her ears to catch the suggestion of any further movement. She was not particularly given to nervous excitement, had slept in many strange rooms up and down the country without even going through the formality of looking in the wardrobe in search of marauders. But this was different. She was not going to have people shuffling about outside her door without knowing the reason why.

Grasping the candlestick, she crept to the door, and suddenly flung it open. As far as she could see, there was nothing at all outside. She stepped into the passage, peering left and right, but it appeared to be empty. Neither could she hear anything, except the creaking noises of an old house beset by a high wind. Baffled, she went as far as the staircase, looked carefully down and up, saw nothing, heard nothing unusual, and returned slowly to her room, on the threshold of which she paused. On the left and right were other rooms the doors of which proved to be locked. And it was only then that she made a survey of the floor, and discovered that the threadbare corridor carpet was laid just as far as her door and not an inch beyond, so that the footsteps of anyone approaching from the other side would be heard upon the polished flooring, to become instantly muffled when they reached the carpet.

So relieved was she at this logical explanation, that the shuffler, whoever he might be, was immediately forgiven. Indeed, she felt annoyed over what she considered her own stupidity, particularly when she found that her forehead was damp with sweat, although she was shivering from the intense cold. What utter nonsense, she thought, to be put out by anything so trivial. If she were not careful, she would be imagining all kinds of absurd things.

Even as she stepped back into her room, she thought she heard a thumping sound. Just to reassure herself, she stopped to listen. She did hear a thumping sound, coming from somewhere above.

It was probably a window become unlatched and swinging in the wind. But it did not sound like a window, nor like a door, nor like anything accidental. It was a steady thump, thump, thump, slow and muffled, more like a signal.

Now this, Dylis decided, was getting more annoying every minute. Did the people in this house never go to bed and stay there? First they shuffled and then they thumped, there was no knowing what they would be up to next. Well, she might be only a stray guest, but she was not going to put up with it. Two could play at thumping. To confirm the enormity of their conduct, she went back into her room, consulted her watch and discovered that it was well past two o'clock in the morning.

Casting a shrewd glance around, she selected the poker as the time-honoured and most likely weapon of attack or defence. Not that she thought she would need it. A few words of reprimand should be sufficient to quell whoever had disturbed her night's rest. But it was as well to take no chances, and even a strong-minded woman feels vastly encouraged when her powers of persuasion are enforced by a poker.

With this aid to combat clutched in her right hand and the candlestick in her left, she swept majestically along the corridor, and up the staircase to the next floor. Arrived there, she paused and listened. The thumping was still going on at short intervals, and appeared to come from the right, beyond a sharp bend in the passage. She made her way thither and found her surmise to be correct, for a dim light showed beneath one of the closed doors and from here the thumping undoubtedly emanated. She rapped softly upon the panelling and waited. The thumping ceased, and a man's voice, weak and throaty, called:

'Come in, come in.'

He sounded singularly out of temper. She entered, to discover a large bedroom, furnished in antiquated style, with a vast four-poster bed predominating. The remains of a fire smouldered in the grate, and in the bed, partially propped up by pillows, lay an elderly man with nearly white hair, a dressing-gown wrapped about his shoulders, his thin hands playing a nervous tattoo upon the coverlet. Beside the bed was a small table, on which reposed a lighted oil lamp, heavily shaded, an array of bottles and medicine glasses, and a walking stick, the top of which was swathed in fabric. The last item Dylis had no difficulty in identifying as that most likely to be used for thumping purposes. The elderly gentleman would, she thought, be Mr Warner Brown. The poker in her hand had become not only redundant, but frankly ridiculous. She stood just inside the room, trying to think of something to say. Mr Brown saved her the trouble by demanding:

'Who the devil are you? I want Ledgrove.'

That, at least, gave her an opening. She moved nearer, hoping she did not look too much like a bad dream, and began:

'I'm Dylis Hughes. I'm staying here the night, and I heard you thumping, so I came up to see what it was all about.'

'Never heard of you,' he interrupted. 'Are you a friend of my wife?'

'Well, in a way. But you see . . . '

'Go away and leave me alone. My neck aches and I can't sleep. I want Ledgrove. Where is he?'

'I really don't know. But I'll find him for you, if you'll tell me where he's likely to be.'

'In his room, of course. Next door. Where else would he be?'

'I'll go and call him,' she said, and went quickly to the door. She had no wish to be involved in an argument with a sick man in the early hours of the morning. Although, upon consideration,

Mr Brown did not look so very sick, nothing like Theresa had said. His face was pale and rather haggard, his eyes extraordinarily dark like those of Inigo. But he seemed to be in full command of his senses. She went out, and found that to the left was a bathroom and to the right a room with the door ajar. She knocked, and receiving no reply, took a few steps inside and looked round. It was a very ordinary room, plainly furnished and apparently lacking an occupant. The bed had obviously not been slept in, but in this room, too, a small fire burned in the grate. She looked beneath the bed, and in all possible places of hiding, for she was beginning to believe that the inmates of Wintry Wold were not bound by normal rules of conduct. She returned next door to announce:

'I'm sorry, but your valet is not in his room. Where else might he be?'

Mr Brown ran a hand over his hair and looked perplexed.

'How the devil do I know? He's never left his room before, not to my knowledge. When I want anything, I thump, and in he comes.'

She thought now that the missing valet was probably responsible for the shuffling. He must have gone down for something or other, but if so, he was a long time returning. Perhaps he was down in the kitchen, making himself a pot of tea. Playing watchdog to Mr Brown must be an arduous business. She asked diffidently:

'Is there anything *I* can do?'

'I can't sleep,' the invalid said morosely. 'Something woke me. All these noises, people coming and going. Who are you? That's what I'd like to know.'

She placed the candlestick and the poker on the ground and sat down on the edge of his bed. She was getting tired of being asked that question. Even though he were sick, there was no need to be so crotchety about everything.

'I can't sleep, either,' she said. 'First I heard someone shuffling past my door, or rather, they seemed to get stuck halfway, and I went out to see who it was. Then I heard you thumping . . . I can't imagine ever getting to sleep again. I've already told you who I am. I came with your nephew, Inigo . . . '

'You did *what*? Why wasn't I told? Where is he? I knew it, I knew it all the time. When I sent Ledgrove . . . Did he get my letter? Where is he, I say? Go and fetch him.'

'It's gone two o'clock,' Dylis said. 'I expect he's asleep.'

Mr Brown leaned forward, peering at her with an expression between resolution and appeal.

'Now listen, young woman. This is a serious affair. Did you, or did you not, come here with my nephew?'

'I did.'

'Describe him.'

'Well . . . he's big, with dark hair and eyes, something like yours, and he laughs a lot, and he's got a sort of cleft in his chin. He likes snow, and he lives in Switzerland . . . '

'Good enough. That's him all right. Did he get the letter I sent him to the Playfair Hotel in London?'

'I don't know about the hotel, but he did mention something about a letter. You asked him to come along and bring a friend.'

'Exactly.' Mr Brown's eyes gleamed with more excitement than the occasion seemed to warrant. 'And you're the friend. Am I right?'

'Yes, in a way. But . . . '

'Good. Then go and fetch him.'

'Now look, Mr Brown. It's past two o'clock in the morning and everyone's asleep.'

'They're not, I tell you. If they were I shouldn't be so restless. You're not asleep and I'm not asleep and Ledgrove isn't asleep, and there are a good many other people not asleep if all this clammering and hammering is anything to go by. Now you go and get my nephew and come straight back here. I've got to see him immediately. There's not a moment to lose.'

He must be mad, Dylis thought, or at least delirious. What in the world could he want to discuss with Inigo at this hour? Perhaps Theresa was right, after all, in not wanting him to be excited. Yet his eyes, although bright, did not look like those of a man whose mind was wandering. Whatever the reason for his strange request, perhaps it would be as well to humour him.

'I'll do what I can,' she said, and her heart contracted a little when she saw his expression of gratitude. Retrieving her candlestick and poker, for she had no way of knowing what lunatic she might meet on the way down, she left him and went on her mission as quickly as she could without danger of tripping over loose bits of carpet and odd stairs scattered about the passages. It was not until she had reached the floor below that it occurred to her she had no idea as to which room Inigo occupied. He might be anywhere either on this floor or the one above. She was certain now that neither he nor Theresa had mentioned it. She could hardly go stumbling into each of the rooms to find out, nor did she favour the course of promenading the passages with the cry, 'Calling Mr Brown.' Yet somebody ought to take over the responsibility. She did not see why, as a guest, she should be saddled with the whims of an invalid. It was really Theresa's job, but again, where was she? She had said that she might snatch an hour or so. It seemed as if she were prepared to snatch the whole night, and at Dylis's expense, into the bargain. She had not explained in which part of the house she was accustomed to sleep. Surely above, somewhere near her husband? But Mr Brown had not asked to see his wife, he wanted to see his nephew.

There remained Ledgrove. Now there was a man who ought to be able to help her. But finding him would entail a search of the whole house, and where would she begin? The bathrooms? She investigated those and found them empty. The kitchen? She made her way to the back staircase leading direct to the servants' quarters and peered down. All was dark below, but that was nothing to go by. Ledgrove might be in the kitchen with the door closed. Treading carefully, for this way was new to her, she went down and began her search, half expecting to see the man in the driver's cap still sitting at the table. But the room was silent and empty, the kitchener remained warm and the boiler hot, having been stoked for the night. The cigarette-ends had been removed, the washing-up cleared away, the whole place looking as if it belonged to a thoroughly well-ordered establishment.

She stood for a few minutes thinking, warming herself by the boiler. The present whereabouts of Ledgrove was a mystery which she did not feel disposed to probe further. She had done what she could, and had no intention of spending the rest of the night searching odd corners. Perhaps she had missed him on the way down, and he had since returned to Mr Brown's bedside, in which case she was certainly wasting her time. And this house was too full of rustling and creaking and rattling noises to encourage even the stoutest spirits towards any nocturnal adventure that was not strictly necessary.

Returning to the floor above, it came to her that if Ledgrove had not yet put in an appearance, it might be as well to try and get the restive invalid to sleep. She would then feel justified in getting back as quickly as possible to the solace of her own bed, and in the morning Inigo could take over his own responsibilities. She was beginning to feel strong resentment towards that young man for daring to sleep, and soundly she had no doubt, while she was left alone to work out circumstances which were really no concern of hers. True, she had earlier offered to take turn in sitting with Mr Brown, but only because Theresa had emphasised the seriousness of his illness. Now, it seemed, he could be left for long intervals to the attention of anyone who might be about.

As for Theresa . . . Dylis directed towards her hostess some very hard thoughts as she went back to her own room, and withstanding the temptation to leap straight into bed, opened her sample case and selected a bottle of Necktar. If she could relieve the pain of which Mr Brown complained, he might be persuaded to sleep the more easily. Abandoning the poker and its implications in favour of the role of ministering angel, she left her room once more with some misgiving, for it seemed to her that the atmosphere was getting colder, if that were possible.

Ledgrove had not returned, she found upon reaching the sanctuary of Mr Brown's apartment. The latter was lying back with eyes closed when she entered, but on hearing the rustle of her movements he sat upright with some force, and demanded:

'Have you got him? Where is he?'

She smiled, in spite of her rising irritability with the whole episode. Anyone would think that she carried Inigo round in her pocket, ready to be produced on request.

'I'm sorry, no,' she said. 'When I got downstairs I found I didn't know which room he has. Of course, I could have hammered on all the doors, but it would mean disturbing the whole house.'

Mr Brown appeared to be thinking about that, and encouraged by his quietness she moved round to the other side of the room, put the candlestick upon the floor and the bottle of oil on the table. In the additional light he looked a little less haggard, but his eyes and hands were still restless. He said, half to himself:

'No, that wouldn't do. That wouldn't do at all.'

She did not know whether he were referring to the disturbance of the house or to some other plan he had been contemplating. He added, looking up at her:

'And you didn't see Ledgrove? Nor anyone else?'

'Not a soul, I'm afraid. I went down as far as the kitchen, too.'

'Everything quiet, eh?'

'Apart from rattling doors and windows, yes.'

'Good.' The intensity of feeling he put into that one word caused her a vague feeling of discomfort. What had he imagined she might find downstairs, if anything? She glanced across at the closed bedroom door, shrouded in shadow, and almost wished that she had taken the precaution of locking it. No, that would not do. She must not allow herself to be infected by the morbid fancies of an invalid. It was, she supposed, the result of a disturbed sleep, the strangeness of her surroundings, and this wretched lamp and candlelight, the unreal quality of which gave her the feeling that she and the man sitting up in bed were completely cut off from the normal world. She suggested, trying to sound bright and easy:

'If you can tell me where I might find Mrs Brown, I could call her and perhaps she could sit with you for a while?'

'No, no. I don't want her disturbed if she's sleeping. Ledgrove will be back in a minute. He's bound to be back. Can't think what's keeping him.' He was silent again, and then suddenly reaching out a hand towards her, he asked, 'Young lady, will you promise me something?'

'Of course. What is it?'

64

'Bring my nephew to me first thing in the morning. First thing, you understand? No delays. Find him and tell him I must see him immediately. It will be better that way, better than getting him up in the night. You promise?'

'I promise,' she said. 'Now, how about you getting some sleep?'

'If only I could,' he said pathetically. 'If it weren't for this infernal pain in my neck ... Ledgrove knows what to do for it. Where is he?'

That gave Dylis her cue. With quiet confidence she sat down on the edge of his bed, and began to tell him, in her soothing, let-me-help-you voice, of the beneficial properties of Necktar, a sample bottle of which, by miraculous foresight, she happened to have beside her on the table. He listened at first in some surprise, then gradually, as she became more eloquent, the drawn anxiety of his heavy brows relaxed a little, and he regarded her with new interest. And when, with a competent gesture, she rolled up her sleeves and uncorked the bottle, preparatory to giving a practical demonstration, he submitted meekly, unwound himself from the dressing-gown beneath which he wore an old-fashioned night shirt, and allowed her to massage his neck with the precious oil, the smell of which, as she pointed out, was unusually fragrant to the nostrils. Indeed, he was forced to admit, when she had completed her ministrations, that her claims were not unjustified, for whatever the curative properties of the oil, her skill as a masseuse was considerable. He said, as he wrapped himself round again and leaned back upon the pillows,

'That's better. Yes, that certainly does feel better. Who did you say you are?'

She told him for the third time, and he nodded as if he had at last absorbed the information.

'How well do you know my nephew?'

'As well as I ever shall, probably. I only met him tonight.'

'Only tonight? I thought you said you were a friend of his? You did say you came here with him?' He looked at her reproachfully, and with just a touch of suspicion.

'So I did.' She recounted briefly her meeting with Inigo, and the circumstances of their arrival at Wintry Wold. He eyed her intently as he listened. He said then:

'Good enough. It's a pity you're not a man, though. I thought he'd bring a man.'

'That's what I thought you'd think, and I told him so, but it didn't make any difference.'

'No, it wouldn't. He always was an impulsive youngster. Friendly and impulsive. Like me. Easily taken in, too tolerant. We're anybody's fools until we find them out. Then we're slow to forgive. Sometimes we never get over it.'

He had closed his eyes, and spoke so softly she had to bend her head to catch the words. She took his hand and put a finger on the pulse. It was slow but regular. She wondered just how rational or otherwise his mental state might be. His fingers closed round hers, and he asked:

'You've met my wife? What do you think of her?'

'Well ...' It was a difficult question to answer. So far, her opinion of Mrs Brown had not reached any great height. On the other hand, if that enigmatical young woman had spent many nights like this, some of her peculiar ways might be excused. Caution and a little temporising seemed to be indicated. 'She's very beautiful, isn't she?'

'Is she?'

A strange remark, Dylis thought, coming from the man who had married her. He opened his eyes for a moment, and she saw in them such a terrible sadness that she was startled. But only for a moment, before he closed them again and appeared to be drifting off to sleep. She sat very still, hoping he had settled down for the night, but just as she thought he really was asleep, he murmured:

'All men are fools. I shall be glad when it's over.'

She felt inclined to endorse his sentiments, but remained silent, and the room became so quiet, apart from the moaning of the wind outside, it was almost oppressive. Only then did she become conscious of the old-fashioned clock upon the mantelpiece, solemnly ticking the minutes away. Its hands indicated 3.15 a.m. A whole hour of her sleep gone, an hour spent chasing ghosts and shadows. But she no longer felt restless or irritable. A strange sympathy seemed to flow between her and the man whose breathing was gradually developing into that of the contented sleeper.

She went on sitting there for another fifteen minutes, but there was still no sign of Ledgrove. Unless he were busy rifling the wine or whisky decanters, she could not imagine where he might be. She had not thought it necessary to carry her investigations as far as the drawing-room. Her own eyes were beginning to close with fatigue, she longed for the warmth and comfort of her bed.

She rose at last, gently disengaged her hand, and seeing that Mr Brown continued to sleep undisturbed, she turned the wick of the oil lamp low, picked up her candlestick and retreated to the door. He looked very peaceful now. He ought to sleep for hours. With a last reassuring look at him, she went out, closing the door quietly, and with some haste negotiated the stairs and regained the security of her room.

Her bed was cold, and the hot water bottle no longer radiated much in the way of comfort. So that it was some time before she recaptured any degree of relaxation, and when she did achieve the solace of sleep, it was peopled by haunting fantasy.

# Chapter V

The wind had dropped by the time Dylis awoke later in the morning. A ghostly light came filtering round the edges of the drawn curtains, and reaching out for her watch she discovered that it was just after eight o'clock. She viewed with much reluctance the prospect of rising, particularly in relation to the night's events, which she considered a good enough excuse to remain in bed for a while longer. Then remembering loyally that disturbances or no, Compton, Webber and Hughes must go on, she rose and put on her dressing-gown and slippers, drawing in her breath sharply at contact with the freezing atmosphere of her room.

With the cessation of the wind, the house had abandoned its groaning and creaking noises, but there were vague sounds denoting that she was not the only one astir. In the light of morning, these seemed natural enough, and with her thoughts now turned to her own affairs, an investigation of current weather conditions was imperative.

She walked to the window and drew back the curtains. Light flooded in, light of a blinding, bluish-whiteness, and the scene outside was awe-inspiring. Her room was in the rear of the house, and from her vantage place she looked down upon a vast undulating mass of snow, beneath which lawns and paths and flower beds had completely disappeared, and the smaller shrubs and outhouses were almost buried. An enormous barn, some fifteen feet high, rose darkly against the white background, the snow massed in a steep bank against its grey stone walls. And in the distance, dwarfing the surrounding heights, towered a hill of immense proportions, rugged and sombre, despite its snowy outline, looking like a threat to the comparatively small belt of cultivation about Wintry Wold. This Dylis took to be Deathleap Sear, and standing there in contemplation it occurred to her forcibly that the name was not without point. A wild and desolate spot, mocking the habitations of man.

Her hands being in imminent danger of freezing, she gathered up her toilet requisites and made all speed to the nearest bathroom. It had ceased snowing for the time being, that was something. She had better make plans for her departure before it started again. First she must get bathed and dressed, then find Inigo and tell him of his uncle's request. After which her own affairs could take precedence.

Enjoying the delightful heat of the water, she congratulated herself on having refrained from arousing her fellow inmates from their beds the previous night. For in the prosaic light of morning, Wintry Wold had lost much of its sinister aspect, and appeared merely as a large, shabby old house, very much neglected. The bathroom, she observed, was not over-clean. A good scouring would do it the world of good. But she had other and better things to tackle than the cleaning of bathrooms. The memory of her poor old car left out in the cold all night worried her not a little. Still, she was only one of many. Local garages would probably find themselves inundated with anxious travellers, as soon as they opened their doors this morning.

She felt refreshed and at ease with herself as she left the shelter of the bathroom to make a rapid return journey. But round the first bend in the passage she encountered Inigo, who came racing up the main stairs, fully-dressed and with a ready smile at sight of her. He said:

'Hallo. I was just coming to see if you were awake and wanting tea or anything. Our autocratic servants have never heard of room service. Was the water hot for your bath? I had one earlier, in fact I was bathed and shaved by seven-thirty. Did you sleep well?'

'If you'll give me time to get my mind functioning I'll tell you,' Dylis said. 'I should certainly like some tea, the water was excellent for my bath, and I did *not* sleep well. Did you?'

'Perfectly, thanks. What was wrong with you?'

'Before we go any farther, *where* did you sleep last night?'

'Same room as I used to have, just at the top of the back staircase. I switched my things over, with Theresa's permission. I like it there. Why?'

'Only that in the night, or rather early this morning, I was charging about the house trying to find you.'

He burst out laughing.

'That's the nicest thing anyone's said to me for a long time. Why didn't you stand and shout? I'd have come like a shot.'

'Don't be an idiot,' she said, suddenly annoyed with him again. He looked so fresh and pleased with himself. 'Do try and be serious for a moment. The fact is . . . '

She had glimpsed Theresa descending the stairs, and instinctively paused, sensing that a description of her nocturnal adventures might not meet with the approval of her hostess. Inigo turned and looked up, and they both stared in consternation. For Theresa, clad in a long black velvet housecoat with a jacket to match, was clutching the balustrade as if for support

70

and dabbing at her eyes with a black chiffon handkerchief. On the bottom stair she came to a halt and looked at them uncertainly. She was very pale, her long curls dishevelled and even more childish in their disarray. She appeared to take a grip on herself then, and said in a voice scarcely above a whisper.

'I'm sorry to tell you, Inigo, that your uncle is dead.'

There followed a silence, during which they continued to stare their incredulity. Dylis was the first to recover, partly because her mind refused to accept the bald statement. She burst out:

'But surely that's impossible? He was all right ... ' Again she paused, purely by instinct. But Theresa did not apparently notice anything unusual in her remark. She said indifferently:

'He was all right last night, I know. At least he seemed so. He was asking for food. But, of course, that's not always a good sign.'

Inigo was looking very distressed. From its former lightheadedness, his face had taken on an expression of deep anxiety, an expression that reminded Dylis of his uncle. He asked:

'But how on earth did it happen? I know he was pretty bad, but surely people don't just die off like that?'

Theresa dabbed at her eyes again, a gesture which Dylis viewed with a certain suspicion, for her eyes, though moist, were not overflowing with tears.

'I don't know,' she said. 'I really don't know what to think. I sat up with him the first part of the night, after all, as I couldn't sleep, and when I went to bed Ledgrove took over. Warner was sleeping then, and looked so very peaceful, I thought there could be no harm in leaving him. And I was so tired, absolutely exhausted. Ledgrove had great difficulty in waking me. He came to my room about four o'clock this morning, or a little after, I think it was, and told me that the Master had passed away in his sleep. You can imagine my absolute horror. If only I'd been awake, I might have been able to do something. Or if not that, at least I should have been with him.'

Here she paused and swayed a little, and Inigo put out a hand to steady her, while Dylis asked:

'When did Ledgrove first notice he'd gone? Was he actually sitting with him when it happened?'

'No . . . no, I don't think he was. My mind is so confused I can't think clearly, but I believe Ledgrove said he left my husband's room for a while, as he was sleeping, and when he returned . . . ' She broke down again, and Dylis, vastly uncomfortable, tried to force her doubts to the back of her mind. But they would keep crowding back, and she felt bound to enquire:

'Where is he now? Ledgrove, I mean.'

'He's gone to fetch the doctor. He started before it was light. Oh, I know it wasn't a sensible thing to do. I told him it would be much better to wait until the doctor arrived. He *said* he would come today, if he possibly could. But Ledgrove was so fond of his master and so very upset, and nothing would stop him.'

'And is that all Ledgrove had to say?' Dylis persisted.

'*Please*, not now, my dear. I don't feel I can discuss it further. This is a terrible blow to me.'

From her pocket she brought a small smelling-salts bottle and sniffed at it delicately. Inigo asked:

'May I go up?'

'But of course, dear. I'll go with you.'

He looked at Dylis enquiringly, but she shook her head. She had sustained too much of a shock to feel capable of staring into the dead face of Mr Brown, whom she had seen so recently alive. Furthermore, she wanted time to think. She watched them ascending the stairs, Theresa leaning on Inigo's arm, and heard her say:

72

'Of course, he was not a young man, and he was seriously weakened by illness. I suppose a collapse under such circumstances is not so surprising. But the doctor will be able to tell us more . . .'

Dylis returned to her room, and began absently to dress. There were several points in this unexpected event that both puzzled and disturbed her. Theresa had said that she sat up with her husband the first part of the night, and then went to bed. That must have been round about two o'clock, for it was past two when Dylis appeared upon the scene. But why, since he was supposed to be taking over, did Ledgrove not sit with the patient instead of shuffling about the house, and where was he all that time while she was with Mr Brown?

She knew, for a fact, that he had not returned before three thirty, because that was the time when she had left Mr Brown sleeping. Presumably, he had resumed his post of duty between then and four o'clock, at which time he discovered that the invalid was dead, and reported the matter to Theresa. But what had happened in that short interval to cause Mr Brown to die? For she was prepared to take an oath that he was merely sleeping, and that quite comfortably, when she last saw him. She had, of course, heard of people dying in their sleep. Perhaps it came as a shock merely because she had never before experienced anything of the kind. And although her acquaintance with him had been brief, she had liked Mr Brown. She realised that now, and a sense of depression weighed upon her at thought of his sudden departure from life. He had been so eager to see his nephew, and now Inigo was up there, but too late to do him any good.

She experienced a further pang over the reflection that it had been in her hands to find Inigo before his uncle died. Perhaps

73

the old man had realised he was going, hence the urgency of his request. No, that would not do. He must have expected to live until morning, because he had seemed quite content to wait until then, when she had assured him that everyone was asleep. Startled by the inferences of that conclusion, she slowed down the process of dressing while pondering upon it. But she was ready, and about to leave her room, when Inigo tapped on the door, and asked if he might speak to her.

'Of course, come in,' she said, and when he entered she saw that his depression matched her own. But she was glad to see him. She wanted to get some of these mysterious details sifted before they became an obsession with her. He said listlessly, 'Well, that's that. Theresa says she's sorry now she didn't let me see him last night, but how was she to know anything like this would happen? She was right, of course. She was only acting under doctor's orders. Still, I wish . . . '

'There's something I've got to tell you,' Dylis interrupted, 'I saw your uncle last night, and although I'm not a professional nurse, he looked surprisingly well to me.'

'Now what can you possibly mean by that?' He regarded her with a somewhat hurt expression, as if he had caught her playing a particularly stupid joke upon him.

'I'm just going to tell you,' she said, and did, and he flopped down upon the nearest chair and lit a cigarette, and listened with many a dubious shake of his head.

'Are you sure you didn't dream it?' he asked, when she ended her narrative with her return to bed at three-thirty. 'It all sounds a bit incredible to me.'

'I'm not in the habit of dreaming,' she retorted, yet trying to exercise patience. 'What's more, I can prove it. Your uncle said he had written you a letter. Well, you told me that. But he also said he had sent it to you at the Playfair Hotel, in London, and you didn't tell me that was where you had been staying, did you?'

He frowned, thought for a moment, and said: 'No, I didn't tell you that. All right, then. So you saw my uncle and he seemed reasonably well and asked to see me. But why in the middle of the night? He couldn't have felt too good to have asked anything so extraordinary. I know it's not your fault, but I do wish you'd managed to call me.'

'That's what I knew you'd say. It's what I've been saying myself, over and over again. But it's no use now. I couldn't possibly guess he was going to die so soon. He didn't look like a dying man. And when I told him I couldn't find you without arousing the whole house, he was quite reasonable about it, except that he made me promise to bring you to him first thing this morning.'

He looked up at her as a sudden thought struck him.

'But why didn't you mention any of this to Theresa?'

'That's a bit difficult to explain. For one thing, she might think I'd been interfering in her affairs, and somehow I felt I wanted to discuss it with you first. I did think of calling her last night, but your uncle said no, I mustn't disturb her. And that's one reason why I *don't* think he could have been feeling very ill.'

'But he was expecting Ledgrove,' Inigo said. 'He probably thought his valet could do as much for him as Theresa and he knew she needed her rest.'

'That's just another thing that doesn't make sense. Where was Ledgrove? Surely if your uncle was as ill as all that, he wouldn't have gone off and left him for over an hour. And I've just thought of something else. Your uncle didn't expect that any one should actually sit with him. All he said was that Ledgrove slept next door, and when he wanted him, he thumped.'

'His mind must have been wandering. Anyway, Ledgrove ought to be back presently, and then we can ask him exactly what did happen. Not that it makes any difference now.' Inigo rose, threw his cigarette end into the empty fireplace, walked to the window, and stared out. 'You know,' he continued, 'I don't like the idea of Ledgrove having gone off to the doctor alone. The roads must be terrible, if our drive is anything to go by, and he's getting on in years, Theresa tells me. He might easily slip and break his neck. Why the devil didn't they get me up, and I'd have gone?'

'Well, why?' Dylis asked.

'Eh? Oh, I don't know. Theresa said she was so upset she didn't know what she was doing. Ledgrove insisted on pushing off, with a lamp to light the way, and all she wanted was to be quiet for a while. I can understand that. I was fond of the old boy, too. D'you mind telling me again what he said to you? I'm being an awful nuisance, but apart from the shock of it, there's something about this business that worries me.'

'Me, too,' Dylis said. She walked up and down the room, partly to warm her rapidly chilling blood, and partly to aid concentration. Throwing back her mind, she tried to reiterate, as accurately as possible, every detail of her conversation with Mr Brown. But it was not an easy task. At the time, anything he had said had not struck her as being sufficiently important to memorise. The unaccountable movements of Ledgrove and her own desire to get back to bed had been foremost in her thoughts.

'This stuff you used to massage his neck,' Inigo said. 'It's all right, I suppose? He didn't get cold while you were doing it?'

Indignation welled up in Dylis then. She could bear any criticism of her own actions. Indeed, she and Inigo had already gone through the routine of self-accusation, supposition, attempted philosophy and ensuing depression common to people full of regret for something unforeseen. But that any aspersion should be cast upon a product of Compton, Webber and Hughes was unthinkable. She told him so, in an icy address lasting some five minutes, at the end of which he said, with the glimmer of a smile:

'Sorry, Dyl. I didn't mean to upset you. It was just the sort of thing anyone might say. You can't remember anything else?'

'No,' she said, not entirely mollified. 'Except that your uncle seemed particularly interested in whether you'd received his letter.'

'Oh, yes. I meant to tell you about that. It's one of the things that are worrying me. Here, I've got it on me.' He brought from an inside pocket a folded and somewhat crumpled sheet of paper, and handed it to her. 'Read it, there's nothing much to it.'

She opened it, inspected carefully the embossed address, and the date, and read:

'My dear boy ... Your father wrote to say that you are in London, and suggests I might like to see you. I need hardly say I shall be delighted. Please come as soon as you can, and *be sure to bring a friend*. Don't trouble to answer this note, and don't mention it to my wife. I want your visit to be a surprise to her. Affectionately ... Your Uncle Warner.'

The handwriting was of the wavering, illegible kind, and it took Dylis some time to decipher it. She looked up at length with a puzzled frown.

'It sounds mysterious to me. What am I supposed to make of it?'

'Oh, it's not *that* I'm worried about,' Inigo said, replacing the note in his pocket. 'Uncle always did have a weakness for intrigue. He would write you a letter about some quite ordinary thing, and finish up, "On no account tell Auntie Mabel". Or, "Please burn this as soon as you've read it". That kind of thing. What I'm worried about is this. Last night, I left my room, before turning in, to go along and clean my teeth and so on, and when I reached the bathroom I found I'd left my toothbrush behind. So back I went, and it seemed to me that someone had been in my room since I left it.'

'How could you tell?'

'Well, I'd changed into my pyjamas and dressing-gown and had left my suit folded over the back of a chair for the time being, and my shoes on the floor beside it. But when I got back, one of my shoes was in the middle of the room. It looked to me as if it had been kicked across the floor by someone who had fallen over it. That aroused my curiosity, and I took a good look round and found that the keys had fallen out of one of my pockets. I might have done that myself, but I don't think so, because there's no carpet in my room and I should have heard them. Then I found that some of my things were not in their right pockets. This letter, for instance, which I'd had on the left-hand side was on the right-hand side.'

'Was there anything missing?'

'Not as far as I could see, unless someone helped themselves to a few cigarettes or loose change. But just the same, it struck me as being very odd. I didn't think of mentioning it before. It's not the sort of thing you go around shouting in someone else's house.'

'I suppose not,' Dylis said thoughtfully. 'Who do you think it was? One of the servants?'

'Possibly. But it seems pretty pointless, to go prowling around someone's room without lifting anything. Unless, coming back suddenly, I disturbed them at it.'

'That certainly might account for the shoe being kicked around. And Vauxhall looks as if he'd rifle the parish poor-box, let alone anyone's pockets.' But she was not thinking of Vauxhall.

Her mind had absorbed and was holding on to a line in Mr Brown's letter . . . 'Don't mention it to my wife, I want your visit to be a surprise to her . . . ' And it had been a surprise, to judge by Theresa's consternation upon their arrival.

'I shouldn't mention it to Theresa,' she said, upon impulse. 'She's got enough on her mind as things are. And I think we'd also better postpone telling her about my seeing your uncle last night. It can't do any good just now, and when Ledgrove and the doctor turn up, we can sort it all out.'

'Perhaps you're right. I didn't tell her I'd had a letter from Uncle, since he asked me not to, although it seemed pretty silly to me.' He regarded her for a moment or two in silence, and added, 'I'm sorry everything's turned out so badly. I didn't realise, in bringing you here, that I was letting you in for such a dismal time.'

'Don't worry about it,' she hastened to reassure him. 'It was better than sitting on the edge of a precipice.' But privately she wondered. He said, taking her arm:

'You'd better come down and have some tea or coffee. You must be frozen.'

# Chapter VI

They found breakfast already laid in the small dining-room, and upon the sideboard tea and coffee and a few hot dishes, to which Charlie Best was liberally helping himself. It seemed that news of Mr Brown's death had already reached below, for when Dylis and Inigo entered, Best paused in his operations to wish them good morning, and to add:

'Awfully sorry to hear about your uncle, old man. Nasty blow, that.'

His face wore just that expression of sympathy becoming to a disinterested party, and his voice was appropriately hushed. Then having said his piece, he returned to his habitually cheerful air, sat down at the table and began an earnest attack upon his breakfast. Dylis could not blame him for that. Whoever died, others had to live, and despite her dejection of spirits, the intense cold had made her more than usually hungry.

The atmosphere in the drawing-room and its small annex was surprisingly warm, considering that the fires could not have long been lighted, but she was glad that she had taken the precaution of donning a green suede jacket over her suit. The curtains were drawn back from the french windows, revealing part of the

80

snowbound veranda outside, a chilling prospect to anyone with an empty stomach. Inigo pulled out a chair for her and moved to the sideboard.

'Tea or coffee?' he asked.

'Tea, please.'

'Can I get you anything else?'

'I'll have some of this cereal,' she said. 'That'll do for a start.'

He poured tea for her and coffee for himself, and brought the cups over to the table. He sat down and stared absently in front of him. Dylis, helping herself to cereal and tinned milk, observed with surprise that a bathrobe hung over each of the chairs that had been occupied the previous night by Mr Howe and his secretary. She asked:

'Did somebody sleep down here, or are they taking a bath on the veranda?'

Charlie Best permitted himself a chuckle, and drank his tea with obvious enjoyment.

'They belong to our friends, Messrs Howe and Raddle,' he said. 'They're out on the veranda now, doing their deep-breathing and other exercises.'

'No!' She turned her head in the direction of the window, but could see no sign of the hardy pair. Inigo said, 'Good God!' and went on drinking coffee. Charlie Best continued:

'You'd think that with the country looking like Siberia they'd give themselves a holiday. But no fear, they're going to show you degenerate folk what real Spartans are made of.'

'What about you?' Dylis asked. 'You're not exactly the embodiment of self-denial.'

'I don't count. Howe regards me simply as a medium of publicity. He told me once that journalists are one of the lowest forms of life that civilisation has begotten, but he admits that if I can write him up and splash him in one of the weeklies, it will be very useful. I will, too. But it may not be quite as flattering to him as he imagines. There are ways and ways of putting these things. Personally, I'd rather die tonight than live as he does.'

Dylis wished that he had not used that particular phrase. She was trying to forget, for the time being, that upstairs was a man whom she had expected to see alive this morning. She rose and helped herself to scrambled eggs and toast, and noticed that Inigo ate but vaguely. Just as she sat down again, the french windows were flung open, admitting the inevitable rush of icy air, and Mr Howe strode in, with his secretary close at heel, both clad solely in black shorts, white singlets and rubber-soled shoes. Mr Howe slammed to the window again, with all the contempt of a man of steel for the protesting occupants of the room.

'A good draught of air,' he said, 'will do no harm to this over-heated atmosphere. They must have kept the fires on all night to have achieved such a temperature. May I wish you all good morning? And it is a good morning, although I doubt whether anyone but Raddle and myself have yet made that discovery.' Each donned his bathrobe, and they sat down at opposite sides of the table. Mr Howe continued, 'Permit me to tender my sincere sympathy in your bereavement, Mr Brown. Your aunt told me the sad news. Raddle, you will please fetch the water.'

Inigo was regarding him with an expression between bewilderment and frank animosity. Then making an effort towards politeness, he thanked the sympathiser, and looked away. Dylis rose to procure fresh tea, and refilled Inigo's coffee cup at the same time. She dare not trust herself to speak. Raddle had also risen obediently, and was on his way out, presumably to the kitchen. She stared after him and back again at Mr Howe as she resumed her place at the table. Neither of them was possessed of an ideal masculine physique. In shorts they looked highly improbable, and were not much better in bathrobes. Mr Howe's face had turned purplish-mauve from the keenness of the cold, but the point did not appear to worry him. He rubbed his thin hands together with an air of sublime content, and reached for a piece of dry toast. Inspecting it critically, he remarked:

'Only the whole wheat can give to bread the sustenance necessary to a high standard of health. This white rubbish is so much poison to the system, but one must eat something.'

Whereupon he proceeded to do so, without the addition of butter or marmalade. Charlie Best said:

'Excuse me, I'm going to have a smoke next door,' and rose quickly and went into the other room. Dylis suspected that he was near to choking. Mr Raddle came back with a glass jug filled with water, and two glasses, which he placed upon the table. Mr Howe dispensed the healthful liquid, and handed a glass to his subordinate in silence. They drank. Cold shivers ran down Dylis's spine at sight of it. She finished her scrambled eggs and avoided looking their way again, until Mr Howe said, turning to Inigo:

'Yes, Mr Brown, I was indeed concerned to hear of your uncle's sudden death. He was, I believe, a comparatively young man.'

'Compared to whom?' Inigo asked.

'Well . . . er, compared to myself, for example. I shall be sixty-eight on my next birthday. Yet I feel vigorous, fit, full of energy. Your uncle, on the other hand, had only just turned sixty, your aunt tells me. Death at such an early age is not only unnecessary, it is inexcusable. Had he lived a healthy, outdoor life, I have no doubt at all that not only would he be alive today, but would have enjoyed a ripe old age, still in possession of all his faculties.'

Inigo, who had been eyeing him stonily for the past few minutes, leaped to his feet. He burst out:

'The man's dead, so for God's sake leave him alone! If he liked to live in a hothouse and pour whisky over his porridge, it's no damned business of yours. And as a family, we reserve the right to die when we please!' He turned to Dylis, and added in a more moderate tone, 'If you've finished, Dyl, let's go and join Charlie.'

'I'm ready,' she said, and followed him into the drawing-room, avoiding the petrified gaze of Mr Howe and Mr Raddle. Those two were beginning to make her feel hysterical. They found Charlie Best seated in the most comfortable chair, enjoying a cigarette. He said in an undertone:

'Thanks, old boy. I've been wanting to say something like that for the last twenty-four hours.'

Inigo shrugged his shoulders and offered Dylis a cigarette, and the three of them sat and smoked in silence, until Theresa appeared, still in her black housecoat, but with her hair arranged and her face freshly powdered. It occurred to Dylis to wonder at her so very appropriate choice of black for her morning ensemble. Was it by accident that she had reached for the black housecoat when Ledgrove had announced his master's death?

Or had she donned it later, with due regard to the air of sadness it gave her? It was a trifle early to rush into mourning. Most men would not notice a detail like that, only the general aspect of it. Evidently she had struck the right note with Inigo, for he rose to get her a chair, and said in a voice full of sympathy:

'Aren't you going to have any breakfast, Theresa?'

'Oh, no, dear, thank you. I couldn't *eat*.' She made the process sound vaguely obscene.

'A cigarette, then?'

She accepted one, and sank back in her chair, sighing wearily. She was still very pale, but Dylis knew something of the art of make-up. She wished she did not have such uncharitable thoughts, that she could accept Theresa for what she appeared to be, as Inigo did. But that brittleness, that insistence upon dramatic effect and predominance of her personality, in any circumstances, were things difficult to ignore. Even before seating herself, Theresa had cast a surreptitious glance at her reflection in the mirror over the mantelpiece, and another into the one on the wall opposite. The sorrowing widow. The woman left all alone. Yet it was not all pose. The slight unsteadiness of her hand as she put the cigarette to her lips looked genuine enough. Perhaps she really had been shocked by her husband's death, but could not resist exaggerating the role in which she found herself.

The men of the party watched her in silent sympathy, until she roused herself sufficiently to ask:

'Have any of you made plans? About your cars, and transport and that sort of thing, I mean?'

'I'm sticking around,' Inigo said. 'You'll want someone on the spot to give you a hand, won't you?'

'So sweet of you, dear. Of course, I don't want my troubles to come between you and ... '

'I'd intended to stay for a few days, in any case.'

Charlie Best said, 'I don't want to trespass on your kindness any longer than is necessary, Mrs Brown. Particularly at a time like this. We intended to get away as early as possible this morning, but I went out and took a look round before breakfast, and believe me, the prospect of immediate transport looks pretty dim. Unless, of course, that break-down gang manages to get through.'

'By the way,' Inigo put in, 'what happened to that van-man, the one who was waiting for his mate?'

'He's still here,' Theresa said. 'Having breakfast in the kitchen, I believe. I told Vauxhall to find him a room last night, when the other one didn't come back. I can't think what has happened. It's all very trying. But I did get him to move the van. Such a silly place to have left it.'

'I'd better get my car stowed away somewhere, if there's room,' Inigo suggested.

'Of course. You left it in front of the house, didn't you? There's an empty garage you can have. We've three garages and only two cars . . .' She broke off and put a hand over her eyes. Dylis said:

'I'd better do something about mine, too. I really ought to be pushing off soon.'

She was trying to be severely practical. It had been kind of Inigo to ask her to stay the night, and apart from a few minor inconveniences, it had been better than sitting in the car. But business was business, and she could not afford to winter in the wilds of Yorkshire indefinitely. It seemed that Theresa shared her opinion, for she said:

'Of course, we don't want to lose you, Dylis, but if you've business to attend to, naturally you'll be anxious to get away as soon as possible.'

'That's all very well,' Inigo said. 'But her car is stuck in a most awkward spot, and even if the roads were clear, she'd need help in getting it off safely. I'll see if I can start mine and make the nearest garage.' But he did not sound very enthusiastic about it. Mr Howe and his secretary entered just then and joined the edge of the group about the fire. Inigo went on, 'I wish I knew what has happened to Ledgrove. I don't like to think of him trudging all that way in the snow. Anything might happen.'

'You could call in at the doctor's and find out,' Theresa said. 'If you don't meet them on the way. Dr Thornton lives just outside Cudge. It's the big grey house. I expect you know it, but anyone will point it out to you if you don't. I'm trying not to worry too much about Ledgrove. He should be all right.'

'And why shouldn't he be?' Mr Howe demanded. 'Fresh winter winds and a little snow never did anyone any harm.'

Inigo glanced up with some annoyance, and asked:

'Have you ever tried walking along a road that isn't a road under several feet of snow for a good many miles, Mr Howe?'

'Are you seriously asking *me* that question, young man? I'll have you know that in my time I've walked and climbed with the best of them. But I am proud to say that my finest mountaineering feats have been accomplished alone.'

'And you never had a mishap?'

'Misadventure, Mr Brown, is liable to overtake the most hardy, upon occasion. But a strong, healthy body need suffer no harm as a result. I remember very clearly spending a whole night on a narrow ledge high up in the Swiss Alpine region, and when the rescue party arrived in the morning, I may say I was none the worse for my experience. Indeed, it was not twenty four hours later that the same heights were again the background for my solitary figure, climbing up into infinite space.'

Which announcement was received by noises of approval from Mr Raddle, and silence from the rest of the company. Dylis and Charlie Best were frankly bored, and Theresa momentarily surprised out of her despondency. Inigo said at last:

'A very interesting story, Mr Howe, but in my own experience solitary climbing is considered too dangerous to be encouraged, and in the Swiss Alpine region rescue parties don't go searching for lone climbers when they get lost. Having broken the unwritten rule they have to look after themselves.'

'Are you suggesting, Mr Brown, that I am a liar?'

'Not necessarily, Mr Howe. But you do seem to have a vivid imagination and a flair for the dramatic.'

'In that case . . . Raddle, you will please attend me to my room.

We have work to accomplish.' At the door he turned for a parting shot at degenerate youth. 'If there is no possibility of moving my car within the next few hours, we shall commence to walk home.'

'Hey, just a minute,' Charlie Best said. 'I'm not letting myself in for that, Mr Howe. I'm sufficiently interested in your theories to write about them, but I'm not aiming to get any first-hand experience.'

'Just as you please, Mr Best. If Mrs Brown has no objection, you can stay here until such time as the car can be moved, when you can drive on to my home, charging all expenses to me. I will give you a map of the route, but if you do not overtake us, you should have no difficulty in finding Higher Uplands. It is known for miles. There is not another house like it in England.'

'That doesn't surprise me,' Best said, as Mr Howe made his exit. 'I'm beginning to wish I hadn't started on this lark. I shouldn't wonder if I finish up with pneumonia. The things we journalists suffer for the sake of our art. And then people think we get an easy living.'

Theresa said to Inigo, with some reproach:

'You shouldn't have spoken to him like that, my dear. After all, the man is a guest.'

'I'm sorry. I didn't mean to fly at him. But the fellow's getting on my nerves. Why doesn't he keep his views to himself? I thought he was harmless enough at first, but now I suspect he's a liar and a charlatan, and I wish I'd never brought him here.'

'It was your idea,' Theresa said. 'Personally, I admire his spirit. And if he wants to walk home, he should be encouraged, not ridiculed.'

It seemed to Dylis that she was still very anxious to be rid of them all. Even Inigo was not beyond criticism. She wondered if Theresa would have done anything to dissuade him, had he said he was leaving that day. But perhaps she should make allowances for Theresa's nervous condition. After all, it was not her business, and in similar circumstances she would not be overkeen on entertaining visitors. Inigo said, rising:

'Well, I'll get out and see what I can do with the car.'

Best offered to help, and Dylis said she would go, too. Mr Howe was right, up to a point. The room did seem uncommonly warm. She would be glad to get some air. Inconsequently, she thought of his supposition that the fires must have been kept in all night. If that were so, could it be possible that Ledgrove had been in the drawing-room all the time she had been searching for him? She had descended to the kitchen by the back staircase and had returned the same way, so she would not have been able to see the light, had there been one in the drawing-room. But why should a conscientious valet, as Ledgrove was supposed to be, sit comfortably by the fire downstairs, while his dying employer knocked for him in vain? She wished she could control her thoughts, so that they would not keep returning to the subject.

'I shall go up to my room and try to rest a little,' Theresa said. 'But I'll send Vauxhall out to give you all the help he can, and he'll show you the empty garage.'

Inigo thanked her, suggested that she should take a sedative to ensure a few hours' sleep, and added:

'What's happened to Mr Carpenter? I haven't seen him this morning.'

'I thought I would leave him undisturbed. He's had so many sleepless nights lately, poor man. And I've no wish to pass on the bad news before it is necessary. It will be a terrible shock to him. He and Warner spent so many happy evenings together.'

She looked very sad and very lonely as she went up the main staircase ahead of them and disappeared into a room situated a few yards along to the right. Charlie Best was accommodated in an apartment almost opposite to the bathrooms. If only, Dylis thought wistfully, she had known just where they all were last night. Best said, when they emerged later dressed suitably for the outside world:

'I bet I know what's wrong with old Carpenter. He hit the bottle once too often. I never saw a worse soak. Sleepless nights my foot! I should say his only trouble is trying to keep awake. Not that I've seen him trying very hard.'

'If they get many winters like this up here,' Dylis said, 'it's not surprising. I'm beginning to see why drinking vodka is an old Russian custom.'

The snow, they found upon investigation, was even deeper than they had imagined. Stepping out from the shelter of the front porch was like plunging into an icy ocean. Furthermore, large flakes were beginning to fall again, in desultory fashion, but the heavy greyness of the horizon promised greater things to come.

Vauxhall joined them, a thick muffler filling the space between overcoat and chin, his hat pulled well down over his eyes. Seen thus in the morning light, he was even less prepossessing, but his manner had undergone a distinct change. Though far from deferential his attitude was one of extreme politeness, and his willingness to help almost embarrassing. This was, perhaps, his method of showing respect to the dead, although last night Dylis could have sworn that he had no respect for anyone. He appeared, also, to have amazing reserves of energy, for it was largely due to his efforts that between them the three men managed to shift the car from its sunken position on the snow-covered flower bed, to the comparative firmness of the equally snow-covered area in front of the house.

90

But when it came to moving it farther, even Vauxhall had to confess himself beaten. For the engine was cold and refused to respond to any kind of treatment, neither did the trio pushing from the rear achieve much in the way of results.

'We'll have to get some of this snow cleared away,' Inigo said. 'How did that fellow manage to move his van?'

'He did it last night,' Vauxhall said. 'Me and Ridley helped. It wasn't so bad, then.'

'I suppose I ought to have done something about it last night, too. But I didn't realise we were in for such a storm. Still, it can't be helped.'

They stood breathing heavily and wiping sweat from their foreheads, for their exertions had been great. Then they began to tramp round and about the immovable monster, frowning, debating, shaking their heads, and Dylis could not help smiling a little, as she always did when witnessing the earnest struggles of men versus machinery.

'I think,' she said suddenly, 'that help is on the way. Unless they're in need of it themselves.'

They all straightened up and looked in the direction she indicated, and saw two men emerging slowly from the tree-fringed drive.

'More trouble, like as not,' Vauxhall observed gloomily. 'This dump attracts it like a magnet!'

# Chapter VII

Dylis, watching the two men approach, was surprised to see that neither of them was Ledgrove. One was tall, and of somewhat nondescript appearance, dressed in a heavy tweed overcoat, a trilby hat and carrying a small suitcase. The other was shorter, broad, and though also muffled up to the chin, he wore no hat and his curly brown hair looked wild and uncombed. He walked with a slight limp and his companion had hold of his arm. Vauxhall said, in a gruff tone evidently meant to be confidential:

'That's the customer that went to get help. Don't think much of what they've sent, I must say.'

'Which one?' Inigo asked.

'One that's lost his hat.'

He had hardly said it before the gentleman thus described hailed him with a shout.

'Watcher, matey! Better late than never, as they say. You wouldn't be 'avin' a spot of trouble, would you?'

He was grinning widely as they reached the group about the car. He had a lively face, good looking in a rather crude way, and exuded health and good spirits. The face of the other man, considerably older, looked pale and desperately tired in comparison, particularly about the eyes. Observing himself to be the main centre of interest, he submitted:

'I just came up to see if I could phone for help. My car's stuck up on the road and I had to kip down in it for the night. But I overtook this gentleman, on the way, and he tells me you haven't a telephone. Is that right?'

'Quite right,' Inigo said. 'I'm very sorry, but there it is. As a matter of fact, there are several people here in the same trouble, and we've been expecting help from the garage at Cudge. But it's a long time coming, unless . . . '

He looked enquiringly at the other man, who continued to grin, evidently deriving immense enjoyment from the situation.

'Should be 'ere any minute, guv'nor,' he said. 'Fact is, I didn't get there meself. I started out all right, but it was gettin' dark, and I slipped with me foot under me, like. Fair turned me up, it did, it was that painful. So I says to meself, Bob, I says, that's me name, Bob Snell, Bob, I says, you'll never do it. So with that I sees a light a bit off the road and I makes for it, and it turns out to be a farm. So up I goes and knocks, and they says come on in, nice and friendly, so in I goes and stops, and I don't 'ave to be asked twice. And when we gets up this mornin', you could 'ave knocked me down to see the snow all piled up, and no chance of gettin' out except by diggin'. Bein' in an 'ollow made it worse, see? So the farmer, 'e looks at me and I looks at 'im, and 'e says, Bob, 'e says, We was nice and friendly by then . . . '

His narrative went on for some time, and from it they gathered that he and the farmer, having called for all male help available, and armed themselves with the necessary tools, finally tunnelled their way out, after which the farmer, who had urgent business to transact in Cudge, which he proposed to reach by means of horse and cart, offered to pass word to the garage that help would be appreciated at Wintry Wold.

'So I come on 'ere to tell me mate, see, so 'e wouldn't be gettin' stewed up. Then this gentleman comes along be'ind, out of nowhere, you might say, you could 'ave knocked me down . . . '

Here Inigo felt bound to interrupt, lest the suggestion to knock him down might be taken literally by one of the group about the car. For the snow was falling in earnest now, and their tempers, already worn thin, were becoming more frayed every moment. And there was no point in continuing, beneath the impact of the wind that had again arisen, a discussion which would be more profitably carried on inside. This idea being carried unanimously, they abandoned the car, and made for the rear of the house in a straggling line, and entered the kitchen, to find the indefatigable Ridley already preparing lunch over a glowing kitchen range, and seated at the table the man in the driver's cap. It was a particular point of interest to Dylis that he should still be wearing it, also that before him were again laid the newspaper, a half-empty bottle of beer, a glass and a pile of cigarette ends in an ashtray.

Upon seeing this sphinx-like personage, Bob Snell emitted many ejaculations of pleasure, shook him by the hand, swore that he had never expected to see him again, and proceeded upon an enlargement of his adventures, not in the least put out that his hearer listened with a marked lack of interest. Indeed, the only time the latter opened his mouth to speak was when he remarked:

'Thought you'd gone and drowned your ruddy self.'

Vauxhall gave them a look of serious displeasure, and stamped out of the kitchen. Charlie Best said:

'I suppose there's no doubt about these Cudge people getting here? I mean, is this farmer likely to slip on the way or lose his memory?'

'Quite likely, I should think,' Inigo agreed wearily. 'In fact, I can't understand a farmer starting out with a horse and cart in weather like this. The best thing I can suggest is to get over there myself. But first we'll all have a drink, because we need and deserve one. I expect you feel the same?'

He glanced at the man with the suitcase, who smiled.

'I could certainly do with one,' he admitted. 'But it seems a bit thick, descending on you like this.'

Inigo politely waved the matter aside, but Dylis, ever conscious of Theresa whether or not she were present, wondered what their hostess would think about it. She was not long left in doubt. Bob Snell, who had sat down on the edge of the table and helped himself to a friendly glass of beer, had just interruped his discourse to say:

'Don't mind about me, Guv'nor. Me and matey'll be all right 'ere,' when the door opened and Theresa entered. She was still very pale, her hair a little untidy, and the shadows about her eyes looked genuine. She asked in a strained voice:

'*Please*, what *is* going on?'

Inigo, Best and Snell all started to tell her at the same time, from which confusion Snell's voice emerged an easy winner. She listened in silence, her hand upon the door-knob, a frown drawing her fine brows together. She was not looking at any of them, but was staring directly at the man with the suitcase, and from her expression Dylis gathered that his presence was not a source of pleasure to her. For once, Dylis could see her point of view. It must be disquieting, to have people piling up on the doorstep at this rate, with no deliveries of fresh food in sight, the weather showing no sign of improvement, and the death of her husband, with all its complications, still in the foreground. The man, sensing her inimical look, turned and said, with the respect usually paid to her:

'So sorry to butt in like this. I understand you've been having quite a bit of trouble round here, and no wonder, with the roads in such a mess. I thought if I could just hang around until I can get help . . . My name's Ashley, by the way.'

His remark called for general, if somewhat vague introductions, and Inigo repeated his suggestion of immediate refreshment. Bob Snell said, waving his glass of beer:

'That's right, Guv'nor. Nothin' like a drop of tiddley'; and burst into loud laughter. Theresa's frown deepened. She said frigidly:

'I must ask you to be a little more restrained. There has been a death in the house.'

If she had said that Death was standing at his elbow, her words could not have been more effective. Instantly the man's face underwent a change. His eyes opened very wide indeed, and his expression suggested the solemnity of funereal rites. He muttered:

'Very sorry, Ma'am. Very sorry, I'm sure. Didn't mean no offence.'

A flicker of interest had entered Mr Ashley's tired eyes. It seemed to Dylis that death must be the one thing that had the power to bring him to life. He, too, offered his sympathy, but made no enquiry as to the identity of the deceased. Theresa turned away, and there was a general move in the direction of the drawing-room. Inigo asked:

'Couldn't you sleep, Theresa?'

'Only for a few minutes, dear. Then I woke up and heard a lot of noise down here, and wondered what had happened. I'm so on edge . . . '

'Why don't you try again? You ought to get some rest, you know.'

'Perhaps I will presently. But I must give Ridley instructions about lunch. We've plenty of stores, thank heaven, but he'll want to know how many will be here.'

She paused and looked as if she were going to faint, and Inigo put a steadying arm about her, and insisted that she should return to her room immediately. The others had already gone ahead to the drawing-room, but Dylis lingered, and as the only female member of the party, felt bound to offer her assistance. Inigo said:

'That's the idea. You take her upstairs and see that she goes to bed, Dyl, and I'll look after everything down here. I'll cook lunch myself if necessary. But we shan't be bothering much about what we eat, as long as we get something.'

'So sweet of you,' Theresa murmured, and allowed Dylis to take her by the arm and assist her up the staircase. Her room proved to be large and very beautiful, furnished and decorated in a style rather more up-to-date than the rest of the house. The curtains were partially drawn, and a fire burning in the extensive grate threw out a cheerful glow. Vauxhall, Theresa said, had insisted upon lighting a fire for her, although she had told him not to bother. He was being so helpful.

She climbed into bed, took three aspirins with a little water, thanked Dylis for her help, and lay back upon her pillows. A quiet, sombre scene, the widow seeking temporary respite from her sorrow. But why, Dylis wondered, passing the open wardrobe, was a man's dark-blue suit thrown carelessly in below a hanging row of feminine garments? An old one belonging to Mr Brown, perhaps. But it did not look old, and it was an odd place to put it, anyway. Mechanically she closed the wardrobe door and glancing across at Theresa, saw that her eyes were closed. Making an effort to dismiss from her mind this young woman and her troublesome affairs, Dylis left her and went below to join the others.

They were sitting round the fireplace in the drawing-room: Inigo, Mr Ashley and Charlie Best, with cigarettes and glasses of whisky in their hands, three men in amiable debate upon the subject of cars. They looked up as she entered, and Inigo said, drawing forward a chair for her:

'You've got competition, Dyl. Mr Ashley is also on the road.'

'Really?' She took the chair and accepted a glass of sherry. She felt very tired and ill-disposed towards polite conversation. She was glad that her fellow traveller also looked as if he were suffering from extreme fatigue and was not, moreover, of that breezy, energetic personality sometimes encountered in commercial hotels.

'Positively. So perhaps you'd like to swap stories while I go and investigate the lunch situation. Although there's not much fear of Ridley walking out on a day like this, it's just possible he might go on strike if someone doesn't say a friendly word to him.' He finished his drink and added: 'We've decided to wait until after lunch, before tackling the transport problem. By then the garage people may have turned up. I don't think so, but we may as well give them the chance. Is Theresa tucked up all right?'

'She was when I left her.'

'Good.' He rose and went to the door, and Charlie Best sauntered after him, saying:

'I'll just nip up and see if old Howe is going to take his grass on toast with us.'

'He'll have to dig it himself then,' Inigo said, with some rancour.

Dylis glanced at the other man when they had gone. He was

98

leaning back in the chair that almost faced hers, his eyes half closed. He really did look very tired. Becoming aware of her scrutiny, he roused himself to say:

'I feel very much the uninvited guest, Miss Hughes. I know a traveller should be used to mixing in anywhere, and I don't mind in a hotel, where I'm paying my way. But you can't help feeling a bit awkward, landing up at a private house where someone's just died. It was one of the family, I suppose?'

'Mr Warner Brown, Mrs Brown's husband.'

'And this young fellow Brown, who's he?'

'Her nephew. By marriage, of course.'

'I see. It's confusing, meeting such a lot of people all at once. You don't like to be rude and keep asking who they are, on the other hand I don't want to put my foot in it, especially as Mrs Brown is so upset. I thought at first she must be the young fellow's wife.' He paused for a few minutes, offered her a cigarette, and went on: 'There's been a lot of sickness and death about here lately, they tell me, with the winter coming in suddenly like this. In my opinion, people ought to wrap up warmer. And I don't say that just because I sell gentlemen's underwear. It doesn't make any difference to me whether they buy silks or woollens, but it's the woollens I recommend this time of the year.'

Thrown thus into the company of a fellow spirit, Dylis felt moved to enumerate her own best-selling antidotes against winter chills, and they embarked upon a comfortable interchange of comments. At the end of fifteen minutes, they had mutually concluded that everyone, in the first place, should wrap up warmly against the cold, but if, despite all such precautions, sickness still descended upon them, then Compton, Webber and Hughes were the people to supply the remedy.

'This Mr Brown,' Ashley said. 'He went suddenly, I take it?'

'Very suddenly. During the early hours of this morning.'

'Must have been pretty bad. The doctor was with him, I suppose?'

'No. He had been here earlier in the day, that was yesterday, and Mrs Brown was expecting him again today. The valet went off this morning to notify him, but he hasn't returned yet.'

'Poor woman. I wish I hadn't had to intrude. She's got enough on her hands with all these people staying here.'

He looked so uneasy about it that she felt quite sorry for him, and hastened to say:

'Well, the rest of us aren't exactly invited. Young Mr Brown dropped in to see his uncle, which of course was all right, but he found me stuck on the road and brought me along with him. And the others just automatically followed. You can hardly drive a hundred yards on the roads just now without running into trouble.'

'That chap who was helping with the car when we came up, not the journalist chap, the other one. Is he in the same boat, too?'

'No, that was Vauxhall, the butler,' Dylis said, and her companion became silent. Vauxhall had that effect upon most people, and in this instance she was glad of it. She did not mind talking shop with a fellow traveller, but had no wish to be reminded of the late Mr Brown. But presently Mr Ashley continued:

'D'you know this part of the country well?'

'No, this is my first visit.'

'And the last, I should think. Times like this it seems to me that we Londoners would do well to stick to our native city.'

'I'm not a Londoner. My people live in Worcester.'

'Well, you look and talk like one. It becomes a habit, if you live there long enough. Compton, Webber and Hughes, Ludgate Circus. Am I right?'

'You are,' she said, somewhat gratified at his identification.

'I can always tell, within a little, where people come from. It's a knack I've taught myself. Very useful sometimes. Now this Mr Brown, the young one, I wouldn't say he came from London. His clothes look sort of foreign, but he doesn't speak with an accent. Would he live in these parts, by any chance?'

'You're wrong,' Dylis said. 'He lives in Switzerland. He's only over here on a business trip.'

'I was right about his clothes. Those Continental tailors ...' He shook his head, as if the thought of them increased his sense of fatigue. His own clothes, Dylis considered, were not so much to shout about. He was not exactly shabby, but his suit had a woe-begone appearance as if, like himself, it were very tired. The result, probably, of a night spent within the confines of a car. Still, it seemed to her not in the best of taste to criticise the clothes of one's host. But then the manners of everyone at Wintry Wold left much to be desired, including her own. She might not criticise her host, but could it be anything but bad manners to regard with suspicion every movement of her hostess? Perhaps there was something in the atmosphere of the house itself that brought out these latent hostilities.

Charlie Best came in just then and announced that he had not seen Mr Howe, but his secretary was in the kitchen preparing a trayload of dry biscuits, cheese and water, which they proposed to consume upstairs, where the air was much fresher than down below.

'It certainly is,' Dylis agreed. 'The air in my room this morning was like blocks of ice.'

'Mr Howe?' Ashley echoed, further wrinkling his already furrowed brow. 'I haven't met him, have I?'

'You've been spared that pleasure,' Best said, with undisguised

101

relish. 'Mr Howe and his secretary live on dried grass, cods' heads and draughts of pure water, tucked away in an eagle's nest up in the mountains. We were on our way to the said nest when, thank God, the car broke down. This house is not exactly civilisation *par excellence*, but it's Paradise compared to what I, as a hard-working journalist, am about to go through in the interests of my readers.'

'It wouldn't be Mr Humphrey Howe, would it?' Ashley asked. 'The one who believes in nature first, last and always?'

'It would and it is. Why, d'you know him?'

'I've never met him. But I've read his books, all of 'em. He got me once, when I was younger and more impressionable. I took one of his courses, the one where you rig up a sort of trapeze in the open air and fling yourself to and fro, day in, day out. I lived on a diet, too.'

'What happened?' Dylis asked, with some interest. She could not imagine him doing anything of the kind. He looked too settled, too stable, ever to have been a Howe disciple. But there was a ring of truth in his voice when he said:

'I got bronchitis. And my wife never stopped chipping me about it.'

It seemed to Dylis the first occasion she had found to indulge in laughter for a very long time. Even so, their mirth was subdued, and they stopped short when the door opened again, half expecting to see Theresa's frowning countenance. But it was only Inigo, come to tell them that lunch was nearly ready.

'We've turned it into a curry,' he said. 'There wasn't very much meat left over, but there's plenty of spaghetti, so you can fill yourselves up with that.'

'How do you like being assistant chef to Ridley?' Dylis asked.

'Oh, we get on all right. We'd have done better still if friend Raddle had not been dithering about out there. By the hungry way he was eyeing our concoction, I should say that man's just longing for a square meal.'

'He won't get that while old Howe is around,' Best said. 'I bet there isn't enough food in his hide-out to feed a hungry mouse. To which he would doubtless reply that in his house there is no mouse problem.'

They were reaching the end of another round of drinks when Vauxhall slid back the communicating door and thrust in his head from the dining-room. Attaining new heights of politeness, he began:

'If the lady and gentlemen are ready . . . ' and paused, looking round at them in some embarrassment. Then with a hasty reversion to his usual style, he added, 'The hash is up.'

# Chapter VIII

By mid-afternoon, Inigo was again agitating for action. They had sat over lunch rather longer than they had intended, or even realised. For Mr Ashley, despite his tired aspect, had a fund of amusing anecdotes and a way of telling them that held attention. And smoking cigarettes and drinking coffee in front of a blazing fire was a pleasant occupation, particularly in relation to the blinding snowstorm that had once more taken possession of the outside world. Dylis, lying back in her chair, taking little part in the conversation, felt inclined to indulge the sense of drowsiness that had descended upon her. But presently Theresa joined them, dressed for the afternoon in a frock of soft blue wool with an angora jacket to match, her hair arranged, her face refreshed from sleep.

'You're looking better,' Inigo said. 'We've been taking it easy, too, but it's time I got to work on that car.' He roused himself, yawned, and glancing towards the window added, 'I'd better work fast, by the look of the weather.'

'It's terrible,' Theresa said. 'I do hope nothing's happened to poor Ledgrove. But perhaps he's staying over at Cudge until the doctor can get away.'

She had left the door open, and round it now sidled Bob Snell. He stood just inside the room, surveying them with his customary grin.

"'Ope I'm not intrudin',' he said. 'But them garage chaps are taking their time, so I thought if anyone 'ere 'as got a car that *works*, we might clear up some of this 'ere snow and get it goin'. The way I look at it, see, if we don't do somethin' pretty quick, we're goin' to be stuck 'ere until Christmas. My matey, 'e wouldn't care, but the chap we works for, 'e wouldn't like it at all.'

'I was just about to say the same thing,' Inigo said. 'If we all give a hand it shouldn't take long. Can you spare Vauxhall and Ridley, Theresa?'

'But of course, dear. I'd be glad to help myself but I haven't the strength, particularly just now. But I don't mind getting tea, and dinner if necessary . . . '

'I'll take over the kitchen,' Dylis said. 'You'd better rest, Theresa.'

'So thoughtful of you, my dear, but really I can't just be *idle*. And I want to help all I can. Let me see, there will be Vauxhall and Ridley, you, Inigo, Mr Best, Mr Ashley, Mr Snell, and . . . and the other one . . . '

'Jackson,' Snell volunteered, 'if you was referrin' to me mate. 'E's not me reg'lar mate, Jackson ain't, and between you and me I'll be glad to get on me way and say good riddance to 'im soon as I can. Fair gives me the 'ump, 'e does. Not a laugh, not a smile. You'd think 'e was at a funeral.' Theresa looked at him sharply, and he added, 'Sorry, lady, no offence meant, I'm sure.'

'How's your foot?' Inigo asked, tactfully leading the conversation to a safer topic. 'You strained it, didn't you?'

'Oh, that. It's all right now, Guv'nor. Nothin' to make a fuss about anyway. Just let me get back into me old box of tricks, that's all *I'm* worryin' about.'

There was a general move, but Ashley, remaining in his chair, asked:

'Don't you think we might give the break-down gang a while longer? They've had plenty of work to do on the roads, I daresay.'

'Break-down nothin',' Bob Snell said. 'They've broken down theirselves, most likely, or that old farmer lost himself. What I says is . . .'

'If you don't feel up to it, old man,' Best cut in, 'why don't you rest up, and take a turn later. Sitting up in a car all night isn't funny.'

'Thanks, I think I will.' Ashley yawned, and leaned back in his chair, the one which Mr Carpenter had occupied the night before. That chair, Dylis thought, must have specially soporific qualities. Best went on:

'I'll look in and see if I can dig out old Howe, and Raddle. This ought to be just their lark, working in the lovely fresh winter breezes.'

But it transpired that Mr Howe was in the throes of dictation and refused to be disturbed, even for the health-giving occupation of snow clearance. Grumbling at what he described as nothing short of chicanery, Charlie Best returned from his mission, and the party set out to accomplish its self-imposed task. Theresa, who had gone out to instruct her servants, came back to the drawing-room and sank down upon a silk-covered pouffe by the fire, and an oppressive silence settled upon the house, broken only by the sound of the elements, and the noises that filtered in from where the men were working with spades and shovels.

'I don't envy them,' Dylis said at last. 'It's terribly cold out there, enough to freeze you to death.'

She was looking at Theresa, upon whose face the flickering firelight was reflected, and she was amazed to see there a fleeting expression of horror. She had not credited the girl with so much feeling. It was gone in a moment, leaving only a brooding look as she said:

'Please don't talk about it. Every time I think of Ledgrove, I blame myself for having let him go. But you can't always be resonsible for another person's actions, can you?'

Dylis, who had temporarily forgotten Ledgrove, was further surprised at the note of serious appeal behind the question. She said:

'Of course not. If anything happens to him, you can hardly be blamed for it.'

'I'm glad you think that.' She sighed and shook her head. Dylis offered her a cigarette, and thought as she did so that it was a novel situation to be sitting by the fire, comforting Theresa, of all people. Mr Ashley appeared to have gone to sleep. Dylis asked:

'What made him go on foot? I should have thought it would have been better to try and make it in one of the cars. You did say you had two?'

'He can't drive,' Theresa said, 'Oh, why don't people *ever* see what's best for them?'

'They don't know, until it's too late, I suppose.'

She seemed a different person to the one who had greeted them the night before. Much of her poise had gone, and there was a helpless look about the nervous movements of her hands. She still peered at herself occasionally in the nearest mirror, but now it was more of an enquiring, rather than a self-satisfied glance. Mr Ashley, coming to life with an obvious effort, remarked:

'It must be pretty lonely here in the usual way of things, Mrs Brown. Unless you did a lot of entertaining?'

'No, we never had many visitors. My husband did not care for company.'

'Shouldn't take to it much myself, I'm afraid. Give me a couple of pubs and a decent cinema, every time.'

'One gets used to it. And the surrounding country is lovely in the spring and summer.'

'All right if you're too old to do anything but make daisy chains. Personally, I prefer a bit of life, travel, getting around. What do you say, Miss Hughes?'

She had it in mind to say that he was being supremely tactless. Mr Brown had not been so very old, but old enough to make it sound like a direct implication. But of course, he was not to know that. Theresa saved her the trouble of replying by rising languidly and saying that she would go and see about tea.

'Why don't you sit down for a while?' Dylis suggested. 'There's no hurry, and we can get the tea together.'

'No, *please*. I would much rather be doing something. My mind won't let me rest.'

'I wonder if I might have a wash?' Ashley asked apologetically. 'I hate to trouble you, but being half-awake all night . . . '

'Of course. It was very discourteous of me not to think of it. I'll show you the way.'

'Don't bother, Mrs Brown. I can find my way all right. I'm used to getting about in strange places.'

'This is a particularly strange place,' she said, with a wan smile. 'People get lost all the time.'

Dylis remained sitting there, after they had gone, watching the shadows gradually take possession of the room, for the day had been unusually dark, and dusk was setting in early. But it was not the pleasant dusk often associated with winter evenings and the romance of firelight. It had a certain eerie quality, as if the shadow of Deathleap Scar were creeping slowly forward to engulf the house. The wind, the falling snowflakes, seemed part of a deliberate plot to hold prisoner the inmates of that house, and the silence within was unrestful, vastly disturbing.

Mr Ashley had been gone so long she began to think he must have lost his way in that labyrinth of passages upstairs. She recalled Theresa's remark, 'People get lost all the time'. Now what had she meant by that? Dylis pulled herself up sharply. This was sheer nonsense. Surely she was not developing into one of those nervous people who cannot be left alone for five minutes, and who read all kinds of things into the most ordinary remarks? Apparently she was, for when it occurred to her that the draught behind her back was due to someone having opened the door silently, she leaped to her feet and faced about almost with a single movement.

A man stood there, and the room had become so dark now she could not see his face, and for no sensible reason her heart was beating violently. Then he stepped farther into the room, and by the light of the fire she saw that it was Mr Carpenter. Even in that dim illumination he looked terrible, his eyes heavy lidded and half closed, his face drawn, his hands shaking.

'All alone, Miss Hughes?' he asked, and his harsh voice brought her back to a sense of reality. Annoyed with her brief attack of nervousness, the triteness of the question irritated her, and she was about to retort acidly. But she refrained, and merely said:

'Yes, the others have gone out digging.'

'How d'you mean, digging?' he asked sharply, and she reflected that his nerves were no better than hers. In fact, everyone in this house seemed just a little on edge, with the possible exception of the two vanmen and Charlie Best. Perhaps it was always like this just after someone had died.

'Shovelling away the snow,' she said. 'They want to get one

of the cars started, so that Mr Brown can drive to the nearest garage.'

'Oh.' He walked across and went into the dining-room, and returned with the whisky decanter and two glasses. He sat down in his usual chair and asked, 'Going to have a tot with me?'

'No, thank you. We shall be having tea soon. Don't you want any?'

'No, I hate it.'

'Well, you might like to eat something.'

'Food ? What would I want with food?'

'People do eat, occasionally.'

'Not me. Not unless I'm driven to.' He drank down half a glass of neat whisky, replenished the glass and put it on the table at his elbow. He stretched his shaking hands towards the fire and rubbed them slowly together. 'This house is like a morgue,' he complained.

She thought about that, and decided there was some truth in the statement. And if it had been true yesterday, it was doubly true today, since, there was now a dead man upstairs. She wondered if anyone had yet broken the news to Mr Carpenter, and risking a rebuff, remarked:

'It must have been a shock to you, Mr Brown dying so suddenly.'

'Shock?' He looked up at her for a moment and back at the fire. 'Oh, yes, a very bad shock. Very bad, very sad. Still, we've all got to die some time. This house is enough to kill anyone. There's only one thing to do when you're in a place like this.'

'What's that?'

'Get as tight as you can as often as you can, and never let the whisky out of your sight.' With closed eyes he tossed back his second measure, shuddered, and refilled the glass.

'Mr Carpenter,' she said firmly, 'that's not the real reason you drink so much, is it?'

'Eh? Drink so much? That's a damned silly thing to say. I don't drink nearly as much as I could.'

'Is it because of Mr Brown?'

He looked up at her again, a queer, sideways look, before returning attention to the bottle in his hand.

'Yes,' he said. 'Because of Mr Brown. That's the idea. Poor old Brown. Good old Brown. As decent a man as ever walked the earth.'

'I know,' she said absently.

'How d'you know? You never met him?'

And that, she thought, was as far as the discussion should go. She said, moving to the door:

'I think I'll go and help Theresa. Will you light the lamp?'

'No,' he said. 'I won't. I like sitting in the dark.'

She went out, without bothering to reply. She did not see why she should be the only one to observe conventions. If Mr Ashley came down now he could introduce himself, and spend an amusing interlude trying to get sense out of Mr Carpenter. She was becoming very tired of the whole business, and much as she liked Inigo, she wished they could have met under less trying circumstances. How pleasant now to be tucked away in a small but comfortable hotel, a good day's business behind her and looking forward to another tomorrow. If she spent much more time loitering around Wintry Wold, her trip would not be anywhere near the success she had planned and Compton would be frankly triumphant at the fulfilment of his prophecy, and dear old Webber would be very disappointed.

So absorbed was Dylis in her thoughts that she did not see Mr Ashley descending the stairs, although the lamps in the passage had been lighted, and was unaware of the proximity of anyone, until he overtook and spoke to her as she reached the door giving entrance to the kitchen. Then she started and turned, annoyed that her heart had again given a furious leap.

'I wish people wouldn't keep creeping about this house as if they were ghosts,' she said. 'Why can't you all tramp around like the butler does? It's so much more lively.'

He said, as they entered the kitchen:

'I'm sorry, I didn't mean to scare you. Who else has done it?'

'Mr Carpenter. He's in the drawing-room now.'

'Who is he?'

'A friend of the Browns.'

'What's that about Mr Carpenter?' Theresa asked, as she came in from the pantry. She was wearing, over her woollen outfit, a blue and white checked overall that made her look very young indeed.

'Only that he's in the drawing-room, sitting in the dark,' Dylis said. 'Can I help you, Theresa?'

'You can open a tin of sardines and some salmon, my dear. I'm going to make sandwiches. So much more sensible for big, hungry men. I'm not very good with tins, I've such delicate wrists. Poor Mr Carpenter. He was absolutely shattered when I told him. Did you want something, Mr Ashley?'

The latter was dressed in overcoat, hat and gloves and carried an electric torch. He said:

'I thought I'd go out and give them a hand. I feel better now, having had a wash.'

'Oh, good. You might tell them that tea will be ready in half an hour.'

'I will.' He went out, and Dylis, closing the door behind him, said:

'How would it be if we were to eat out here, Theresa? It's quite warm, and it'll save carting things in and out.'

'A very good idea. I shan't want anything myself, but if the rest of you don't mind ... '

'You ought to eat something,' Dylis said, busy with the tin-opener. 'You'll make yourself ill, if you don't.'

'I *couldn't*, my dear. Just now I feel as if I shall never eat again.'

Dylis thought that might be due to her having already finished a meal in private, if the crumbs adhering to the top part of her pinafore were anything to go by. Unless, of course, she had deliberately put them there to give added effect to her childish appearance.

# Chapter IX

Not only did they partake of tea in the kitchen, they also ate a light supper there. By the evening, they had cleared the whole length of the driveway and part of the road beyond, but as Inigo pointed out, it was then too late to attempt the journey to Cudge, since even if he reached there, it would be unreasonable to expect either the garage hands or the doctor to turn out at such an hour. Particularly the doctor, since for him it would not be a question of saving life, but merely to sign a confirmation of death. There was, therefore, only one sensible course open, to eat the meal that Dylis had prepared, snatch some well-earned sleep, and make an early start in the first light of morning.

Theresa, after preparing tea, had retired to the drawing-room to sit with Mr, Carpenter, consigning the kitchen to the care of Dylis, who, nothing loth to see her go, was at the same time somewhat surprised to find herself in the position of head cook and bottle washer. She was still further surprised at the way the men, having put away their spades and shovels for the night, came in and settled down at the kitchen table so amicably. She supposed it was the result of working together in the common cause and in the teeth of a biting wind.

Vauxhall, finding his domestic duties temporarily taken off his hands, gave up attempting to be a butler and became almost convivial, amusing himself and the rest of the company by a demonstration of card tricks. Inigo was, for the most part, silent, likewise Ridley, and Jackson the vanman, but Bob Snell kept up a running commentary on anything and everything, affording Dylis and Charlie Best much entertainment. Ashley, though still looking very tired, joined in the conversation from time to time. No one had mentioned it, but Dylis supposed that he would be found a room for the night.

The only jarring note occurred when Mr Howe, with his secretary in tow, appeared in the doorway of the kitchen, to enquire, somewhat acidly, what plans, if any, had been made for the evening meal. To which Inigo replied, as politely as he could, that they had already partaken of theirs, but if Mr Howe cared to help himself to anything he fancied, he was very welcome. He had, until then, completely forgotten the existence of Mr Howe, but refrained from saying so.

'Thank you,' Mr Howe said. 'We have no wish to disturb you, and our wants being simple, we will satisfy them later when the atmosphere is free from cigarette smoke. I have spoken with Mrs Brown, and have agreed to accept her kind invitation of another night's lodging, after which Raddle and I will start upon our trek for home.'

'We've cleared the driveway,' Inigo said. 'And providing it doesn't snow a few more feet in the night, we might be able to get something done to your car tomorrow.'

'I thank you again. But I have no intention of waiting upon the vagaries of local mechanics. We shall walk, and Mr Best can bring the car along later.'

'I'll give you a lift if I catch you up on the way,' Best said magnanimously. 'Have a sardine sandwich, Mr Howe, or a nice bit of tunny fish on toast. It's the nearest we've got to a cod's head.'

'Young man, if I thought there might be a hint of levity in your remarks, I should no longer require your services. Come, Raddle.'

'Lord save us!' Best exclaimed, as the door closed behind them. 'If I get through without murdering that old devil I'll deserve to be buried in the Abbey. And if I do ever get that car of his started and catch them up on the road, I'll go right ahead and pass them at sixty.'

'You'll be lucky if you pass them at five on that road,' Inigo said.

Bob Snell chuckled. 'Proper old death's 'ead, ain't 'e? "Our wants is simple," says 'e. I bet they are an' all. I bet 'e tucks in a nice bit when you ain't lookin'. That kind always does. Take advice from a fool, Guv'nor, and lock up all the grub when 'e's on the loose.'

But Inigo was not in the mood to take advice from anyone, neither did he care whether Mr Howe stripped the pantry bare or went supperless to bed. He was, he said, going to get some sleep, without further delay, and Vauxhall having agreed to stow Mr Snell and his mate away somewhere for the night, he and Dylis, along with Ashley and Best, left the warmth of the kitchen to plunge into the icy temperature beyond.

Ashley, too, said he would be grateful to get a decent night's rest, and Dylis was so tired she stayed only to say a brief good night to everyone, before making a dash for the stairs and her own room. Only one more night, she thought, as she lit the candles and looked about her with a sense of deep depression. Providing she did not meanwhile die of cold, this time tomorrow

116

she would be tucked up in a cosy hotel. Well, if not cosy, at least an hotel, full of normal people doing normal things. There came a tap at the door, and opening it cautiously, she saw Inigo standing there, the inevitable oil lamp in hand. She was beginning to hate the smell of burning oil. He said:

'I just wanted to thank you for getting supper, and for everything else you've done. I'm sorry it's all so flat. I invited you here as a guest, and turned you into a general help.'

'Don't worry about it,' she said. 'I expect it's good for me. I can see now why Vauxhall and Ridley don't smile sweetly upon visitors. That kitchen range . . . !'

'I know. They're not a bad couple of blokes, are they, when you get to know them? This place ought to be brought up to date. But I expect Theresa will sell it.' He paused and they both looked and felt uncomfortable. He went on quickly, 'I forgot all about your hot water bottle. Shall I get it now? I'll only take a couple of ticks.'

'No, don't bother. I just want to tuck up in bed and forget all about everything.'

'Me, too.' They were talking in hushed voices, which was unnecessary, because no one had yet retired. And since Mr Brown was dead, it could not make any difference to him whether they whispered or shouted. She had always regarded these outward gestures of respect to the dead as somewhat affected, until this moment. Now she discovered that it was an instinct, rather than a convention. Inigo said, with a fleeting smile:

'I'll leave you to it, then. But if you can't sleep, knock me up and I'll tell you a fairy story.'

'I shall sleep,' Dylis said. 'Just let anyone try to stop me.'

But something was stopping her, she discovered later, when she had been lying beneath her pile of blankets for a very long time, and getting more wide awake every moment. It was not the cold. She had been warmed by her sojourn in the kitchen, and had not noticed the absence of a hot water bottle tonight. It was not the wind, for it had dropped again, giving place to a lull that was curiously unsoothing. She was still tired, but each time she closed her eyes they had a tendency to open of their own accord, and her mind felt clear and watchful. She had heard the rest of the household moving about, coming upstairs, talking, saying good night in subdued voices, the creaking of somebody's shoes as they went past her room, soft footsteps to and from the bathrooms, a man's cough. And eventually silence descended upon the house, a silence in which anyone should be able to sleep.

Suddenly she knew why she was lying awake. She was listening. Unconsciously she had been listening all the time, even after the house was quiet. Particularly after the house was quiet. She leaned out and reached for her watch, and saw that the hands pointed to 1.30 a.m. A nice time to be awake when everyone else was sleeping. And a nice wreck she would look in the morning, if she did not do something to counteract this ridiculous attack of insomnia.

She put the watch under her pillow, relaxed her whole body, and forced her eyes to close. When she looked at the watch again it indicated ten minutes past two. She was surprised and indignant at the depth of her relief. What had she been waiting for, then? Someone to shuffle along and pause outside her door, or the sound of thumping . . . ?

Her heart gave a furious leap as from the passage came a low, sharp cry, a gasping sound, followed by silence. Without even asking herself what she was going to do, she leaped out of bed, flung on dressing-gown and slippers, fumbled for and found the torch which tonight she had placed conveniently upon the bedside table. This time she was not going to be content with surmises. She was going to get to the bottom of it.

But if her strength of mind did her credit, it also served her a bad turn. In her eagerness to reach the door, she caught her foot in a few projecting strands of the threadbare rug, tripped, and fell headlong across the floor. Undaunted, she picked herself up, grabbed the torch which she had dropped in her confusion, made a dash for the door, wrenched it open and plunged out into the passage.

Her single beam of light did not go very far in the way of illumination, but sweeping it like a searchlight this way and that, she was in time to see the figure of a man, in dressing-gown and slippers, bent almost double, and groping with one hand against the wall towards the bend in the corridor. As the light from Dylis's torch reached him, he half turned his head, let out a low moaning sound and disappeared from view. Hot in pursuit, her enthusiasm again betrayed her. This time it was not the carpet, but something metallic that rolled between her feet, causing her for a split second to lose her balance. She recovered, stooped to investigate, and discovered it to be a small electric torch with a chromium case. Mechanically she picked it up and went on, moving with more caution. Around the bend, the passage was in darkness and deserted, all doors closed and not one with a light showing beneath. Carefully she walked on round another series of twists and turns, and reached the back staircase.

Here she leaned against the wall and considered the position. The man in the dressing-gown had been real enough. So had been the sound that brought her out of bed. But was it he who had cried out like that? And who was he, anyway? She had not been near enough to catch a glimpse of his face, or to see any part of him clearly, but she had the impression that he was elderly, or ill, or both, or . . . well, that cry had sounded as if someone were being stabbed in the back.

She looked over the banisters into the black well of the staircase. She looked up. Only Mr Brown was upstairs, and he was dead. At least, he was supposed to be dead. She realised suddenly that it is difficult to believe in the death of a person without clear evidence before the eyes. And she had not seen Mr Brown dead. She had only seen him alive, and that not so very long ago.

Without making any definite decision on the point, she began to walk slowly upstairs. She moved the switch of the torch she had picked up, and found that it was working. That and her own made two pleasing circles of light upon the stair-carpet. She would have given a lot to be able to flood the corridors and stairway with good, sane light, to send it searchingly into all corners and alcoves. But mere lack of light was not going to drive her cowering back into her room, just as she had something concrete in place of all the mysteries and suspicions of the last twenty-four hours.

She reached the landing of the next floor, but had some difficulty in finding her way, since previously she had approached via the main staircase. But this floor was not so very different from the one below, and in triumph presently she located the main stairway and the sharp bend to the right beyond which lay her objective. Yet around that bend she paused, for as on the previous night a dim light issued from beneath the door of Mr Brown's room and she had not expected that.

Her heart began to play strange tricks again, and she could not make up her mind whether to march boldly up to the door and open it, or if it would be more seemly to knock. But if Mr

Brown were dead, there could be no point in knocking on his door. Unless someone were in there with him. And while she stood hesitating, the issue was decided for her. There came a muffled sound from within, and she moved back quickly into one of those alcoves, the existence of which she had hitherto condemned.

The door opened, and momentarily she saw Mr Ashley, fully dressed, complete with overcoat, scarf and gloves, silhouetted against the subdued light of the interior. Then he stepped into the passage and closed the door, and they were alone in the darkness with only a few yards between them. She was almost certain that he could not have seen her, but just the same she pressed as close as possible to the cold wall, until he had switched on an electric torch, and made his way to the head of the staircase with a swiftness and silence admirable considering the house was strange to him.

She did not hear him descend, but creeping to a strategic position, she watched the bobbing light until it disappeared from view. She rubbed her hands together and found that they were damp, though cold. Without giving herself an opportunity to retreat, she moved quickly to Mr Brown's room. She did not knock. She opened the door and glanced round. It was just as she had seen it on the previous night, the oil lamp burning low on the bedside table, but now there was no fire in the grate and the room was bitterly cold. She closed the door and stepped across to the bed. It had been re-made, the banked up pillows removed, and a sheet drawn up over the face of the occupant. She hesitated. It seemed wrong to disturb him. But she must know, she must find out what was happening in this house. If he were dead, he would want her to find out. There was something he had wanted to tell Inigo.

Gently she drew back a corner of the sheet, and stood looking down upon the face of the man she had seen only once before. But now it was no longer fretful and anxious. It had a curiously mask-like look, remote in its pallor, and somehow, she felt, just a little reproachful. Unless she were being extraordinarily imaginative. She became aware that her eyes had a stinging sensation, and her breathing was difficult. She replaced the sheet and turned away.

A faint and familiar perfume had reached her nostrils, and glad to concentrate on anything that would turn her thoughts elsewhere, she made an effort to analyse it. Of course, it was the oil with which she had soothed away the pain in his neck. What had she done with the bottle? She frowned, trying to recall her actions, finding the memory blurred. She had not taken it back to her room. No, she had left it on the table. She went round to the other side of the bed and carefully inspected the medicine bottles and other items. The oil was not there, but the unpolished wood of the table had a fresh and pungently smelling stain of grease upon it, as if the bottle had been overturned. Someone must have upset it, and put it somewhere. Theresa, possibly. But if so, she must surely know that someone other than Ledgrove had been with her husband last night? Would she have guessed who that person was? Dylis tried hard to recollect, but could not be sure whether she had told Theresa the nature of her business. She rather thought not. In any case, it was more likely that Ledgrove had found the bottle. She searched everywhere, including the medicine chest, but could see no trace of it other than the stain upon the table.

It came to her then that this was leading nowhere. From starting out to investigate a cry in the corridor, she had closeted herself with a man who was past telling anything, and become involved in a search for something that did not matter much one way or the other. What did matter was that somewhere in the house was the man who had uttered that disturbing sound, and Mr Ashley, whose behaviour was extraordinary, to say the least. Unless he, too, had heard the sound, and had come up here from the same motives as herself. But why should he be wearing his overcoat, gloves and muffler? Surely it was not so cold in his room that he went to bed fully dressed?

She glanced again about the room, but could see nothing that might interest a stranger. Nothing appeared to have been disturbed. She had the uncanny feeling then that perhaps he and she were not the only ones who had visited Mr Brown that night. Someone had lighted the lamp. Alert now, she made a thorough search of all likely places of concealment, but drew a complete blank.

With stealth matching that of Mr Ashley, she left that ice-cold room, and turned her attention to those on either side. Ledgrove's room was just as she had seen it last night. So was the bathroom. Yet a new suspicion was beginning to invade the confusion of her thoughts. She must tell someone about this. If she kept it to herself any longer, she would begin to think she had gone crazy.

She had no difficulty in locating Inigo's room. It was very much isolated, set at an odd angle on the floor below near the back staircase. She had passed it on her way up. She might have awakened him then, had she thought about it. Well, she could not think of everything. She tapped softly on the door and waited. She tapped louder, and waited again. She bent down and called through the keyhole:

'Inigo! Are you there?'

Of course he must be there. Where else was he likely to be?

She was getting into the habit of saying the most insane things. It must be due to the lack of sleep. Yet she was startled when the door was flung violently open, and Inigo, in pyjamas and with bare feet, shot past her and began to dash madly up the corridor. She hissed after him:

'Inigo! What do you think you're doing?'

In the light of her two torches, he looked fantastic. At the sound of her voice, he swerved, turned and came slowly back, rubbing a hand over his face and blinking. He said sleepily, 'Is that you, Dyl? I was having a nightmare. I thought I was in a coffin, and someone was knocking nails into it.'

'That was me knocking on the door. I wanted to talk to you. But for heaven's sake go in and put something on. You'll catch pneumonia.'

'So will you,' he said. 'You're shaking with cold.'

'I'm not cold. I'm just upset.'

'Why, couldn't you sleep?' He had taken her advice and returned to his room, and she followed, closing the door. He lighted the candles that stood beside his bed, thrust his feet into slippers, and wrapped himself in a warm dressing-gown.

'No,' she said. 'What's more, I'm not the only person in this house suffering with insomnia.'

'No? Well, let's hear about it. But you mustn't catch cold. Every time I get out of bed in this room I feel I'm in cold storage. Have an eiderdown.'

He took it from the bed and wrapped it round her and she sat down in a wicker chair and accepted the cigarette he offered. By the number of ends piled up in the ashtray on the table, it appeared that he, too, had not been sleeping well. He still looked only half awake as he seated himself on the edge of the bed, and asked:

124

'What's the idea of the two torches? Have you been hunting ghosts again?'

'I found one of them on the floor of the passage outside my room.'

'What, a ghost?'

'No, a torch. This small one. Look, Inigo, I didn't come here knocking you up to try and make you laugh. It was about ten past two, and I hadn't been to sleep, and I heard a cry out in the passage . . . '

'What sort of cry?'

'Well, it was kind of sharp, not very loud, and broke off suddenly, rather as if someone had been stabbed in the back.'

'Did you ever know anyone who was stabbed in the back?'

'Of course not. But I've a certain amount of imagination.'

'That's the trouble, Dyl. You've a lot of imagination, and that's probably why you can't sleep.'

'But I *can* sleep,' she said, with some indignation. 'In an ordinary house I can outsleep anyone. But if you think I just sit up at night imagining things, then there's no point in discussing it further.'

'Now don't get belligerent,' he said. 'I didn't mean it like that. I just thought your nerves might be on edge, that's all.'

'I never had any nerves until I came here. Do you want to hear this story or not?'

'Yes, please. If people are crying out loud in the corridors, I suppose I should take an intelligent interest.'

Already she had forgiven him for his veiled scepticism. It did sound rather tall, put into so many words, and she was beginning to doubt her own common sense, until she came to the part about Mr Ashley; She recounted that with triumph. But she was disappointed when Inigo asked, regarding her in perplexity:

'Well, what am I supposed to do?'

'I should think that was obvious. You'd better see Ashley and ask him what he was doing up there.'

'But it was you who saw him. Why didn't *you* ask him?'

She found that difficult to answer. Sitting here in the dim candlelight, with Inigo watching her, puzzled and concerned, her nocturnal wanderings seemed ridiculous. And his concern, she felt, was entirely for herself, not in the least connected with anything that might be happening in the house. Impossible to explain the fear that had come over her when she had seen the light beneath Mr Brown's door, or the moment of panic that had caused her to hide in the shadows when she saw that door open, and Ashley emerge. She did not remember ever being afraid of anything before, and she was not going to admit it now, especially in face of Inigo's unhelpful attitude. She knew that in similar circumstances she might have taken the same view, but the knowledge did nothing to assuage her ruffled feelings. She began to be annoyed with him again. She said:

'It's not my house. If I'd asked him what he was doing, there was no reason why he shouldn't ask me the same thing.'

'That's just what I mean. Then you could have cleared it up nicely between you.'

'And left you to sleep in peace,' she said bitterly. 'But it still wouldn't have explained the man in the dressing-gown who dropped his torch, if it was his torch, nor the sound I heard, nor the light being on upstairs . . . '

'I can answer that one. Theresa told me she had left the lamp alight. She said it seemed so cold and dark up there. As for the man in the dressing-gown, there are plenty of people it might have been. Howe or his secretary, Charlie Best, one of the servants, they all sleep on this floor.'

'It didn't look like any of them.'

'But you said you weren't near enough to see clearly.'

'I wasn't. But he was stumbling along, all huddled up, groping his way by the wall. And on the floor was the torch he'd dropped, or someone had dropped, and why should he hurry off like that when I shone a light on him?'

'Perhaps he didn't like the idea of a woman seeing him in his dressing-gown. Some men are funny like that.'

'And a lot of them aren't,' Dylis retorted. 'Besides, he couldn't have known I was a woman, because I was behind the light. Do you mean to say you're just going to sit there and let people run about the house making noises, without doing anything about it?'

'What do you suggest? That I go and knock up everyone and ask them if they're all right?'

'Why not?'

'For one thing, they'd think I was crazy.'

'Not if it turned out that one of them wasn't all right.'

He stubbed out his cigarette-end, and sat staring ahead of him, his hands thrust into the pockets of his dressing-gown. She could have screamed at his placidity. And then she recalled something his uncle had said, something about he and Inigo being too tolerant, until they found people out. That was all very well in the ordinary way of things, but what was the use of sitting around being tolerant, and finding out too late? She was further exasperated when he said:

'Couldn't it have been Ashley? The one who cried out, I mean? He might have been having a nightmare, like me, and ... '

'The man I saw was wearing a dressing-gown,' she said. 'A dark one of some kind, while Ashley had on an overcoat, a scarf and gloves. You may think I'm graduating for the nuthouse, but nothing will convince me that he dashed back to his room and changed, before going upstairs. Why should he?'

'I don't know, I'm sure. I'll ask him tomorrow, if you insist upon it. Though I can't pretend I like it. I suppose, being in the hotel business, I'm used to people having funny ways. Back home, if guests wander about at night we don't take much notice.'

'This isn't an hotel, it's a house.'

'Yes, but it's not my house.'

'How do you know it isn't? Did Theresa say anything about a will?'

Ordinarily it would never have occurred to her to ask so blunt a question. But she was not feeling ordinary. She felt unreal, unnerved, and possessed of a longing to rouse Inigo to some kind of action. But she experienced a flicker of remorse when he turned melancholy eyes towards her.

'No,' he said. 'We haven't discussed anything like that. We've both been feeling too down to go into the material side of it. I naturally assumed that his estate, such as it is, has been left to her. Not that it matters. I wouldn't want any of it, and neither would my father.'

'But he was fond of you,' Dylis persisted. 'And he wanted specially to see you about something. He said so.'

'Suppose he did? Where is all this leading us now?'

'I'll tell you. It's been at the back of my mind all the time, and now it's come to the front. I don't think your uncle died naturally.'

'Eh?'

'I said I don't think he died naturally. In fact, I think he was murdered.'

Inigo did not move. He remained sitting there and staring at her, and with neither of them speaking the silence of the house crept in and enveloped them. Then mechanically he reached out for another cigarette and lighted it. He asked, between the first few inhalations:

'Is there anything you know that I don't, anything you haven't told me?'

'No, not as far as I can remember. I've nothing definite to go on, nothing that any reasonable person would regard as evidence. But I'm not feeling reasonable. Since this morning, or rather yesterday morning, I've had this idea and tried to argue it away, but it would keep coming back, until it's become a certainty.'

'But who would do a thing like that, assuming it were possible?'

'I told you I've nothing definite to go upon. But it seems to me that Theresa is not quite the little angel she would have you believe.'

'Theresa? But she's so small.' It occurred to both of them at the same time that it was her lack of physical strength he had queried, not her will to murder. He added hastily, 'It's preposterous, anyway. Why should she want to kill the old man?'

'I don't know. Unless he was going to alter his will in your favour.'

'But apart from this property and the other, it must have been such a small amount he had to leave.'

'If you read the newspapers, you ought to know that people commit murder for less than that.'

'He was a sick man. He probably wouldn't have lived so very much longer. And how would it be done? You've seen him tonight. He looked perfectly normal, didn't he?'

'How do I know? I haven't made a study of it. A doctor would be able to tell, I expect.'

'Exactly. And Theresa has sent for the doctor. So that rules *that* out.'

'Does it? Suppose Ledgrove didn't go for the doctor? We've only her word for it. And by the look of things, if he did start out he certainly didn't get there.'

'Well, if he didn't go, where is he?'

'Say I'm mad if you like, but I've a strong feeling he's somewhere in this house. It's big enough. And I've another feeling, though less strong, that it was Ledgrove I saw staggering about in the corridor.'

'You and your feelings,' he said, and got up and began to pace to and fro. 'I'm willing to believe that somebody's mad, and I'm not sure that it couldn't be me. This is worse than my nightmare. What makes you think it might have been Ledgrove careering about in a dressing-gown?'

'Because from what I saw of him the first night I was here, he's not exactly young and could look old in a poor light, and he stoops rather.'

'But why should he cry out?'

'I don't know. Unless someone was after him and attacked him in the dark. Or perhaps he's gone mad, or was mad all the time. He let out a very strange noise as he disappeared. And according to Theresa, it was he who found your uncle dead, although I left him alive only half an hour before.'

'But why ... ?' Inigo paused, and stood looking down at her in exasperation. 'Dylis, you're fantastic. I'm not going to listen to any more of this, not tonight. I'm going to take you straight back to your room and you're going to sleep. And we'll discuss it all tomorrow, if there's anything to discuss. First thing I shall drive over and get that doctor ... '

'And right beside you will be Dylis Hughes. So far I've played the lone wolf and got a kick out of it, but Wintry Wold has done something to my nervous system.'

'Right. You come along, too. I was going to suggest it anyway. We'll pick up the doctor and Ledgrove . . . '

'Providing he's there.'

'If he's not, no doubt it will mean he's gone into a drift or had some sort of accident, poor devil. In that case we'll have to search for him.'

'I should start with the house,' Dylis said.

'Before we follow up any of your theories, we'll see what the doctor has to say.'

'I know. And his decision will be final and legally binding. But don't be surprised if it all turns out differently to how you expect. What about Ashley?'

'I was coming to him. What shall I say? That you were hiding on the landing and consider that he was loitering there with felonious intent?'

'Say anything you like, or nothing at all,' She rose abruptly, flung the eiderdown upon the bed and walked to the door. 'But if you don't like hearing horror stories, you shouldn't invite people to wake you up in the night.'

'Just a minute,' he said, as she was on her way out. 'I'm coming along, too.'

'It's all right, thanks. I know my way. If ever Theresa wants to open this as a show place, I'll be glad to act as a guide.'

'You're being nasty,' he said, following her out into the passage. 'But I'm coming along to see fair play just the same. This fiend in a dressing-gown might take it into his head to whistle through his teeth or tweak your ear. You can't be sure.'

In injured silence she allowed him to accompany her back to her room, subduing the natural urge to point out to him the exact spot where she had found the torch and the corner where the disturber of rest had disappeared. She opened her door and thanked him coldly and was turning away, when he caught her nearest hand and held it for a moment between his own. He said:

'I'm sorry if you don't like me any more, Dyl, but I can't help being me.'

'Don't be absurd,' she said, and snatched her hand away. But she smiled a little after she had closed the door upon him, and it was only when she was preparing to get back into bed, that she was once more assailed by a sense of misgiving. Suppose they started making noises in the corridor again? Without asking herself specifically whom she meant by 'they', she hastily procured a chair and wedged it beneath the doorhandle, and upon it she placed a miscellaneous collection of toilet articles, all of which could be relied upon to make a fine clatter should anyone attempt to intrude upon her.

Somewhat ashamed of this action, for she had never done such a thing before, she blew out the candles, and then, upon impulse, went to the window, drew back the curtains and peered out. It was another dark night, dark and heavy with silence. She could not even make out the nearest objects in the grounds beyond. Impossible to believe that in a few hours it would be daylight. That, at least, would be a comfort. The whole character of the place seemed to change with the dawn.

She was moving away when her attention was caught and held by a pin-point of light that had suddenly appeared some way off to the left. It was bobbing up and down spasmodically, as if held by someone whose progress was anything but smooth. She watched for a while, fascinated. The snow would still be thick out there. They had only cleared it in front and along the driveway. Again she felt triumphant and inclined to rush straight back to Inigo. But caution stayed her. By the time she had aroused him from his bed, the light would, in all probability, have disappeared, and he would have no doubt then that she was suffering from hallucinations. Better to go down and investigate herself. Better still, on second thoughts, to ignore it and turn in to bed. She was tired enough, and why should she spend her nights trying to unravel mysteries which Inigo did not consider mysteries at all? She would not even bother to mention this one, since he was so little interested. The light had disappeared now. She let the curtain fall back into position, yawned, and felt her way to the bed. It was wonderful to get beneath the warmth of the blankets, to pile the quilt on top and to stretch out in comfort. Let them all yell their heads off. She was not going to turn out again. She fell asleep.

# Chapter X

'Are you awake, Dylis?' Through slowly returning consciousness, she heard Inigo's voice, his light rapping upon the door of her room, and made an effort to rouse herself. Daylight streamed round the curtains, and her glance, moving sleepily in the direction of the door, encountered the chair she had placed against it and the pile of articles on top. It looked incongruous in the light of morning. She laughed, and called out:

'All right, half a minute.'

She was becoming adept at leaping out of bed and donning dressing-gown and slippers with the minimum of delay, but it took her a few minutes longer to draw back the curtains and to remove the obstacles before opening the door.

'I put up the barricade after you'd gone last night,' she said, smiling at his surprised face as he stood there, fully dressed, balancing a small breakfast tray on one hand. 'Now laugh your head off.'

'I'm not in the mood,' he said, entering and closing the door with his free hand. 'I've lost my sense of humour. Tell me you heard people galloping up and down the corridor wailing like banshees and I'll believe you.'

He did look worried, she thought, standing with his back to the door, still balancing the tray in absent-minded fashion as if he had forgotten its existence. She asked:

'Is that for me? Or did you bring it up just to prove that even Wintry Wold can provide room service?'

'I'm sorry. Of course it's for you. I thought you might like some tea and toast as it's gone ten o'clock.'

'Has it really? I'd no idea. Why did you let me sleep so late?'

'It seemed a pity to wake you earlier, after you'd had such a rotten night.'

He carried the tray round and put it on the table, and she wrapped a blanket about her for extra warmth and comfort, sat down on the bed and poured herself a cup of tea. He lit a cigarette and began to walk restlessly about the room. He said:

'I've been trying to get the car to go.'

'Really? I thought we were going to make that journey together?'

'So we are, or rather, we were. But I thought there was no harm in getting the engine warmed up a bit by the time you were ready. But it's no use. It's out of action.'

'I expect it's cold,' she said, enjoying her tea, and wishing that the men of her acquaintance would not take such a morbid interest in engines. By Inigo's harrowed face one might have thought that somebody else had died.

'Of course it's cold. But that's not the point. Someone's been messing about with it.'

'Well, you were all having a go at it yesterday. I don't wonder it's packed up.'

'With the interior,' he said. 'Someone has deliberately jammed the works. Now I know something about cars ...'

'But I don't, so it's no good trying to explain it to me. As far

135

as I'm concerned, a car either goes or it doesn't and if it doesn't, then I leave it in the hands of a mechanic until it does. Can't you borrow one of Theresa's?'

'I thought of that, too. In fact, I found it difficult to believe, at first, that someone had really been having a go at mine. I couldn't imagine anyone being so damned silly. So I came in and asked Theresa, and she said I could borrow one of hers, the smaller one, the other hadn't been so good the last time she took it out. She gave me her keys and I went over to the garages, and I found that *both* her cars had also been tampered with. By the time I'd stamped around and shouted a bit, Bob Snell came out and had a look at his van, and that isn't working, either.'

'But it was out of order when they brought it in, wasn't it? I thought that was what all the fuss was about.'

'Not really. The brakes were faulty, and they didn't care to risk it on these roads. Snell is in a proper wax about it. I didn't know he had it in him. You should have heard his language, or perhaps it's as well that you didn't. But what he isn't going to do when he catches up with whoever did it . . . And what *I'm* going to do . . . '

'What are you going to do?' Dylis interrupted, hiding her interest behind an air of indifference. Perhaps it was petty of her, she thought, but she was glad that something definite had occurred to arouse Inigo from his usual calm. And he had been so trying over her own misgivings. Now he could see for himself that something was wrong somewhere. As a further stimulus, she added, 'You're absolutely certain about all this? I mean, you're not getting imaginative, like me, for instance?'

He sat down on the nearest chair, and said, with a half smile:

'I'm sorry about last night, Dyl. I ought to have realised you've too much sense to go knocking on doors just for the fun of it. But let's forget about that for the moment. If you'll just let me explain the basic principles on which a car runs, or doesn't run, I'll soon convince you . . . '

'You've convinced me already,' she said hastily. 'I believe every word you say. All the cars are out of action. And for what it's worth, my opinion is that it was done round about the time I came back to bed.' She had finished her breakfast, and walked across to the windows and looked out. She saw, with approval, that the sun was trying to pierce the enveloping clouds above Deathleap Scar. The temperature seemed to have risen, too, unless it was the effect of the tea Inigo had brought her. To the left of the house was grouped a series of outbuildings, still thickly embedded in snow. She asked, nodding in that direction, 'Is that where the garages are?'

'Yes, but you can't see them from here. We've cleared a way round to them from the front of the house, and Best and I have stowed my car under cover. I'm going to work on it presently. Why?'

'Because last night, after you left me, I saw a light bobbing about over there, like someone carrying a torch.'

'You did? Why didn't you tell me?' Then seeing her look of derision, he added, 'All right, I know. You thought I'd say it was someone calling the cat in. But who *would* do a thing like that?'

'Well, to my knowledge there were four people wandering about last night. Me, but I couldn't have done it because I wouldn't know how. You, but I take it you're not in the habit of playing practical jokes on yourself. The man in the dressing-gown, but he was hardly dressed for the part, and Mr Ashley, who was wearing an overcoat.'

'Have a cigarette,' Inigo said, as if the problem of Mr Ashley and his overcoat called for a stimulant. He went on presently, 'It does look like it, doesn't it? But why?'

'I can't answer that. But if you remember, he's the only one who hasn't seemed keen on getting away from this place, apart from you and the rest of the people who've reason to stay here. He put off helping you clear the snow as long as possible, and only went out about half an hour before tea yesterday. He said he was tired . . . '

'Did you say half an hour before tea?'

'Yes, about that. Theresa and I were in the kitchen and he said he was going out to give you a hand. So she said to tell you that tea would be in half an hour. And later you all came in together.'

'But he only joined us in time to tell us that tea was ready, and we all flung down our tools and came in straight away. What was he doing all that time, I wonder?'

'Perhaps he was doing the job then.'

'Hardly. Someone might have seen him.'

'And you said these garages were locked, didn't you?'

'So they were. I hadn't thought of that. Theresa herself gave me the keys.'

'Has anyone else got a key?'

'That I'll have to find out.'

'But if anyone has another key, it would only be one of the servants, wouldn't it? Or . . . well, your uncle might have had one, or his valet. It looks as if we're coming back to my first argument.'

'What was that?'

'It seems as if someone doesn't want you to go and get that doctor.'

'Oh, Lord!' he said, and rubbed his chin in perplexity. 'This is all so damnably unpleasant. And it isn't very logical, either. Sooner or later the doctor is bound to arrive on a routine visit.'

'Suppose she just cooked up that story about the doctor, and there never really was one?'

'Then there'd have to be an inquest, and that would be even

more awkward if . . . you know what I mean. Besides, we know that the old man did have a doctor when he had pneumonia, because later he wrote to my father and said so.'

'And then he was supposed to have a relapse. Oh, I don't know what to think. It's all so confusing. I thought I liked Mr Ashley at first, but now I'm not at all sure.'

'He does seem a nice enough sort of bloke. That's why last night, when you were so worked up, I just couldn't see stepping up to him and saying, "Mr Ashley, will you please keep to your room," or whatever you thought I should say.'

Dylis sighed. She said, 'You'd think the devil himself was a nice sort of bloke, providing he kept his horns hidden. Odd things have been happening here all the time that you just wouldn't see. There was that person creeping about in your room while your back was turned, the first night we arrived.'

'There was nothing much I could do about that,' Inigo said. 'And it can't have anything to do with Ashley, even if he did mess up my car. He wasn't here that night.'

'No, that's true.' Thoughtfully she turned again to stare out of the window. The snow looked curiously blue-tinted and sparkling. She was beginning to hate the sight of it. 'What about Mr Carpenter?' she asked. 'He's a pretty strange person.'

'He looks like just an ordinary dipso to me.'

'And Charlie? You don't think it might be his idea of humour?'

'I shouldn't think so. He seems a decent sort of bloke . . .' He broke off when she started to laugh, and amended, 'I don't imagine he'd run around messing up cars, anyway. He seemed as fed up about it as anyone.'

'They all seem to be something or other, but are they? Mr Ashley seems to be a commercial traveller, but I'm getting the idea that he's nothing of the kind.'

'Why not? He looks like one, doesn't he?'

'That's just it. He looks too much like one.'

'Now, Dylis, do be reasonable. The night before last you were raving against Vauxhall because he doesn't look like what he's supposed to be, and now you've turned against Ashley because he does.'

'I told you before, I'm not feeling reasonable. But we won't go into that again. The question is, what are we going to do?'

'My first instinct was to go round threatening everyone with physical violence. But having cooled down a bit, I'm going to get that car fixed if it's the last thing I do. In the first place, it's not my car, and secondly, I want to get hold of that doctor.'

'You'd better make sure, then, that fixing the car is *not* the last thing you do. I think I'll come down as soon as I'm dressed to see that no one knocks you on the head while you're fiddling about.'

'Would you mind?' he asked, on his way to the door.

'Not a bit. I might be tempted to do it myself one of these days. But just now I don't want any more complications. Is the water hot this morning?'

'The water here is always hot. We've our own methods of keeping the pipes protected in winter.'

'Good. I'll have a bath, then. I feel terrible.'

'You look wonderful,' he said, as he went out, and she avoided glancing in the mirror, in case, to her critical eye, his statement might have been disproved.

# Chapter XI

It was approaching noon when Dylis came downstairs. She had put on her camel hair coat and snowboots in anticipation of a sojourn in the garage, for though the day was definitely warmer, she was taking no chances. Wintry Wold was not the sort of house where one could nurse a cold in comfort.

The house seemed strangely deserted this morning, and though recent events did not suggest any necessity to stand upon ceremony, at the same time social instincts demanded that she should exchange greetings with someone. Hearing voices in the drawing-room, she went in, and discovered Theresa and Charlie Best in conversation. Mr Carpenter was also present, sunk deep in his customary chair, and to judge by the liberal dose of his favourite potion to which he was clinging with both hands, for him the day was already well started. Obviously, too, he had decided to save the precious minutes usually wasted in decanting the whisky, for a bottle, three-quarters full, stood on the table beside him. A casual nod in Dylis's direction was all the interest he took in her entrance. Not so Theresa, who with Charlie Best was leaning against the mantel, and turned immediately to say:

'We were wondering what had happened to you, my dear. Inigo said he thought you were over-tired. I hope you slept well?'

Dylis did not answer for a moment, considering many things. Was there just a hint of suspicion in Theresa's manner? She did not look as if she had slept any too well herself. Her eyes were brilliant, but shadowed, and her face, though carefully made up, had a suggestion of real anxiety about it. She was jumpy, too. The fingers of one small hand beat a light tattoo upon the mantelpiece, and she was smoking a cigarette with quick, nervous movements. She had abandoned, in part, the role of sorrowing widow, and was dressed more as a woman of action, in the kind of costume worn for winter sports even down to a very small pair of black leather boots. Dylis almost expected skis to be lying negligently somewhere in the background. She said with due caution:

'No, I didn't sleep very well. Did everybody else?'

'I did, for one,' Best said, smiling. 'But that doesn't go for everybody. Have you heard we've got a saboteur in our midst?'

'Inigo did say something about it, if you're referring to his car.' She was trying to sound as casual as possible. She sat down on the arm of a chair and lighted a cigarette. Theresa said:

'Not only his car, but both of mine. *And* the van, although I'm not worrying too much about that. As far as I'm concerned, it's been nothing but a nuisance all the time. The sooner they take it away, the better I shall be pleased. What I *am* worrying about is that anyone staying in my house could be so despicable. Really, I can hardly believe it, yet. It's positively insane. With everyone working so hard yesterday to get the snow cleared away, and then ...'

'Have you found out who did it?' Dylis asked.

'I have not. I find it difficult to imagine the mentality capable of such an outrageous thing. And as hostess it places me in

142

a particularly awkward position. I can hardly *accuse* one of my guests.'

But her eyes, glancing from one to the other, did accuse them, in a veiled way. Real or simulated, her indignation was very effective. And not unbecoming. Best was regarding her in frank admiration. Dylis said:

'We're none of us guests in the accepted sense of the term, Theresa, so I shouldn't bother too much about that side of it. In fact, we're pretty conspicuous by our absence this morning. Did Mr Ashley oversleep, too?'

'I really don't know. With all these extraordinary things happening, I'm completely confused. But he's not down yet, as far as I know.'

'A pity. I was going to offer to tidy some of the rooms for you. It must be difficult, with so little help about the house. I've done mine. Which is Mr Ashley's room, by the way?'

'Next door to the second bathroom,' Best said. 'Almost opposite mine.'

'Oh. And you managed to sleep fairly well, you say?'

'I always do. Why?'

'Only that I wish I slept your end of the house. My end was pretty noisy last night.'

'How do you mean?' Theresa asked.

'People were chasing each other about the corridors.' She had put out her cigarette, and was sitting with her hands in the pockets of her coat. She withdrew one, holding the torch she had found in the passage upstairs, and began idly to switch it on and off. Neither Best nor Theresa appeared unduly interested. The latter said:

'It was probably someone going to the bathroom. Or did you actually see anyone, Dylis?'

'I saw a light bobbing about in the grounds,' she hedged, replacing the torch in her pocket. 'Some time after three, I should think it was.'

'That was our man, I'll bet you,' Best said, and Dylis was about to add, 'Or Woman,' but refrained, having the impression that Theresa was longing to say the same thing. Since they were the only two women in the house, it would hardly have improved the situation. She said instead:

'And where is Mr Howe? I thought he was going to walk home this morning?'

Best laughed. 'You didn't swallow that yarn? Believe me, he won't stir out of this house until his car is ready and waiting. Sorry to disappoint you, Mrs Brown, if you thought we'd be on our way sooner. I went along to have a chat with him this morning, and all I saw was Raddle's feeble face peering round the door. Howe is giving out that he's in the middle of something so terrific that he can't be disturbed at any price, and won't even see me. I asked wasn't he going to do his exercises on the veranda, and Raddle said no, he did not care for the vulgar curiosity of certain people in this house, and preferred to do them by the open window in his room. It sounds phoney to me. What's more, I wouldn't be surprised if it was either him or his secretary who fixed the cars so nicely.'

Theresa opened her eyes very wide. 'But why should they? I thought Mr Howe was most anxious to get home.'

'So did I. But that man is a fanatic, and you never know what his breed is up to. He might have done it out of spite, intending to walk out of here when it suits him. Or maybe he's not as anxious to get home as he makes out. That mountain retreat sounds like hell on earth to me. And if he has much more of his nonsense, I'm not going to write him up at all. I'm not sure it wouldn't be better to write something about this place. There's more human interest in it, for one thing. *Winter comes to Wintry Wold.* Or, *Snowed in at Deathleap — a saga of the Yorkshire Dales.* How would that be, Mrs Brown?'

He was obviously talking for the sake of it, smiling down at her, but she moved uneasily, and remarked:

'You might write it, Mr Best, but would you get anyone to print it?'

'You bet I would. Or if not, I'd print it myself, complete with photographic studies of you in that outfit. And if that didn't fetch them . . .'

He was interrupted by a choking sound from behind, and turning, stared in surprise to see Mr Carpenter struggling to his feet. The face of that gentleman was a deeply mottled red, and he swayed to and fro, clutching at the mantelpiece for support. His speech was thick and uncontrolled, as he blurted out:

'What do *you* know about printing anything?'

'There's not much I don't know,' Best said, still with an expression of mild astonishment.

'What are you? What d'you call yourself?'

'I'm a free-lance journalist. Any objection?'

Theresa whispered, tugging at Best's arm: 'Don't take any notice of him. He's not well. You can see that.' And raising her voice: '*Mr Carpenter!* Do control yourself.'

But Mr Carpenter was beyond all control. Waving his empty glass beneath Best's nose, he rushed on:

'I've every objection. Every objection in the world. I was twenty years in the printing trade and never met a journalist who knew a damn thing about it.'

Best said, grinning, 'Maybe you didn't look in the right places. All journalists don't hang around saloon bars, you know. Were you ever on the press?'

For a few seconds Mr Carpenter stood and glowered at him. Then he muttered:

'To hell with you! What right have you to ask me questions?'

'Mr Carpenter,' Theresa said again, and moved to take him by the arm. 'Please remember that you're speaking to one of my guests.'

But he shook her off, and seizing the whisky bottle, tucked it under his arm, and made his way unsteadily to the door. He said over his shoulder:

'Damn sight too many guests about, if you ask me. Place is like a ruddy hotel, no peace anywhere.'

He slammed the door behind him, and Theresa sank down in a chair, and looked up at Best appealingly.

'I'm so sorry,' she said. 'But you must try to forgive him. He's been terribly worried lately. And then this other unpleasant business has upset us all.'

Her appeal was not made in vain. Best leaned over and patted her shoulder, which gesture seemed to afford him immense satisfaction. It also made Dylis feel slightly *de trop*. He said:

'That's all right. We journalists are a tough race. I must say the old boy's moods are a bit sudden, but we won't hold it against him.'

'I must go and see about lunch,' Theresa said, easing herself away with admirable skill. 'I've sent the servants out to see what they can do with the cars.'

'I'll come and lend a hand as soon as I've had a word with Inigo,' Dylis offered. 'He's in one of the garages, isn't he?'

'Yes. Poor boy, he's very troubled about that car because it's only on loan. Mr Best, will you show Dylis the way?'

Reluctantly he let her go and accompanied Dylis out through the french windows of the dining-room. Outside the air was still bleak, but the crispness had gone, leaving a moisture in the atmosphere suggestive of a slight thaw. Round by the garages they came upon a scene of great activity. In one stood a long black car built on singularly modern lines, and over this symbol of the age of speed Vauxhall and Ridley, each clad in overalls, were poring with anxious faces.

Dylis called out, 'Good morning,' in response to which Vauxhall raised his head for a second, grunted, 'Is it?' and continued with the task in hand. Ridley said something under his breath that might or might not have been a greeting. Dylis rather thought it was not. Still, one could hardly expect these Jacks-of-all-trades to be in a state of high humour. One moment tending pots and pans, laying tables and making beds, the next, grappling with the problems of locomotion.

The garage to the left of them was closed and padlocked, but the one on the right was open, and in there was the car Inigo had driven, with its bonnet up and spare parts mixed with tools all over the stone floor. The front wheels were jacked up, and from beneath the body of the vehicle sprawled Inigo's long legs, and the sight of them lying there inanimate caused Dylis's heart to leap. She said, stooping to get a better view of him:

'Inigo! Are you all right? You're not dead or anything?'

Charlie Best laughed, as Inigo came sliding out, his face smeared with oil, and in his eyes the light that comes to man in his greater moments.

'Not yet,' he said, scrambling to his feet. 'But I'm beginning to find out what this is all about.'

'That's fine. How long do you think it will take?'

'How long?' He exchanged a look with Best, the look of men who know something about cars. 'A job like this might take any time.'

'Only the weather looks as if it's breaking, so the roads ought to be better presently.'

'Don't you be too sure. It's just as likely to freeze up again, and then look out for trouble. They'll be like an ice rink. Charlie, come here a minute.'

Best moved in closer, and they went into a confabulation lasting many minutes, during which they inspected the long-suffering car from all angles, crawled about the floor, twisting their heads this way and that, took sections apart and put them together again. Dylis felt certain that, had they been small enough, they would have crept in amongst the works and pulled the bonnet down over their heads. She said at last, grasping Inigo as he was about to wedge himself beneath the vehicle again:

'Did you find out about those keys?'

'Eh? Which keys? Oh, yes, the garage keys. Theresa says hers were the only ones as far as she knows, but there may be others about somewhere. The old man never drove himself. Did you say something, Charlie?'

Best, all but standing on his head at the rear of their problem child, straightened himself and remarked:

'As far as I can see, old man, it would be quicker to walk.'

'I'm afraid you're right. I was thinking the same thing myself.'

'In that case,' Dylis put in, 'I'm walking right beside you.'

'Don't be silly, Dyl,' Inigo said. 'You couldn't walk all that way in this weather.'

'Couldn't I? You'd be surprised how far and how fast I can walk when I feel like it. And after last night I feel very like it. So get on with the good work, boys, or you can expect to see me streaking down the drive any minute.'

Observing the enthusiasm with which they rushed back to their conference as she turned away, she wondered whether the motive behind last night's deed of sabotage might have been to keep everyone occupied this morning. If so, it had been highly effective, for as she came round to the back of the house she saw the pantechnicon drawn up in the vicinity of the barn, and upon it Bob Snell and his mate were working with extraordinary absorption. What was there about a car, she asked herself, that caused otherwise reasonable men to turn into fidgety fanatics?

It was almost a relief to get back to the kitchen and to Theresa who, far from preparing lunch as advertised, was sitting on a corner of the table, smoking a cigarette and gazing thoughtfully into space. She looked up, startled, when Dylis entered, jumped to her feet, and asked:

'How are they getting on? The men, I mean?'

'Oh, they're having a lovely time. What shall we give them today? Something out of a tin, or something on toast?'

'Anything you like, my dear. I really don't care about food any more.'

Dylis went to the store cupboard and ran an expert eye over the vastness of its contents. Apparently she was now caterer-in-chief. She said:

'It's handy for you, having servants who are also expert mechanics.'

'That's one of the reasons I keep them. I'm absolutely helpless where cars are concerned. I can drive, but that's about all. But I expect you yourself are an expert, aren't you? Running about the country as you do, you must know *all* about cars.'

Her eyes met those of Dylis's in an expression of undisguised insinuation. Dylis shrugged. She remarked:

'If my knowledge were written down, it wouldn't cover a postage stamp,' and went in search of the tin-opener.

# Chapter XII

Lunch was an even more unorthodox meal than Dylis had anticipated. Theresa took a trayload of coffee and a few sandwiches into the drawing-room, as she said she wished to be alone. Vauxhall came in later, gathered up a couple of bottles of beer and two pieces of cold pie and went out again without a word. Evidently he and Ridley were lunching al fresco. Then Charlie Best appeared, followed closely by Jackson, wearing his inevitable oilskin and driving cap pushed back off his forehead. Best said:

'I just thought I'd snatch up something to eat. Inigo will be in presently.'

He cast a significant glance at Jackson, who had sat down at the table and was helping himself to tinned salmon and boiled potatoes. Never a talkative man, he had so far withdrawn from his fellow beings that they might have been speaking in a foreign language for all he appeared to notice.

Dylis felt depressed. Gone was the camaraderie of yesterday evening, and in its place was an atmosphere heavy with mistrust. It seemed that none of them had any intention of again leaving their respective cars unattended. But if that were the reason for lunching in relays, whom did they suspect, and why? She said, as Best took a seat at the table:

'I may as well have something, too. The way Inigo had his head stuck into that engine, he'll be ages. How's it going?'

'It's not,' Best said, piling odds and ends of food promiscuously on to his plate. 'Whoever bungled up that car knew what he was doing, all right.'

Jackson, who had absorbed himself in a twopenny weekly spread out beside his plate, raised his head and stared at Best blankly for a moment, before returning attention to his lunch and his reading matter.

'Seen anything of Howe?' Best went on, turning obliquely to the vanman, with one elbow on the table.

'Mr Raddle came down earlier,' Dylis said, 'He took up a collection of stuff looking like a vegetarian's nightmare. Mr Howe sent down word that he'd like to pay Theresa for her hospitality, as he'd no intention of being under an obligation to anyone. She said she'd never heard of anything so revolting in her life.'

She smiled a little at the memory of Theresa's indignation. Whatever her fault, she never failed to play the role of hostess to the best of her ability.

'Good for her,' Best said. 'Trust old Howe to say the wrong thing at the wrong time. I've met a few tactless old fools, but he's the last word.'

'He's not very good at practising what he preaches, either. Remember how he said that they share the housework between them when they're home? Yet it's always poor old Raddle who has to take up the meals here.'

'All right in theory,' Best said. 'But when it comes to it, his motto is, "You help me and I'll help myself."'

They fell silent after that, until Jackson pushed back his chair, lighted a cigarette, and stood looking at Dylis for a moment as if he were about to say something. Then he folded up and pocketed his paper, took his plate, knife and fork and deposited them in the sink, and went out as silently as he had entered.

'There goes a rummy bird,' Best said. 'If he's always like that I don't wonder Snell is fed up being on the road with him.'

'What are they carrying in that van of theirs?' Dylis asked. 'There's no name or address on the outside of it.'

'I don't know exactly. Toys or something, I believe Snell said.' Best yawned, and got to his feet with some reluctance. 'I suppose I'd better get back. Thanks very much for the lunch. Cigarette?'

'Thank you.' She accepted one and the light he offered. 'I feel I'm running a good pull-up for carmen.'

'Not to mention journalists, and other irresponsible characters. Where's Mrs Brown? Gone back to bed?'

'She's in the drawing-room. I shouldn't disturb her, if I were you. I believe she's getting a little tired of her uninvited guests.'

'I wouldn't wonder. Cheerio, see you at teatime, if not before.'

She drew up the most comfortable chair to the fire, when he had gone, and sat brooding upon the absurdity of everything. To be camped with a collection of strangers in an isolated spot, not knowing when she would be able to get away, was a situation that exasperated her, beside the many puzzling aspects of the place. She did not want to be puzzled and exasperated. She wanted to finish her business and return home. She was thinking wistfully of brightly-lighted London, its telephones and taxi-cabs, its buses and underground railway, when her solitude was again invaded. She looked up, hoping it might be Inigo, but it was Bob Snell who entered, hair ruffled, face ruddy from his exertions in the keen air. Evidently his ill-humour had spent itself, for he grinned at her cheerfully as he asked:

'Got any grub for me, Miss? My matey says you got 'im a nice bit of fish. It's a lot of trouble we're puttin'you to . . . '

'That's all right,' she said. 'Sit down and help yourself. It's cold, I'm afraid, except the potatoes. There wasn't much time for cooking.'

She was wishing she had not stayed in the kitchen, being in no mood for enforced conversation. But it would look so rude if she got up and walked out now, and Bob Snell was a pleasant sort of person, pleasant and easy to talk to. No, she was being too tolerant. She was getting into Inigo's habit of accepting people at face value. She looked at him critically as he loosened his coat and sat down in the same place that Jackson had occupied, took a plate from the pile at hand and began to delve about in the dishes she had prepared.

His table manners, she noted, were vastly superior to those of his mate, completely at variance with the roughness of his speech. He might, she thought, have washed some of the grease from off his hands, but none of them seemed to be over fussy on that point. He helped himself to a glass of beer and drank half of it before starting on his lunch.

'Thirsty work, Miss,' he said, grinning again as he glanced up to find her watching his movements with interest. 'Me and matey 'ave been on that old box of tricks since breakfast. Not that 'e's much 'elp, Jackson ain't. Got a 'ead like a board, and don't know the insides of a car from 'is own. Stiffen the crows, you should 'ave seen 'is face when we found 'er all mucked up. "Now what are we goin' to do?" 'e says. "You mean," I says, "what am I goin' to do while you fiddle about lookin' like a wet Wednesday." Proper fiddler, Jackson is, without the word of a lie.'

'Is it going to be a long job?' Dylis asked, feeling bound to say something.

'Not with me on it. Leave Jackson to 'isself and 'e'd be creepin' about out there till Christmas. But I likes to get a job done.'

'I wonder, if you're so good at it, you don't do the brakes as well, instead of waiting for the garage people.'

'Ah, that's just what I can't do, Miss. It's like this, see. If you know anythin' about cars ... '

Too late she realised she had let herself in for yet another technical tirade. And once Bob Snell got into his stride, stopping him was not easy. Feeling idiotic, she listened and nodded and smiled, and broke in at last:

'Yes, I quite see the difficulty you're in. How's the lunch?'

'Nice bit of fish, Miss, very nice. As I was sayin' ... '

'It's salmon,' she said. 'Out of a tin. I prefer it fresh, myself.'

'Can't tell the difference. Never could. It's the same with meat. One meat's as good as another to me. Any place I eat I just asks for 'ot meat and veg. It all goes down the same way.'

Deciding quickly that a discussion of meat and menus was preferable to brakes and gears and engines, she launched with enthusiasm into a discourse on the relative merits of beef, lamb and veal, the seasons in which pork should and should not be eaten, and the best methods of cooking fresh-water fish. At the end of which Bob Snell had finished his lunch, and rose from the table with scarcely concealed boredom.

'Much obliged, Miss,' he said, buttoning his coat. 'I'll get back and finish the job now, then when them mechanics get 'ere ... '

'Mr Snell,' she interrupted, upon impulse, 'have you any idea who messed up your car?'

He stood looking at her in silence for a while, hands thrust deep into his pockets, brows drawn together in a frown that completely obliterated his usual good humour. He said then, 'I've got ideas, Miss. Plenty of 'em. But I ain't sayin' anythin'. There's one thing I do know, I ain't bein' caught rotten again.'

With which ambiguous statement he took his departure, leaving her with the uneasy feeling that his suspicions might, in part, be directed towards herself, and the impression that he was not a man who forgave lightly. Not that it was any concern of hers, and there was no reason why she should worry about it.

But she was worried. Furthermore, she was oppressed by a feeling very akin to a headache, from which she rarely suffered. For want of something better to do, rather than any liking for the job, she washed up, and since there was still no sign of Inigo, she left the remains of the food upon the table, picked up her coat and went upstairs to her room.

As usual, it was bitterly cold, but the bed looked inviting. Here was a chance to demonstrate the efficacy of one of her own cures. A couple of Nurelief tablets and an hour in bed, and she ought to be feeling wonderful. She poured out half a glass of water from the carafe, and opened her case of samples. She was in the act of taking out the little phial of white tablets, when it occurred to her that there was something missing from the orderly row of bottles. One bottle of Necktar, that was all right, she had used it on Mr Brown. But it did not take much of a mental effort to realise that two bottles of Quickease had also disappeared. Since when? She sat down on the side of the bed to think about it.

She had not opened the case since the night she had seen Mr Brown, of that she was positive. But somebody had, and had also lifted two bottles of her special curative oil. Now why should they want to do that? They could have had it for the asking. She put a hand to her head and tried to visualise the motive that might lie behind so petty a theft. She could think of nothing sensible.

Obviously the person concerned wished to keep his or her identity secret, but why? Two possibilities came to mind, either that there was someone in the house whom she had not yet seen and who had no intention of being seen, or that the person who took the oil had some sinister reason for doing so. Whichever it was, she did not like it. Moreover, it angered her to think of someone coolly going through her possessions.

She extracted two of the white tablets and swallowed them with a draught of water, before beginning a systematic search through the remainder of her things to ascertain whether anything else had been rifled or disturbed. She could not be sure, but having spent some time over the investigation, it seemed as if the interest of the intruder had not strayed beyond the sample case. Thoroughly perplexed and annoyed, she locked it away inside her travelling case, and abandoning all thought of rest, she went out into the passage.

The house was enjoying one of its sombre silences. Automatically, her mind turned to the early morning, to Ashley, to Ledgrove, and to the man who had dropped the torch. She walked slowly along the corridors, and at the head of the main staircase she paused. Inigo was ascending, two at a time. Reaching her side, he said:

'Hallo, Dyl. I was just coming to see where you'd got to. I was worried about you.'

'Why should you be?'

'Oh, I don't know. I've been on edge since this morning, I suppose. Has anything happened? You look grim.'

'I'm feeling grim. About one and a half times as grim as you did when you discovered your car. Someone has pinched a couple of samples out of my case.'

'Samples of what?'

'Oil. The stuff we call Quickease. No, don't laugh, Inigo. This isn't a bit funny. I believe there's a lunatic at large in this house.'

'I'm sorry. I wasn't really amused, but you look so murderous.'

'That's exactly how I feel. It's not the loss of anything so trivial. I'd have given it to anyone, had they asked for it. But the idea of someone sneaking about my room . . . It's too much. And don't ask me if I'm absolutely sure, or I'll scream.'

'I wasn't going to. I told you I'd believe anything now. But where's the sense in it?'

'There isn't any. Unless . . . ' She lowered her voice. 'You know what I suggested about your uncle's death. I left a half-empty bottle of oil on his table, and that disappeared, too. I noticed that when I was up there this morning. Suppose I'm right, and someone is trying to pin this thing on me?'

She expected him to protest, but he merely frowned and said:

'But I don't see how it could be done.'

'Neither do I, but I'm going to find out before this goes any further.'

'How?'

'I'm going down to have a little talk with Theresa.'

'I shouldn't do that just yet.' He put a hand on her arm, and she was surprised to see that his face wore a strained expression unnatural to him. 'I should have told you this earlier, but it didn't seem very important. I don't know that it is now. But this morning when I first went downstairs, I heard Theresa talking to someone in the drawing-room, a man, with a voice I couldn't place.'

'How do you mean?'

'Well, I could have sworn it was a voice I hadn't heard around here before. That's what made me hesitate as I was about to barge in. And then as I opened the door, I heard someone go out by the french windows, although naturally I didn't see him. So I asked Theresa who she was talking to, and she said it was one of the servants.'

'And you don't think it was?'

'At the time I didn't think much about it. But this oil business, well, it just crossed my mind that there might be someone in this house not accounted for.'

'That's what I've been thinking. What kind of a voice was it?'

'Not very loud, cultured, quite pleasant. I didn't hear what they were saying.'

'It certainly doesn't sound like one of the servants.'

'No. So I'd rather you didn't have a showdown with Theresa just now. If she has been up to anything, she's hardly likely to admit it. When we've got the car going, we'll find that doctor, and then I'd like to go into this thing thoroughly.'

'How long is it likely to take?'

'Any time now. Charlie's a wizard with cars.'

'Are you sure you can trust him?'

'I'm not sure I can trust anyone, except you. But if not, he can hardly get up to any tricks while I'm away, because I should know then that he'd done it in the first place.' He was silent for a while, and then asked suddenly, 'Have you seen Ashley yet?'

'No, he didn't come down to lunch.'

'That's funny, isn't it? I can understand him skipping breakfast, as he was tooling about last night, but you'd think he'd be up by now. Let's give him a knock.'

'On what excuse?'

'We can ask him if he'd like coffee or something. That man intrigues me.'

All was silent inside and outside Mr Ashley's room. Inigo knocked, and they waited. He knocked again, several times,

158

called, whistled and made other noises indicative of his presence. There was still no reply. He tried the handle of the door and found that it was locked.

'Is he one of the lucky ones supplied with a key?' Dylis asked.

'I suppose so. Some of the rooms have keys, and some haven't. But it's a damned queer thing to lock the door of his bedroom, isn't it?'

'A sensible thing in a house like this,' Dylis said. 'Although he didn't strike me as being afraid of the dark. Have a look through the keyhole. It's not done in the best circles, but we'll overlook that.'

'Can't see a thing apart from the furniture,' Inigo reported a minute later. 'He must have gone somewhere or other. But where?'

'Perhaps he's gone altogether,' Dylis suggested.

'What, skipped out without so much as a "Thank you for having me"?'

'Well, he wasn't too shy about skipping in. Don't you think you ought to force that door? Something may have happened to him.'

'Good Lord! You don't think . . . ?' They stood and stared at each other. A prickly sensation crept up and down Dylis's spine. Her head felt better, though. If ever she got out of this mix-up she could add her personal testimonial to those which already upheld Nurelief. 'I was marooned in a House of Death, but Nurelief brought me true relief.' Webber would be pleased with that. But meanwhile, something had to be done, and Inigo, transformed into a man of action, was about to do it.

'I've got a better idea than that,' he said. 'There's a ledge runs along outside from the bathroom to Ashley's room. I can nip along that, and get a good view in through the window.'

'But suppose he *is* in there? It'll be a shock for him, seeing a man suddenly peering at him through the window.'

'Can't help that. I've got to get this thing settled. And I need only peer a little way to see, well, whatever it is we're trying to see.'

'But someone may see you from below.'

'Not very likely. This side of the house is sheltered. Come and have a look.'

Dylis was doubting her wisdom in having urged Inigo to do something. Turned into a man of action, he was a trifle disconcerting. Her doubts increased when, having followed him into the bathroom, she discovered that the ledge he had described running from the window there to that of Ashley's room was scarcely a foot wide and built above a sheer drop of more feet than she cared to think about. As he had said, the windows here were screened by trees, and set at an angle whereby they could not be easily overlooked. She stared out and down and along the snow-covered ledge, drew in her head and shook it with some vigour.

'It's silly,' she said. 'You might fall and break your neck.'

'Not me. I've negotiated trickier things than that. You haven't much faith in my climbing prowess. And you yourself said something might have happened to Ashley.'

'If it's happened, it's happened,' she said, suddenly callous towards that gentleman. 'And it won't help if anything happens to you.'

'Nothing will,' he said, opening the window wide and preparing to ease his person on to the ledge.

'Inigo!' She grasped a portion of his coat and held on. 'I'm not going to let you do anything so crazy.'

One leg already out upon the sill, he regarded her in amazement.

'Why, Dyl, you're quite agitated. That's not like you.'

'Wouldn't you be agitated if I suggested turning myself into a mangled corpse?'

'I'll answer that when I come back,' he said. 'Shan't be a tick.' Firmly he disengaged himself and drew up his other leg, and stood for a moment testing his weight upon the ledge. 'You never know with these old houses,' he explained. 'They sometimes give way in the most unexpected places.'

'If you must commit suicide,' she said, 'I'm not going to watch you. I'll be out on the landing.'

She withdrew from the window and went out, closing the door of the bathroom upon the scene of action. She listened again outside Mr Ashley's room, but all remained silent. In some agitation, she lit a cigarette, and began to pace up and down the corridor, muttering things uncomplimentary to the character of men in general, and Inigo Brown in particular, asking herself why she had to get involved with anyone so completely foolhardy. One moment he was all calmness and tolerance, ready figuratively, if not literally, to let anyone get away with murder, the next he was up in arms and balancing on window ledges, and prepared to lay down his life in all directions. No one had asked him to take any such risks. All she had said was that he should not allow people to run about the house making strange noises, without looking into it.

Pausing again outside Mr Ashley's door, she was relieved to hear a thud which could only be Inigo entering through the window. At least, she hoped so. She was about to call out to him, when another sound reached her ears. Someone was approaching along the corridors from the direction in which lay her own room, someone who whistled in a tuneless sort of way. It sounded like a man's whistle. She moved quickly away from the door, took a few steps forward, hesitated as the man appeared. It was Mr Ashley. Her emotions at sight of him were somewhat confused. She could not have said now exactly what she had expected Inigo to find on the other side of that locked door, but Mr Ashley had figured vaguely in her imagination as a man lying drugged upon the bed, an inanimate body stuffed beneath the bed, a figure bound and gagged and locked inside the wardrobe.

But here he was, looking very much alive, though still tired as if he had not slept for a week, and whistling. In face of these indisputable facts, her fears appeared not only groundless but senseless. Furthermore, at any moment now Inigo would fling open the door of that room . . . She raised her voice and called out:

'Why, Mr Ashley! I was wondering where you were. We had lunch ages ago.'

To her own ears, her voice and words sounded highly artificial and unconvincing. But he did not appear to notice anything wrong, as he came abreast of her and remarked:

'I expect you did. Sorry I wasn't down. I had a bit of a head this morning, and didn't fancy anything.'

'Oh.' She regarded him with some suspicion. If her tablets had disappeared she could understand it. But he would hardly have wanted the oil to massage his head. 'I could let you have some tablets for it, if you like. They're very good.'

She was standing in the middle of the passage, so it would be difficult for him to get by without deliberately pushing past her. And Dylis was not the sort of woman whom a man might push, except in the gravest extremity.

'Thanks very much,' he said. 'But I feel better now. I've been having a talk with Mr Howe. He's quite an interesting chap, when you get to know him.'

'You're the only one who thinks so.' She hoped that her

expression would pass as a smile. Could Inigo hear all this, she wondered? At least he must know she was talking to someone. He had not opened the door, that was a good sign. But of course he could not open the door, because Mr Ashley had the key. She was still thinking in terms of inanimate bodies. If she could only keep this conversation going long enough, Inigo would take the hint and hop out by the window again and along the ledge to the bathroom, providing he did not fall in the process. The thought of his large feet slithering about on that slippery surface sent a chill all over her. But she continued, 'I didn't know Mr Howe was up, or rather, down? He sent word to say he was keeping to his room today.'

'So he is. I went along there to see him. Have a cigarette?'

'Thank you.' If she was in no hurry to move, neither, it seemed, was Ashley. Yet he had been making for his room, of that she was certain. Perhaps he did not wish her to know that he kept it locked. It would be rather a blatant admission of mistrust on his part. And whom did he mistrust, and why? More likely he had something in there he did not want anyone to see. She said, still very loudly:

'You won't have heard about the cars being put out of action last night? Or did Mr Howe tell you?'

'No. What cars?'

'All the cars.'

'Not my car?'

'I meant all those here. Mrs Brown's, and Inigo's, and the van. Someone messed them all up so they can't be driven.'

'That's very strange, isn't it?'

'It is, isn't it?' He must, by now, be thinking she was half-witted. She felt rather like that, and blamed herself for having got into such a ludicrous position. She had given up blaming Inigo, for right now, if nothing worse had happened to him, he was probably struggling to climb through the bathroom window and getting stuck in that restricted space.

'Haven't you any idea who did it?'

'None at all. At least, I haven't, but everyone else is going about hinting darkly.'

'What an extraordinary thing. And we were all getting along so nicely last night, too. Most upsetting, isn't it?'

'Yes, isn't it?' She thought she heard a faint noise come from the bathroom. She added, 'I suppose you didn't hear anything in the night, Mr Ashley? Someone must have been prowling around.'

'No, not a thing. Did you?'

'I saw someone in the grounds. Or rather, I saw a light which must have been attached to someone.'

'And you didn't go down to investigate?'

'Why should I? It didn't strike me as important at the time.'

'I suppose not. But you must have heard something, to have got you out of bed.'

'I did hear something . . . ' She hesitated. This discussion was not moving along the right lines. It was she who ought to be asking the questions, since it was he who had been walking about the house in his overcoat. She added, 'At least, I thought I heard something, but I believe now it was just imagination. These old houses . . . '

'And then you went back to bed?'

'Yes.'

They were silent for a moment. He appeared to be pondering on something, and she was watching him with close attention. He said at last, edging towards the bathroom to which she was turned obliquely:

'I think I'll have a wash and brush up and come down and get some tea. I could do with a cup.'

She had a mental vision of Mr Ashley bending over the

washbasin, and Inigo blithely stepping through the window on to his back. She said, barring the way:

'You can't go in there. Mr Brown is having a bath.'

'Oh, I didn't know that. Do you always wait around while he has a bath?'

She could not be sure, in the dimness of the passage lighting, but she thought there was a hint of amusement in his weary eyes. She said hastily:

'I only came up to see where he was. He seemed to be gone such a long time. He got all messed up doing the car.'

In miraculous confirmation of her words, there came from the bathroom the sound of splashing water, and Inigo's voice rose softly on the air, singing, 'Rub-a-dub-dub, one man in a tub,' to an improvised tune. He had got back safely, then. The shadow of inanimate bodies vanished completely, and she became severely practical. When Mr Ashley said:

'Well, the other bathroom's free, isn't it?' She took him by the arm, and began to urge him in the direction of the staircase.

'The water's not very hot this afternoon,' she said. 'Mr Brown told me it goes off like that sometimes and then comes on hot again later. Now you come downstairs and I'll make you a nice cup of tea. I should like one, too.'

She thought he looked at her rather queerly, but she no longer cared. She had steered a way through the worst of the business, and Inigo could look after himself for a while. She hardly heard Ashley say, as they went downstairs together:

'It's nice of you to take so much trouble.'

She was wondering whether, now that they were out of the way, Inigo might be climbing back into that room for any reason. She was relieved to find Theresa in the kitchen, vaguely poking at the fire, above which the large black kettle was steadily coming to boiling point. Dylis said, and it sounded rather as if she were handing over a prize:

'Here's Mr Ashley, Theresa. He's not been feeling well, and could do with a cup of rea. It's early yet, but I thought ...'

'I was just going to make it,' Theresa said. She had a mink coat draped about her shoulders, and looked like a cinema star posing in her kitchen for the benefit of a photographer. 'I've been to see how they're getting on. It's wickedly cold outside.'

'It's not too warm in here,' Dylis said, quick to grasp the opportunity. 'I think I'll get my coat, too. Will you look after Mr Ashley?'

Theresa turned, the poker held in one delicate hand. It may only have been coincidence, but her voice did not sound very pleasant as she said:

'Yes, I'll look after Mr Ashley.'

Dylis did not stop for further altercation. She returned quickly upstairs, and was in time to meet Inigo on his way down. He had washed and combed his hair, and showed no trace of his recent exertions.

'So much for housebreaking,' he said. 'Thanks for holding the fort, Dyl. You were marvellous.'

'I felt like a fool. Did you find anything?'

'I didn't have much time. As far as I could see, there were no bodies tucked away anywhere. But what was the name of that oil you say disappeared?'

'Quickease?'

'No, the bottle you left up in my uncle's room. Necktar, wasn't it?'

'That's right. Why?'

'There's a bottle of that, practically empty, in Ashley's room. What do you make of that?'

'At first guess I should say he lifted it from your uncle's bedside table. You didn't see any sign of the other?'

'No, but as I say, I didn't have much chance to look. D'you think the man could be a kleptomaniac, or something?'

'Possibly. He said he'd been talking to Mr Howe. What part of the house is his room?'

'A little farther on from yours.'

'He was coming from that direction.'

'Perhaps we ought to ask old Howe if he's missed anything.'

'I'm not sure about that. I'm wondering whether there isn't something between those two. They weren't on visiting terms yesterday, and Howe wouldn't even see Charlie this morning.' And then, as another thought struck her: 'Inigo! You don't think anything can have happened to him, do you?'

'Who, Charlie?'

'No, Mr Howe. It seems funny to me that yesterday he was planning to walk home, and today he won't leave his room or see anyone.'

'He saw Ashley.'

'We've only got his word for that.'

'But what could happen to him? Raddle has the room next door, and he's been spoon-feeding the old boy all day.'

'So he says. But it looks very queer, all the same.'

'Queer or not, I've no intention of climbing along any more window ledges to find out.'

'Nobody asked you to. That was your own idea. But we could knock on his door and ask if he's all right.'

'And be greeted with one of his delightful speeches? Not me. Let Mr Howe work out his own troubles. I'm going back to the car. Where's Ashley now?'

'In the kitchen with Theresa.'

'D'you think it safe to leave that man with anybody?' Inigo asked, beginning to hurry down the stairs. 'He might be dangerous.'

'So might Theresa,' Dylis said, following close on his heels. 'She's got the poker, and I don't think she'd hesitate to use it.'

Inigo, pausing in the hallway to retrieve the overcoat he had left there, remarked in a low voice:

'I shouldn't mention this oil business to anyone just yet. Let things take their natural course for a bit. I'll be in as soon as I can.'

It was only when they entered the kitchen, and Ashley, seated at the table, looked up with a faint smile, that Dylis realised the coat she was supposed to fetch was still hanging in her wardrobe.

# Chapter XIII

Allowing events to take their natural course, at Inigo's suggestion, Dylis found that they moved suddenly to a head. Darkness had fallen, and she and Theresa and Mr Ashley were still sitting round the kitchen table, when Charlie Best came in. Dylis was glad to see him. They had finished a not very companionable tea, and having exhausted all general topics of conversation, were smoking cigarettes in an even less companionable silence. Charlie, smiling through a film of grease and dirt, was like a beacon breaking up enveloping gloom.

'Must get me a wash,' he said, peeling off his coat and flinging it over the nearest chair. 'Any tea going?'

'Plenty,' Theresa said, the picture of listlessness. 'How's the job?'

'Almost done.' He removed his jacket, rolled up his sleeves and turned on the hot water tap. 'You don't mind me washing here? I don't feel I can face the arctic regions upstairs.'

'Just as you please.' Theresa lighted another cigarette. 'Has Vauxhall finished my car yet, do you know?'

'I couldn't say. Haven't been able to get a word out of him. He's not exactly a happy sort of fellow, is he?' He had covered his face with soap suds and was rubbing vigorously. 'Not that we've had much time for talking. It's been the devil of a job, and I've got a crick in the neck that's killing me.'

Dylis had risen to add fresh tea and water to the pot. She said:

'That's what comes of knowing too much about cars.'

'Or not enough.' He finished his ablutions, put on his jacket and took a seat at the table. Rubbing the back of his neck with one hand, he went on, 'Here's your chance to trot out your little bag of cures, Dylis. After what I've been through, I could do with a spot of massage by a beautiful lady.'

'What you could do with and what you'll get are miles apart,' Dylis said. 'Here's your tea.'

'Thanks very much.' He took the cup and proceeded to stir in sugar. 'You don't mean to say you're going to turn down an opportunity for practical demonstration? I'm disappointed in you. I thought you were a saleswoman.'

'So did I, up to a couple of days ago. Have a sandwich.'

'What *are* you two talking about?' Theresa asked, looking from one to the other in bewilderment. Best grinned.

'I'm trying to persuade our Dylis to massage my aches and pains away, but as you see, she's crying off. Why, I don't know, because she gave a wonderful harangue on the subject the other evening. But, of course, you weren't there, Mrs Brown. You should have been. Old Howe went nearly mad, because he maintains no one would suffer with anything if they all followed his fresh-air-and-water diet. I'd like him to try crawling about under a car, and see what that did to him. He's a horror. I wouldn't be surprised if he hasn't had something to do with giving me a pain in the neck. What was that stuff you recommended for necks, Dylis, some sort of oil?'

'Oil?' Theresa repeated, and now there was definite interest in her eyes.

'A curative oil,' Dylis said. 'My firm sells those things.'

She was not sure that she approved the direction in which this conversation was heading. She took a sideways glance at Mr Ashley and saw that he was lolling in his chair, looking tired and rather bored. Theresa, on the other hand, was staring at her intently across the table. Charlie Best was consuming sandwiches and drinking tea with immense satisfaction.

'How very amusing,' Theresa said, not looking at all amused. 'I'd no idea you travelled in anything so practical.'

Charlie Best was taken with a sudden spasm of laughter. He said, recovering and helping himself to a second cup of tea:

'You don't know the half of it. Dylis has almost cornered that particular market. You ought to hear her when she really gets going. She completely floored poor old Howe, and she had me so worked up I'd have chased out to the local chemist right away, if we'd been anywhere near civilisation. But since she refuses to go to work on me I'm thinking it was so much sales-talk.'

'You're not being very fair to Miss Hughes,' Ashley pointed out. 'She may consider you're not a suitable test case.'

'He isn't,' Dylis said. 'A crick is not the same as a stiff neck, by any means.'

Best waved the point aside. 'That's just subterfuge. I've a good mind to try some of old Howe's gymnastics, to prove how badly you've let down the faith of one of your admirers.'

It *was* subterfuge, Dylis admitted to herself, and suddenly she was very tired of it all. She had intended to steer the conversation into a more general course, but now she was not going to try any more. At that moment she felt there were things she would like to do to Charlie's neck other than curing it. She said:

'Well, it seems I still have one admirer in this house, since someone knocked off a couple of bottles out of my sample case.'

'More sales-talk,' Charlie scoffed. 'Why should anyone want to do that?'

'Why, indeed? That's just what I've been wondering.'

There followed an uncomfortable silence, as she glanced quickly round the table. Ashley's face was impassive, Theresa still looked at her with an expression between interest and perplexity, and Charlie Best lighted a cigarette. He said at length, no longer smiling:

'You're not serious, Dylis? It's such a damned silly thing for anyone to do.'

'Of course it is. So silly, that I wasn't going to mention it, if you hadn't brought up the subject. It's the principle of the thing, or rather the lack of it, that annoys me. I'd have given the stuff to anyone who'd asked for it. I'm practically at the end of my trip, so it isn't very important.'

'In that case, there's not much point in discussing it,' Theresa said. She put up a hand to stifle a yawn, rose, and wrapped her mink coat about her shoulders. 'I'm going out to see how the servants are getting on. They've been quite long enough, heaven knows.' She reached up to a shelf and brought down a hurricane lamp, lighted it from the fire, and went out, looking incongruous in a graceful fashion. Ashley also rose then, and said:

'I think I'll see about that wash. The water's hot now, isn't it?'

He was addressing Dylis, but Best answered:

'Been hot all the time, old boy. Miraculously enough, it always is.'

Dylis, avoiding Ashley's eyes, began clearing the table, and continued to do so until he had left them. Her feelings towards Best had reached a pitch of exasperation when she dare not trust herself to speak. He seemed quite unaware of it, as he helped her remove cups and saucers and plates, and putting on his overcoat, remarked:

'I'll be getting back to the grindstone. Inigo will want his tea.'

'Tell him to help himself,' Dylis said. 'I'll leave the teapot on the stove. I'm going to have a one-woman strike in the drawing-room. This kitchen bores me.'

Half-way to the door he paused to look back at her.

'You're not mad at me or anything, are you? I was only trying to cheer things up. Old Carpenter's right, in a way. This place is getting like a hotel, a particularly frowsty one where everyone looks daggers at everyone else. I wish I knew what it was all about. There is a story in it somewhere, I'm certain.'

'You get that car going, and never mind about stories,' Dylis said. 'I'll leave the lamp on for Inigo.'

She found the drawing-room in darkness, and the neglected fire burning low. She groped her way to the lamp, lighted it, drew the curtains, closed the door communicating with the dining-room, and put a couple of logs on the fire. She walked over to the bookcase, selected a volume at random, and sat down in an easy chair. Whatever games the others might be playing, she was determined to have a little relaxation. But at that distance the light was too dim for reading, and she did not fancy sitting within the comparatively cold vicinity of the single illumination. Neither did she fancy the book, on learning its title, *The Loveliness of Yorkshire*. She was quite prepared to believe that Yorkshire, under ideal conditions, could be lovely but was not in the mood to go into the question. She laid it aside and sat staring into the kindling fire.

She was not surprised when Theresa joined her. She had not expected to be left in peace for long. And that little lady certainly did not look like a messenger of peace, rather was her face set in the expression Dylis had come to recognise as a cover for her more pointed remarks. Unsmiling, she flung her coat over the back of an armchair, and crouched down upon the edge of it. She said, with a casualness that did not deceive Dylis for a moment:

'I've been thinking about those samples you say have disappeared. It's not very important of course, but I don't *like* things like that happening in my house.'

Dylis eyed her with an indifference that was not assumed. She had reached the point when Theresa's likes and dislikes no longer interested her. She said:

'Neither do I. But since it is your house there's not much I can do about it.'

'Have you any idea when it happened?'

'Some time between this afternoon and the first night I stayed here.'

'I daresay it's just someone playing a joke on you.'

'Probably. There does seem to be someone about with a strange sense of humour, doesn't there?'

'There does. What makes it so difficult is not *knowing* one's guests. Have you missed anything else? Any of your other samples, for instance? Only Mr Best was talking about stiff necks, and I wondered . . . '

'If he did it? I shouldn't think so.'

'Is Necktar one of your products?' Theresa asked, so suddenly that Dylis wondered if she had really intended to ask the question, or whether, having seen the bottle, her curiosity was too much for her. She said, also casually:

'It is. We recommend it for massaging the neck.'

Theresa leaned over and took a cigarette from the open box upon the table, and as an afterthought, offered the box to Dylis.

She picked up a wooden spill, held it to the crackling logs, and lighted their cigarettes as carefully as if they were charges of dynamite. She asked:

'I suppose you carry samples of that, too?'

'I had one sample of it, but I haven't got it now.'

'Oh. I thought you said you hadn't missed anything else?'

'I haven't. I used that one myself.'

'Taking your own medicine?' Theresa asked, with a laugh that was entirely forced. And this, Dylis decided, was where the gloves came off. She was not going to hedge any longer. Very deliberately, she said:

'No, I very seldom have anything wrong with me. As a matter of fact, I used it to massage Mr Brown's neck, a very short time before he died.'

The effect of this statement was not remarkable, except that for a minute or so Theresa seemed to have some difficulty in breathing. She took the cigarette from her mouth, stared at the burning tip of it, and slowly put it back again. She said:

'My *husband*? You mean you were actually with him before he died?'

'I was. Up to half an hour before, if your statement as to the time he died is correct.'

Theresa ignored this implied doubt of her veracity. She rose up from her chair and became several things at once, a child on the verge of tears, an outraged wife, a slighted hostess, a widow whose sorrow had been profaned. The outraged wife predominated.

'You *dare* to tell me that!' she burst out. 'You were with him almost until the last moments of his life, and you kept it to yourself. You kept it from me, his wife, and from Inigo, his nephew.'

'I may have kept it from you, his wife, but I told Inigo, his nephew,' Dylis said. 'Now suppose we cut out the high drama,

175

Theresa, and you tell *me* something. Where was Ledgrove between about two-fifteen and three-thirty on that morning? Because he wasn't with your husband.'

'How should I know? And why should I believe anything you say, a woman who would come between a wife and her husband?' But she sat down again and looked at Dylis intently before adding, 'You say you told Inigo?'

'Yes.'

'Then why didn't he tell me?'

'I advised him not to.'

'But *why*? I had a right to know. It was *my* place to be there if my husband needed anything. And what were you doing in his room? Was he conscious then, and did you speak to him? Don't you see how important this is to me? What right have you to sit there, keeping these things to yourself?'

'I'm trying to tell you,' Dylis said. She was, but in her own way. Theresa, she judged, was seriously disturbed about something. Not just the fact that another woman had been with her husband during his last moments of life. It went deeper than that. Her first spasm of indignation over, she looked as if she were waiting for a jury to bring in a verdict of guilty or not guilty. Watching her carefully, Dylis began to describe the events in the early hours of her first morning at Wintry Wold, but she did not get beyond her arrival in Mr Brown's room, before Theresa interrupted:

'But why didn't you call *me*? He was dying, and it was my place to be there. I could have done something. I might even have prevented his death.'

'He wasn't dying,' Dylis said. 'He was able to hold a perfectly lucid conversation.'

It had not been perfectly lucid as far as she was concerned, but she was not going to admit that just now. Beneath her façade of injured wifehood, Theresa was cracking up, and if there was anything to give away, she was liable to do it at any moment. She said, with a pathetic catch in her voice which the hostility of her eyes belied:

'Tell me exactly what he said. I've the right to know.'

'He said one or two things that puzzled me at the time. In the first place, he was very anxious to see Inigo, although I pointed out to him that it was past two o'clock . . .'

'How did he know Inigo was here?'

'I told him.'

'*You* told him. After I'd stressed the point that he must not be excited in any way. With your interfering nature you couldn't resist it, I suppose. Taking it upon yourself to massage his neck too. I didn't guess it was you. I thought Ledgrove had left that bottle there. If Mr Best had not brought up the subject, I might never have known. Why, you practically *caused* his death.'

Dylis waved aside this tirade. 'He was in pain,' she said. 'It was the least I could do, and I didn't see any harm in mentioning Inigo. They were bound to see each other later in the day, or some time.' She paused, thinking about that. Since Inigo had taken that journey specially to see his uncle, he would hardly have gone away without doing so. Theresa knew that, too. If there were anything she did not wish Inigo to hear from his uncle, the latter had died at a most convenient time. 'You've talked a lot about rights,' she went on. 'What about Inigo's right to see his uncle, and Mr Brown's right to see *him*? You didn't hesitate to do a little interfering yourself, there.'

'I knew what was best for my husband in his weak condition. I was his nurse. I should know. And the doctor said he was not to have visitors.'

'Yet you sent a letter asking Inigo to come.'

'I sent it? I did nothing of the kind. I knew nothing about it until . . . '

They both saw her mistake at the same time. Dylis, who had been leaning back with half-closed eyes, but watching Theresa none the less closely, observed the fleeting look of consternation that crossed her face. Dylis did not give her time to recuperate. She cut in:

'Until you went through Inigo's pockets and found the letter his uncle wrote to him in London. I can't remember the exact wording, but it finished up something like, "Don't mention it to my wife, I want your visit to be a surprise to her."'

Theresa was on her feet, glaring down at Dylis with undisguised fury.

'You've no right to say such things,' she raved. 'How dare you sit there, insulting me, your hostess? First you accuse my husband's valet of neglecting his master, then you accuse me of intrigue and . . . worse. It's the kind of low, crawling, unspeakable thing you would do yourself, going through a man's pockets. How do *you* know what was in that letter, unless you've been prying about in other people's rooms, which seems to be a habit of yours?'

'You're not very consistent,' Dylis pointed out, with composure. 'If you wanted me to believe you knew nothing about that letter, you shouldn't have made it so obvious that you did. And now you ask how I knew about it. Well, Inigo gave it to me to read.'

'Oh, he did? And may I ask why he should take you into his confidence? What is there between you two, a conspiracy?'

'You're being melodramatic again,' Dylis said. 'Inigo knew someone had been through his things, because they were all put back in the wrong places, including that letter. Showing it to me was just incidental when he was telling me about it.'

178

'And how do you know he didn't show it to me?'

'Because he said he didn't, as his uncle asked him not to. And you wouldn't have got so bothered about it, if he had.'

'You think you're being very clever, don't you? Well, there's such a thing as being too clever, my dear.'

'I don't doubt it. Was your husband too clever, by any chance?'

Theresa shot her a glance full of venom, and began to move nervously about the room. She said suddenly:

'Suppose I did happen to see that letter? I've a right to know what's going on in my own house, haven't I?'

'Be damned to you and your house!' Dylis exclaimed, losing her temper. 'All I want is to get out of the wretched place.'

'You were glad enough to take shelter here.'

'And I'll be equally glad to take shelter somewhere else, where people aren't dying and disappearing and messing about with cars and creeping into each other's rooms. Who started this conversation, anyway? I didn't and I've no particular wish to go on with it.'

She got up from her chair, and would have left then, had not Theresa caught her arm, saying with a touch of hysteria in her voice:

'You can't go before you've told me what my husband said to you.'

'Can't I?' Dylis looked down at the little hands clinging to her arm, brushed them aside, and pushed Theresa down into the chair she had vacated. 'It would take more than you to stop me.'

Theresa looked up at her, made an effort to rise, and thought better of it. She said:

'But I've a *right* to know.'

'If you say that again I'll slap you,' Dylis threatened. 'What difference does it make what he said or didn't say? If he was as ill as he was supposed to be, someone should have been with him. You say you were sleeping, and left Ledgrove in charge of him. Personally, I don't believe a word of it. Why did Mr Brown have a walking stick to thump on the floor with, if someone was accustomed to sit with him all the time? You're not all deaf, are you? I asked him if he wanted to see you, and he said no. I couldn't do more. I'll tell them what he said at the inquest, if anyone wants to know.'

'There won't be an inquest.' Theresa was slowly regaining her lost dignity. 'My husband died a perfectly natural death.'

'If you're so sure of that, why the anxiety over his last words?'

'He was my husband. I devoted my life to making him as happy as I could. I've . . . '

'All right, you said it before. You've the right to know. Well, here it is, for what it's worth.' Dylis lighted a cigarette and leaned against the mantel. She was, she realised, on delicate ground. If Theresa really had nothing to do with her husband's death, her own veiled accusations were most unseemly. At the same time, Theresa had more or less admitted that she was not above prying into people's pockets. But that did not necessarily imply that she was also capable of murder. Theresa sat very still in her chair, the anger gone from her face, leaving it pale and earnest in expression. Uncomfortably aware of growing doubt, Dylis returned to her narrative where she had left it, and continued up to the time of three-thirty of that fatal morning, when she had come back to her own room.

There followed a silence, during which the two women scrutinised each other with minute care. Theresa drew a deep breath at length, and asked:

'Is that all? Are you sure that was *all* he said?'

Dylis shrugged. 'Pretty well. Except that he finished by asking me what I thought of you.'

'And what did you say?'

'I said I thought you were very beautiful, and he said, "Is she?" And then he fell asleep.'

A faint smile curved Theresa's mouth. 'So his last words were of me. I'm glad of that, and thank you for telling me.'

But Dylis was not listening to this sad little speech. She was calling herself several kinds of an idiot for having bungled the situation. Theresa had been expecting her to say something entirely different. But what? A little bluff might help matters along. If Theresa were the innocent soul she made out, it could do no harm, and if not . . . Dylis said:

'That's all, as far as I can remember at the moment. But suppose, later, I were to remember something else your husband said, something he would have told Inigo, *if he hadn't died*?'

'I wish you wouldn't talk in riddles,' Theresa said irritably, but she was on guard again. Dylis continued:

'There *was* something, wasn't there? Something you didn't want Inigo to know?'

'I don't know what you're talking about. But I shall certainly speak to him about your extraordinary behaviour.'

She glanced at her small wristlet watch and made a movement to rise, but Dylis leaned over and pushed her back into the chair again. She found that pushing Theresa into chairs was a stimulating experience.

'Don't waste your time,' she said. 'It's no good asking him. If you've any common sense you'll know that had I told him, he wouldn't be taking it so calmly. But then you don't know him very well, do you? He's easy-going up to a point, but beyond that he gets mad.'

'What is this "something" you keep talking about?' Theresa almost shouted, reaching the end of her control.

'Hasn't it occurred to you that your husband might have given me a message for Inigo, because he *knew* he was probably going to die?'

'How could he know? He wasn't so very ill.'

'You admit that now? Earlier you said he was.'

'I didn't say anything of the kind. I said . . . Oh, you're impossible.' She sat staring into the fire for a while, and gradually a calm settled down over her features. She looked like someone who had been through a bad time, and who realises with relief that things are not beyond all hope. She had evidently come to a decision.

'My husband died a natural death,' she repeated. 'And he could not have known he was going to die. All the same, since you and Inigo have seen fit to keep this to yourselves for so long, I should be glad if you'd go on doing so. I shouldn't like Ledgrove to be censured for negligence.'

'That's hardly likely, is it?'

'And why not?'

'He's dead, I imagine,' Dylis remarked, and watched for the effect that might have, if any. It failed to register. Theresa said:

'I hope not, poor man. I also hope you won't be *too* disappointed if he turns up safe and sound. It seems to me you've a flair for melodrama yourself. Have you anything else to say to me? Because if not, I should like to get a little air. This room is stifling.'

'Go ahead,' Dylis invited her. 'I don't find talking to you particularly amusing.'

With a vague feeling of frustration, she watched Theresa gather up her coat and walk across to the door communicating with the dining-room, and fling it back. She had certainly not made much headway. Well, what did it signify? If Theresa had not started anything, she had been prepared to let the whole matter slide.

Theresa took a few steps into the other room, halted, and emitted a scream, the shrillness of which reverberated through Dylis like an electric shock. For a moment she stood petrified by the mantelpiece, her mind unable to impel her body to action. But from the darkness of the other room came further screams, madly hysterical, redolent of fear. Kicking aside the footstool that obstructed her way, Dylis moved quickly into the dining-room, and caught Theresa by the shoulders, where she stood leaning against the table.

'For the love of heaven, what's the matter?' she demanded.

But Theresa could not or would not tell her. She was sobbing now, and in between her sobs she went on screaming.

# Chapter XIV

With Theresa clinging to her like a lost child, there was not much Dylis could do. So she stood in the semi-darkness and waited for whatever came next. Fortunately, it was not long before relief arrived in the shape of Mr Raddle, who came quietly in through the drawing-room, a lighted candle in his hand, and asked:

'Is anything wrong?'

'No,' Dylis said, with some bitterness. 'Nothing at all. We're just playing Postman's Knock.'

She did not mean to hurt the man's feelings, but to be clutched in a fervent embrace by the hysterical Theresa was too much for her equanimity. By the light of Mr Raddle's candle, she could see now that the dining-room was empty, save for themselves. What she had expected to see she hardly knew, but Theresa's screams had conjured up something horrible to the mind. The dining-room door burst open then, and Mr Carpenter appeared, rubbing a hand over his eyes, and demanding:

'What the hell's going on? I never heard such a God-damned noise.'

Theresa chose that moment to abandon her frenzied hold upon Dylis, and to cast herself upon the ground, where she proceeded to bang the carpeted floor with her fists, and to scream even louder.

'I'll get her a glass of water,' Mr Raddle said.

'Make it a jug,' Dylis advised him. 'A large one.'

'Indeed I will. The more water absorbed into the body, the better the constitution.' He retreated, and Mr Carpenter said, moving to the sideboard:

'Brandy.'

By the unsteadiness of his gait and the careful economy of his speech, his occupation for the past few hours could be readily guessed. Nevertheless, his suggestion was not unsound.

'Theresa!' Dylis shouted, bending down and making an effort to raise her from the ground. 'What's got into you?'

She was somewhat put out by this unexpected climax to their conversation. She knew that Theresa had been on edge, but up to the time of opening the communicating door, she had apparently regained her composure. Perhaps it was just a natural reaction to nervous excitement. Whatever it was, she declined to be raised from her prostrate position, she declined to stop screaming. Mr Carpenter, a glass of brandy in his hand, tottered across the room and dropped down on one knee beside her.

'Here,' he said. 'Do you good.'

She reached out a clenched fist, knocked it from his hand, and pressed her face more firmly into the carpet. Between wrath and sorrow, Mr Carpenter surveyed the fallen glass with its contents spilled across the floor. He swore softly but with feeling. Dylis, who had temporarily given up trying to find a solution and was leaning against the table, looked up with relief as Inigo, with Charlie Best following, came charging in through the french windows. Inigo held a hurricane lamp above his head, and the rays falling upon his dishevelled hair gave him an appearance of unreality.

'Dylis!' he exclaimed. 'Are you all right? Whatever's happened?'

He dashed round the table and put an arm about her, saw Theresa, and was about to go to her aid, but Charlie was before him. Without much effort, he lifted her in his arms and carried her into the drawing-room, where he laid her on the couch, just as Mr Raddle entered with a glass jug filled with water.

'Give me that,' Dylis said, took it from him and went to where Theresa lay, sobbing and still letting out spasmodic screams. Dylis was about to pour it over that young lady's tear-stained but still lovely face, when the latter forestalled her by sitting upright, and saying in a choking voice:

'I'm ... I'm all right now. Please don't bother. It was silly of me.'

She gave a quick, enveloping glance at the faces crowding round her, Inigo, Charlie, Mr Raddle and Dylis, and Mr Ashley, who had unobtrusively joined them. Mr Carpenter, who had remained in the dining-room long enough to close the french windows and to help himself to the despised brandy, now came forward with a further glass of that ancient means of revival, and said:

'Chuck this down her throat. Do her good.'

Best took it from him and handed it to Theresa, who accepted it with a grateful smile.

'Thank you,' she said, and sipped a little. Mr Carpenter remarked:

'Ruddy lot of nonsense,' and retired to his favourite chair by the fire.

'But what happened?' Inigo asked. 'Charlie and I heard you screaming as far away as the garage. We rushed up thinking someone was being murdered, at least.'

'Nothing. Nothing at all, really. Dylis and I had been talking, and I went into the dining-room to open the window. It was dark in there, and as I flung back the door, I saw . . . a man.'

Dylis raised an eyebrow. She could have pointed out that there were four men bending over Theresa at the moment, and none of them seemed to be causing her any alarm. She refrained. The heads of the four men in question raised themselves an inch or so and they stared enquiringly into each other's faces. Best asked:

'Who was it? And what was he doing?'

'I don't know. I didn't see him clearly. And he wasn't *doing* anything. That's what frightened me. He was just standing by the door, the other door that opens on to the passage. Oh, I know it was silly of me, but my nerves are so strung up . . . ' She suppressed a sob, and took another sip of brandy. Charlie Best patted her hand. Inigo said:

'Well, who the devil was it? Charlie and I were out in the garage. Where were you, Mr Raddle?'

'I, sir,' that gentleman said with dignity, 'was with Mr Howe in his room. We heard screams of a violent and uncontrolled nature, and Mr Howe requested me to come down and ascertain their cause. On arriving . . . '

'All right. What about you, Mr Carpenter?'

The latter said, without even turning round:

'In bed.'

'With all your clothes on?'

'With all my clothes on. Except my shoes. D'you mind?'

'I was having a wash,' Ashley volunteered. 'What's happened to the servants, the butler fellow and the other one?'

'They were out in the garage,' Inigo said. 'They heard Theresa screaming, too. Vauxhall said . . . well, never mind what he said, but I thought they were following Charlie and me.'

'I expect they didn't want to leave the car,' Theresa said, and gave him a look full of meaning. Dylis, who had been thoughtfully surveying the circle of faces, asked,

'What about the two vanmen? They're the only ones not accounted for.'

'They're over by the barn,' Inigo explained. 'They probably wouldn't have heard anything, at that distance. Feel any better, Theresa?'

'Much better, thank you. But I'm a little cold. Would someone get my coat?'

Charlie Best fetched it from the dining-room, where it lay upon the floor, and wrapped it about her shoulders. She finished the brandy, and sat huddled up there, looking forlorn and pale. Dylis, who had regretfully abandoned the water jug, walked over to the fire and warmed her chilled hands. She was feeling sceptical towards the whole episode. Theresa's screams had sounded genuine enough, but were out of all proportion to the incident that had caused them. She may have seen someone standing by the door, but Dylis doubted it. A shadow, seen in a light bad, could look quite substantial to the imaginative. And suppose she had seen someone? Who was there in that house, the sight of whom could send her into hysterics? Having caught her out in one form of deception, it was difficult to put much credence in anything she said.

The gathering about the couch was breaking up, the men preparing to go their separate ways. Theresa, again glancing round at them, said:

'Please don't go. Now that you're all here, I think there are one or two things we should go into.'

'You ought to rest, Theresa,' Inigo said. 'You're all in. Charlie and I have finished the car, and we're just going to run it round to see how it goes. We've cleared up some more of the snow out there, too, so it should be all right. Why don't you lie here quietly? Dylis will be around if you still feel scared. Won't you, Dyl?'

Dylis said she would, and smiled with much amusement when Theresa did not show any sign of joy or gratitude. Charlie Best warmly seconded Inigo's suggestion, but whether out of solicitude for his hostess or because he was longing to get back to the car was by no means certain. But Theresa was adamant. Before either Mr Ashley or Mr Raddle could make a move or add their voices to the discussion, she said:

'I'm perfectly all right now, thank you. It was just an attack of nerves, brought on by someone who may only have been playing a practical joke, and now has not the sense to admit it. I could understand that, if we'd not had other evidence that there is someone amongst us with a very strange sense of humour. You are all staying here under the most trying circumstances, but I have done my best to make you as welcome as possible. But frankly, I don't like this kind of thing happening in my house, and really Inigo, since you're the only male member of the family present, I think it is up to you to put a stop to it.'

Inigo sat down and looked at her with a mixture of emotions. The others, aware of the tenseness that had crept into the atmosphere, did likewise, all except Dylis, who continued to lean against the mantelpiece, wondering what Theresa might be up to now. Mr Carpenter was the only one who took no interest in the proceedings. He blatantly snored. Inigo said at last:

'But my dear girl, what can I do? You don't expect me to tail everyone about the house in the hope of catching them making an apple-pie bed, or something indicative of a perverse sense of humour?'

'You're a man, aren't you?' Theresa asked, eyeing him with

unusual coldness. 'Surely you don't have to be tinkering about with cars *all* the time?'

'I'm a man all right,' he said. 'And as such I use a little logic. The quickest way to clear up this situation is to get one or all of the cars in working order.'

'After which, I suppose, you will find some other excuse for playing about in the garage. With your uncle lying dead upstairs, I should have thought your first concern would be to find out who is making free of the house and grounds in so extraordinary a fashion.'

What exactly was she getting at, Dylis wondered. Her own surprise was reflected in the faces of the other interested occupants of the room. This attack upon Inigo was so out of place, particularly in view of his recent concern for her. If she were trying deliberately to antagonise him, she was doing very well indeed. There was an angry bitterness beneath the restraint of his voice when he said:

'Do you think I've *forgotten* that he's dead? If there were anything I could do to bring him back, do you think I'd overlook it? But I don't see that it will help for me to go running round the house chasing shadows. I'm doing something practical. We've got to get the doctor here, and I want to find out about that poor fellow Ledgrove. As for the other things that have been happening, I agree, they're odd. We'll hold an enquiry on them, if you like, but I don't think it will do any good. Have you told Theresa about your samples disappearing, Dylis?"

'Yes. As a matter of fact, I've told her everything.'

'And I do think,' Theresa said, 'that you might have taken me into your confidence before, Inigo. After all, this *is* my house, and ... '

'You've a right to know what's going on,' Dylis finished for her.

'While we're all overstepping the bounds of etiquette, Theresa, I suppose you're sure this *is* your house. There's a will in your favour?'

Theresa sat up very straight, and her tone was contemptuous, as she answered:

'There is a will, and naturally my husband's property passes to me. That will all be settled legally in due course. But I did not ask for a debate on my personal affairs. I was merely saying . . . '

'I think,' Mr Raddle interrupted, in his soft voice, 'if you'll excuse me, I had better return to Mr Howe. He will be wondering where I am.'

'Ah . . . ' Theresa turned her hostile gaze upon him, where he sat uncomfortably on the edge of a high-backed chair. 'And how *is* Mr Howe? We have not had the pleasure of his company lately.'

Dylis, feeling that her own nerves were none too steady, was seized with a strong desire to burst out laughing, and to sing, 'Oh, how are you, Mr Howe, how's your mother, Mr Howe?' She could see no sense in Theresa's behaviour. Having started an argument about cars and people hiding in the dining-room, why drag in Mr Howe? With the best will in the world, Dylis could not imagine him doing anything of the kind. The secretary was looking acutely ill at ease.

'He is very well, Madam, very well. I'm sure he would have been most concerned had he known it was you who were screaming. I'm sure he *will* be concerned . . . '

'Why didn't he come himself then, when he heard me scream?'

Mr Raddle rose, and if he did not actually stand to attention, he gave the impression of doing so.

'Mr Howe,' he said, 'is engaged upon a work of vital importance, work of a creative nature which he cannot, at the moment, disturb. Were it otherwise, he would have left your house this morning, Madam, as he had no wish further to inconvenience you.'

'And how long is this work likely to take?'

'He has dictated to me in the past twenty-four hours some ten thousand words, and should be ready to leave the day after tomorrow.'

'Really?' She looked at him with undisguised irony. 'It's nice of him to let me know. But there's a limit to my kindness. I hope you'll tell him that.'

'I shall, Madam, never fear.' And Mr Raddle bowed himself out of the room, as if leaving the presence of royalty. Dylis had been watching the two of them with a curious sensation of disbelief. At last Theresa had abandoned her role of amiable hostess, and as her more natural self Dylis found her almost likeable. Almost, had it not been for that unjustified attack upon Inigo. But there was more to come. Theresa leaped to her feet and began to pace about the room, her hands clutching nervously at the edges of her coat as it swung out from her slender shoulders.

'My guests!' she exclaimed, with unsuppressed bitterness. 'I was glad to take you in, all of you, because you were stranded and had nowhere else to go. My hands were full, but I did not mind a little extra work and worry. And what do I find? Disgraceful behaviour. People sneaking in and out of each other's rooms, playing practical jokes of a most malicious kind. You all stare at me so innocently. None of you had anything to do with it, of course. And you, Inigo, whom I thought I could trust. You allowed yourself to be a party to a conspiracy . . .'

'That'll do, Theresa,' he said, getting to his feet. 'We've heard quite enough. I'm sure we're all agreed that we shall be glad to leave your house as soon as possible. But you're only hindering us, carrying on like this. Are you coming, Charlie?'

'You bet,' Best said, rising also. He had been following Theresa's speech with astonishment and regret. He paused, as she took a step towards them and said:

'No, wait. I've something else to say to you.'

They hesitated, but what she would have said they never knew. For at that moment there came the sound of the french windows opening and shutting, heavy footsteps through the dining-room, and Bob Snell appeared in the doorway. He carried an electric torch in one hand, and his face, begrimed with dirt and oil, was very grave.

'Sorry to bust in,' he said, 'but I got somethin' to say and it won't keep.'

'Well, say it,' Inigo invited irritably. 'What's stopping you?'

Bob Snell looked across the room at Theresa, and Dylis was interested to see that she returned his gaze with something akin to fear in her eyes.

'I got to talk to the lady,' he said. 'I knows what I knows, but I ain't sayin' anythin' except to 'er. In private.'

But at that there was a general protest. Inigo said, 'If you've got anything important to say we'd all better hear it. Mrs Brown has seen fit to accuse us, in a vague kind of way, of making free of her house and grounds. If it's anything to do with this car business . . .'

'Nicely put,' Best said.

'The cars haven't been messed up again, I hope, Mr Snell?' Dylis put in. It had just occurred to her that Inigo and Charlie had left their treasure unguarded. And where were Vauxhall and Ridley? And where, as an afterthought, was Mr Ashley? A moment ago, he had been leaning with his elbows on the back of an armchair, listening to Theresa's tirade. Now he had disappeared, although she had not seen him go out of the room. He must have left very quietly, while their attention was fixed upon Bob Snell. No one else appeared to have missed him.

Theresa said, with a quick return to her best behaviour,

'Of course, Mr Snell, if you've something important to say to me . . .'

She stepped across the room, and in so doing knocked against Mr Carpenter's chair. He sat up, passing a hand over his face, and muttered:

'*Now* what the devil is it? Can't sleep for five minutes in this perishing house.'

Bob Snell had retreated into the dining-room, lit solely by the hurricane lamp which Inigo had left upon the table. Theresa, at the communicating door, was forced to pause, since Inigo stood in her way. She said:

'If you're going to behave like a thwarted schoolboy, my dear, I shall have to call the servants.'

But she had no need to do so. As if taking their cue from an unseen callboy, Vauxhall and Ridley came at lightning speed through the french windows, much as Inigo and Charlie had done earlier. They were breathless and almost inarticulate, but Vauxhall managed to say:

'It's Jackson! He's gone off with the van.'

'Since when?' Bob Snell asked, his expression struggling between incredulity and consternation.

'Since you left it. We heard him start her up, and thought he was just trying her out, until we saw him heading for the drive.'

"E must be barmy!' was Bob Snell's verdict, as he made a dash for the open spaces again. 'But 'e won't get far. Stuck in the drive already, most likely.'

He was through the french windows in an instant, with Vauxhall and Ridley following. Precisely what they intended to do was not apparent, should Jackson fail to fulfil Snell's prediction, but their will to action was infectious. Without exchanging a word, the group gathered in the drawing-room went hurriedly after them, Theresa struggling into her coat, Inigo snatching up his hurricane lamp in passing, Charlie looking alert and interested, and finally Mr Carpenter, flushed of face and knocking into furniture as he moved, muttering, 'To hell with the lot of them!'

Only Dylis remained, because she had no coat, and saw no reason why she should subject herself to the unpleasantness of a cold. But curiosity prevailed, and with a regretful glance at the brightly burning fire, she ran upstairs to fetch her coat from the wardrobe in her room. If the disappearance of a van were of sufficient importance to arouse Mr Carpenter from his lethargy, she could not just sit back in the role of amused spectator. And she had the feeling that she might need a coat from now onward, if people were going to rush in and out of the french windows for the rest of the evening.

Returning quietly along the first floor corridor, she paused at the head of the stairs and drew back into the shadows. Someone was ascending, slowly, a trifle faltering, as if weighed down by a cumbersome burden. Against the dim light filtering from the passage below, the figure of a man came into her line of vision, bent almost double, carrying over one shoulder the limp body of another man. The face was hidden from her, but Dylis caught a glimpse of tousled grey hair, a dark overcoat, heavy boots wet with snow, and the man who carried him was Ashley.

A few seconds more and they had merged into the darkness shrouding the upper staircase, and only the light of the torch which Ashley had switched on showed her their progress. A strange choking sensation assailed her throat, and she stood with her back pressed against the cold wall, straining her eyes, seeing the small point of light turn off in the direction of Ashley's room, hearing him mutter something as he moved away from her.

Without giving herself time for reflection, she followed, hardly breathing, fumbling her way along the wall, pausing when Ashley paused, going on with a sickening sense of mounting nightmare. At a safe distance from Ashley's room she stood and waited while he unlocked the door and stumbled inside. The door closed softly.

# Chapter XV

The party that eventually returned to the drawing-room was cold, dishevelled and frankly argumentative. The van driven away so unceremoniously by Jackson had not broken down in the drive. They had, in fact, reached the end of that slippery surface in time to see its rearlight disappearing along the way that led past Wintry Wold, to join eventually the road to Cudge. And though the roads must still be in a highly dangerous state despite the evidence of a slight thaw in the atmosphere, the point did not appear to be worrying Jackson.

But it was worrying Bob Snell, to judge by the vitriolic language in which he cursed his renegade mate, as they grouped once again about the fire in the drawing-room. Inigo said, slapping his cold hands together:

'I don't see how he can get very far, with those brakes. You said yourself they were in bad shape. The best thing we can do is to get out my car, and I'll give you a lift until we catch up with him. Then I can go on to Cudge, and that'll be killing two birds with one stone.'

He had made the suggestion before, on the way back to the house, but no one was very enthusiastic about it, except Charlie

Best, who had offered to go along, too. As far as Mr Carpenter was concerned, the incident was closed, for he had already poured himself a drink and retreated to the comfort of his chair. Theresa said, trying somewhat hopelessly to restore her hair to its usual tidiness:

'I think you'd better stay here, Inigo, while *I* drive to Cudge. The car is working, Vauxhall?'

That versatile man admitted grudgingly that it was, but added that since he now knew the inside of it better than his own, it would be more practical for him to take the wheel, with Ridley for company, and as a possible helpmeet. Ridley, who was wandering about the room, smoking a cigarette and looking singularly ill at ease, nodded several times but said nothing. Theresa frowned.

'When I want suggestions from you,' she said, with all her old dignity, 'I'll ask for them. I shall drive alone.'

'This ain't gettin' us anywhere,' Snell said. 'If you're drivin', lady, p'raps you wouldn't mind . . . '

'Don't be so damned silly, Theresa,' Inigo interrupted. 'You'll only make a mess of it.' He moved to the door. 'I'm getting the car out, and anyone who likes to come along will be welcome.'

'That'll be me,' Best said, rising from the arm of the chair where Mr Carpenter reposed in happy oblivion. 'But we'd better put a jerk in it, if we're going to catch up with that van, brakes or no brakes.'

Bob Snell hesitated, caught, as it were, between opposing camps, and Theresa said, drawing on her gloves, 'You all do what you please, but I'm driving my own car.'

'Where's Dylis?' Inigo asked, realising with sudden alarm that he had not seen her for some time.

Theresa laughed, and remarked, 'Poking her nose into someone else's business, I daresay, in her usual delightful manner.'

'And what about Ashley?' Best put in, with an enquiring glance round for the other missing guest. 'He was with us when we went down the drive, wasn't he? I thought he came with us.'

'So did I.' With the assurance of a general issuing commands, Theresa turned to her servants. 'Vauxhall, go and get the car started, and take Ridley with you, and look out for anyone you may see around.' She put peculiar emphasis upon the last words and added, 'Where are you going, Inigo?'

Halfway to the door leading on to the passage, he paused. 'To look for Dylis. I expect she's in her room. Charlie, d'you mind fetching out the car? I'll be with you in a minute.'

'Surely,' Best said. 'If this is going to be a neck-and-neck race, I'd like to be in at the start.'

He followed in the wake of Vauxhall and Ridley. Inigo went out the other way, observing, as he did so, that Theresa, despite her bravado, seemed to be in no particular hurry. He grinned a little as he raced up the stairs. She was a complex character. He wondered if she would take Snell with her, or whether she would really start at all. If she changed her mind, he and Charlie could take Snell with them. But he must find Dylis first. Quickly he made his way along to her room.

But a rapid inspection of it only added to his anxiety. Her coat, he observed, was missing, and it was possible she had gone out into the grounds to look for him. He called her name as he retraced his footsteps, and paused at the head of the stairs, still holding firmly to his lamp. He was about to descend, when he heard her soft answering call, and a moment later she came running lightly along the corridor, to catch him by the arm, her expression distressed and urgent.

'Dylis!' he exclaimed, seizing her in turn. 'What have you been up to? I was worried.'

'Prepare to worry some more,' she said. 'It's becoming my normal state of mind. We've got to do something quickly, but I'm not sure what. I'm convinced now your uncle was murdered.'

'But why . . . ?'

'Don't shout, and don't ask me if I'm sure I'm all right. Quickly, this way.' She was dragging him along towards Ashley's room. 'It's Ledgrove. He's turned up. He was unconscious, but he's just coming round.' She paused outside Ashley's door. 'I saw Ashley carry him up just after you all went out. He didn't see me, so I waited till he'd gone again, and then I forced the door, because he'd locked it. I always did have my suspicions of that man.'

She opened the door, and Inigo followed her in, closing it behind him. It was a large room, furnished in the same old-fashioned style as the others, illuminated now by two candles standing upon the mantelpiece. Ledgrove lay on the bed, a mound of bedclothes over him, his grey hair in wild disarray, his face drawn and pallid, with a stubble of beard about the chin.

'He was like this when I came in,' Dylis whispered. 'His hands were cut and burned, so I bandaged them, and I've been trying to bring him round with brandy. But I can't think why Ashley should have taken off his boots and tucked him up . . . '

Frowning, Inigo sat down on the edge of the bed, just as the valet opened tired, bloodshot eyes, to stare fearfully up at them. But his expression changed as Inigo said, 'It's all right. You're quite safe now. I'm Inigo Brown, and this young lady's a friend of mine.'

'Thank God, sir!' Ledgrove reached out a thin hand to clutch at his sleeve. 'I'd know you by the likeness to Mr Warner. Very alike, you are. They got him, didn't they? I was trying to get up there to see, but I came over funny. Is he dead? Just tell me that.'

'Yes, he's dead,' Inigo confirmed sombrely, and sighing, the valet closed his eyes for a moment. The next, and they were wide open, staring with a bitter anger, and his voice, though weak, was urgent.

'It was murder, sir, and I'd take my solemn oath on it. Mr Warner was a prisoner, in his own house, you might say, ever since his last illness. He got me to post that letter to you, without his wife knowing, because he wanted to alter his will and leave everything to you. He was afraid she'd get wind of it, see, if he got his solicitor along. So he thought if you came on a chance visit, as it were, with a friend, he could alter his will on the sly, and me and the friend could be witnesses, and you'd be able to see him right in case of trouble. He reckoned he wouldn't live long, even if they let him, and he wanted it all squared up nice before he went. He was a good man, sir, and now he's gone it's up to you to see they get what's coming to 'em.'

'I intend to,' Inigo said, and Dylis was startled at the change in his face. 'Why did my uncle marry her?'

Ledgrove sighed again. 'She made a dead set at him, and he didn't stand a chance. I saw what was coming, with him feeling twenty years younger and her making up to him something awful to watch. And after they were married, you never saw such a happy couple, or so people thought. But not me. I knew she'd got her fancy man around, even while she was running after Mr Warner. She guessed I knew something, too. She hated me like poison, but Mr, Warner, he was obstinate in some ways, and wouldn't let me go.

'The trouble started soon after we got back from abroad. He didn't want to come back, said it would be too quiet for her. He didn't know that was what she'd married him for chiefly, this house here and the one over the border. I don't know the real

201

rights of it, but he must have come to some arrangement with her, for he sacked the woman and her two daughters who used to look after the place, and instead we had two menservants. That's what *she* called them, but they looked more like gaolbirds to me.'

'Vauxhall and Ridley?' Inigo asked.

'That's what they call themselves. But I reckon the police know 'em by other names. I can't tell you just what's been going on, but it's something dirty and there's money in it, you mark my words. They knew I'd never shop them, because of Mr Warner. He was that far gone on her at first he gave in to her over everything. But money was what she wanted, and not being a wealthy man, I suppose he gave in again over this funny business. That's how I figure he came to turn over his two houses to her and her friends. Old Carpenter's in it, too. I don't mind him so much, because he doesn't put on airs. But he'd sell his own grandmother for the sight of a whisky bottle.'

'He wasn't a friend of Mr Brown, then?' Dylis queried.

'Never saw him before *she* came here. No, he'll be another of her nice friends, Miss, and he'll go on being her friend, so long as she doesn't stop the drink. She's too canny for that.'

Inigo asked, in a tone of suppressed emotion, 'Who killed my uncle?'

'The one I've been telling you about, sir, her fancy man. He turns up here every so often, to keep an eye on things, and on her, if you ask me.'

'What is his name, do you know?'

'Crane, they call him. Don't know his other name. It's always Mr Crane this, and Mr Crane that. "Get Mr Crane's room ready." . . . Oh yes, he always sleeps here, or almost always.'

'What sort of voice has he?' Dylis asked, recalling that Inigo had heard Theresa in conversation with someone whose voice he could not place.

'Just an ordinary sort of voice, I'd say, Miss. Quite pleasant, nicely spoken . . . '

'What does he look like, then?'

'That I can't tell you. I never saw him face to face. He's a bit shy, is Mr Crane. But I've heard him talking to her, because there was only one room they used, and that was hers, after Mr Warner was taken so bad. It's not right to be talking like this to you, Miss, but what is, is, and there's no way of getting round it.'

'Don't you worry about me,' Dylis said. 'My opinion of Mrs Brown was not too good in the first place.'

'A woman's instinct. You can't beat it. She's a wrong 'un all right, although I don't say she'd ever have gone as far as murder, if it hadn't been for *him*. But as Mr Brown was about her, so she was about this Crane. What he said was law, and she'd have married the devil and murdered him, too, I expect, if Crane had told her to.'

'So he told her my uncle had to go, and that was that,' Inigo said bitterly.

'She didn't need too much persuading to agree to it. Things had been awkward ever since Mr Warner found out about her and Crane, just after his first illness. He got me to help him dress that day. Wanted to surprise her, he said. And surprise her he did. He found 'em together, and then the lid was off with a vengeance. The next thing we knew he was back in bed with a relapse. But he wouldn't give in. He was going to live, he told me, until he'd got his will straightened out. He had great faith in you, sir. Well, a day or so after the letter was posted, he was that on edge, expecting you every minute. I knew *she* was expecting Crane, but I didn't let on to Mr Warner, not wanting to worry him.

'When you dropped in as it were from nowhere, she must have been properly flummoxed. Mr Warner heard the bell ring, and sent me down to find out who it was. She and Vauxhall were below, getting drinks ready, and she said it was just some stray people who'd got stuck in the snow. And the same that time I saw you in the kitchen, Miss. You didn't look like one of *their* lot, so I thought she might be telling the truth for once. I sat up for a bit with Mr Warner, after she'd brought his supper, then I made him comfortable for the night and went to my own room next door.'

'There was no need for anyone to sit by him all night?' Dylis asked.

'No, Miss. Once he was on the mend, he wouldn't have anyone with him, not after he'd found out about her. But he had a stick and knocked on the floor if he wanted anything. He wasn't much trouble. He went off to sleep all right that night, but somehow I couldn't do the same. Around one o'clock I thought I heard a car drive up. I hadn't undressed, and at last I couldn't stand it any longer. I felt there was something going on. So I went downstairs . . .'

'That was some time after two, wasn't it?'

'About that, Miss. How did you know?'

'I heard you go past my room. You were wearing slippers, weren't you?'

'Yes, Miss. I didn't want them to hear me, see? They were all in the drawing-room, her and him and their two precious servants. I saw the light under the door and I got down on the ground and listened. It was this Crane who'd driven up in the car I'd heard; a big, powerful car it is, or he wouldn't have got through in that weather.'

'That'll be the one Vauxhall and Ridley were working on today,' Inigo said. 'She told us it was hers.'

'She never had more than one, sir, a smart blue one that Mr Warner gave her. The other is Crane's, all right. He was in a proper stew over you getting here before him. She said how you'd brought a friend along with you, but she'd fix you both and get you away without any trouble.'

'Oh, she did?' Dylis said, with some annoyance. 'So she thought she'd fix us? She'll find she has to think again before she's much older.'

'I hope so, Miss, I'm sure. But you watch out . . . '

'We'll watch out,' Inigo said grimly. 'What happened then?'

'Well, they kept it up for quite a while, trying to work out ways and means, but Crane got his way in the end. He reckoned it would be easy. Mr Warner was still very weak, so it wouldn't take much to smother him in his sleep. They wouldn't have to use much strength on him, and seeing the doctor had been coming regularly, if he called in a day or so and found his patient had died, why shouldn't he sign a certificate? It wasn't easy, he said, for a doctor to tell if someone died of suffocation in a case like that. She'd always taken good care to look like a loving wife when the doctor was around. Only she and her friends knew that Crane was here, or so they thought, and it was convenient the weather being so bad. It often takes off the invalids, coming in suddenly like this, and it was a good excuse for not getting the doctor at once. And if by any chance he did want an inquest, the verdict was bound to be accidental death, Crane said.

'There was me, of course. I was supposed to be in the room next door, but Ridley was told off to keep an eye on me, in case I woke while Crane and Vauxhall were doing the job.'

He fell silent, and Inigo and Dylis exchanged glances. Before either of them could speak, Ledgrove went on, with an attempt at a smile, 'You've done me good. I'm getting hungry. I haven't eaten since they got me.'

'Good heavens!' Dylis exclaimed. 'You were ...'

'I was in the barn. They chucked me in there to be out of the way. They didn't want two dead bodies on their hands. They were going to take me out in the car, as soon as they could and throw me over somewhere so it'd look as if I'd fallen, on my way to fetch the doctor.'

'But why?' Inigo asked.

'They caught me listening. That woman's got ears as long as a donkey. I got cramped up, crouching by that door, and I just shifted a bit, didn't think I'd made any noise, but she was on to me in a minute. It was all up then. Crane had slipped out, when they grabbed me in, but those two dirty gaolbirds fixed me up nicely with ropes and a gag to stop me raising the roof, and they even thought to put boots on my feet instead of slippers, and a coat, and a hat to chuck down after me so I'd look all of a piece. The faithful valet come to a sticky end. That Vauxhall made a joke about it, but to give *her* her due she was looking a bit sick and had to have a couple of drinks to pull her round. Then they stuck me out in the barn, because I'd got to be alive when I went over, or it might look fishy. They fed me with water, and nothing else ...'

'I'll get you something,' Dylis said. 'If you think you could eat it.'

'I can eat all right. I'm a lot tougher than I look. But you'd better go carefully, Miss. I'm warning you ...'

'I'm warning you, too, Dyl,' Inigo said rising. 'You've taken enough risks for one night. We've got to work this out together.'

She looked from him to Ledgrove and nodded, apparently calm. But her throat felt dry as she asked, 'Just one more thing. How did you get out of the barn?'

Ledgrove looked ruefully down at his bandaged hands. 'They've got an oil heater in there, Miss. They use the barn, d'you see, for their goings on. I was too weak to do anything when they first chucked me in . . . when that Vauxhall knocks you out, you stay knocked out for quite a while. But tonight I got desperate, and being a bit stronger, I held my wrists over the stove until I'd burned through the ropes. Then I got the rest of me loose. There's a small window at the back covered in canvas, so I smashed it and managed to get through. It was as much as I could do to walk, but I got under cover. I saw lights flashing about, and knew they were after me. So I hid under a bush, and a bit later I heard a lot of shouting and running, but not my way, so I thought it was too good a chance to miss of getting into the house and seeing if Mr Warner was alive or dead. And I knew you were about somewhere, sir, but when I got as far as the dining-room, I came over funny, and I don't remember any more.'

He closed his tired eyes and Inigo said in an undertone, 'Ashley must have picked him up then. We wondered where he'd got to.'

'I don't like it at all,' Dylis whispered back. 'I've a nasty feeling he might be . . . '

'Crane? Surely not. Theresa's been anything but pleasant to him.'

Dylis shrugged. 'She's a smart little actress.' She glanced at Ledgrove, lying so still and pallid that he appeared to be with them in the flesh only. 'I *must* get him some food. He looks terrible, doesn't he?'

'He does. But I think you'd better wait a bit first. They're all at sixes and sevens downstairs. I'll try and get them out into the grounds, so that you can slip down and do your stuff. Then I'm going to talk to Theresa . . . '

'Don't you think you'd better get the police? This isn't a one-man job, I should say.'

'And leave you here alone with all this business going on? Not likely.'

'Couldn't you send Charlie?'

'I suppose so. But he's a journalist, and this is a family affair. I don't want it broadcast to the nation.'

'Maybe not. But you can't hush up a murder, can you?'

'I don't know. I was never mixed up in one before. But I don't want to raise a hue and cry until I know positively who did it. Particularly with the local police.'

'And you propose to find out by asking Theresa?'

'She'll tell me,' Inigo said. 'Just give me fifteen minutes alone with the little lady.'

'Well, you'd better work fast, or I shall start walking to the police station myself.'

'We've got the car going now.'

'How do you know someone hasn't busted it up in the meantime?'

'Oh, Lord!' He clutched a hand to his forehead. 'I'd better get below and see what's going on. You stay here with Ledgrove and keep the door barricaded, in case anyone comes looking for him. It's better for him to be hungry than dead.'

'All right,' Dylis said wearily. 'But don't leave me too long. If there's going to be a scrap, you may find me right behind you with a poker.' She added, as he opened the door and looked out, 'Inigo! Do be careful.'

'You bet. Watchful Willie, that's me.'

He went out, and somewhat reluctantly, she closed the door and put a chair under the handle, with another on top of that. Ledgrove had fallen into an uneasy doze. One of his eyelids twitched spasmodically. Dylis lighted a cigarette from the candle flame and sat down to wait.

# Chapter XVI

Inigo, reaching the head of the stairs and about to descend at a run, paused as Theresa, accompanied by Mr Carpenter, appeared round the bend in the corridor from the direction of Dylis's room. Mr Carpenter was weaving from side to side, and his shadow, cast upon the walls by Theresa's candle, looked like that of an eccentric dancer. She called out:

'We've been looking for Dylis and Mr Ashley. But we haven't seen either of them. Have you?'

'Ashley's not in his room,' Inigo said truthfully. 'They're somewhere downstairs, I expect, or in the grounds. I was just going down to see.'

'So mysterious of them, isn't it?' Theresa said. He noted, as she came abreast of him, that she had regained her composure, on the surface at any rate, and her eyes, looking up at him above the light of the candle, were blankly innocent. He found it hard to realise that she had any other side to her nature. He countered:

'No more mysterious than the behaviour of some other people around this house. We've all been diving in and out like a lot of lunatics.'

'Lunatics is right,' Mr Carpenter said thickly. 'Damned lot of lunatics is what I've said all along.'

'*Please*,' she admonished him. 'You've been so helpful up to now, don't spoil yourself.'

Exactly how Mr Carpenter had proved so helpful was one of the things Inigo intended to find out. He said:

'I want to talk to you, Theresa, alone.'

'Of course, my dear, but not now. We're just going to look in these other rooms ...' She waved the candle in the direction where lay the rooms of Best and Ashley. Not while he could stop them, Inigo thought. It was on the cards that they were really looking for Ledgrove, if the whole thing were not just a mad dream, and he did not want the valet to be discovered immediately. He said:

'I've already told you, I looked and there's no one there. Why should anyone be?'

'I really don't know. Except that all my guests seem to be a little eccentric. And you were anxious about Dylis, weren't you?'

'I still am. I thought she might be in her room, but she's not, and Ashley isn't in his ...'

'So you think I must have hidden them away somewhere? I'm afraid your family is inclined to be theatrical, Inigo. But I haven't time to discuss such things now, my dear. I'm going to drive to Cudge. Come, Mr Carpenter.'

But she did not wait for her drunken escort. Leaving him to follow at his own unsteady pace, she went down the stairs at a rate which in any other woman could have been described as tearing. But Theresa did not tear. She kicked up the heels of her little Alpine boots and appeared to fly through the air, so rapidly did she reach the hall below, yet withal gracefully. Inigo, now frankly furious, followed, but Mr Carpenter, with waving

210

arms and unsteady legs, meandered in his way, all but tripping him up in the process. At the bottom, Inigo thrust him rudely to one side, sprang clear, and made for the drawing-room door through which Theresa had disappeared. On the other side, he found that luck was with him, for Theresa was venomously eyeing Charlie Best, who was impeding her progress by leaning in the communicating aperture. Charlie said in an injured way as Inigo appeared:

'What's going on, old man? People rushing in and out, and lights flashing about in the grounds. Have you all gone nuts, or what?'

'Something of the kind,' Inigo said, and got a firm grip on Theresa's mink coat as she was about to dive beneath Charlie's arm.

'Well, if you prefer playing touch to driving to Cudge, don't let me stop you,' the journalist said. 'But I got the car out and ran it round to the front and it's all ready when you are. I didn't want to freeze to death out there, so I just nipped in for a warm.'

'Mr Best,' Theresa said, through gritted teeth, 'will you please stand out of my way? And Inigo, I must ask you not to molest me in this undignified fashion.'

'Has it come to that, old boy?' Best asked, with a grin and a reproving shake of the head. But the grin faded as Theresa reached up and smacked him smartly across the face, twisted out of Inigo's grasp and streaked through the dining-room and out of the french windows. Inigo plunged after, calling over his shoulder:

'Sorry, Charlie. We're having a slight family argument. See you in a minute. We may need that car later.'

Theresa must have the eyes of a cat, he thought. Outside it was pitch dark, and the snow was sloshy and slippery underfoot. But over to the left, where they had cleared a broad driveway as far as the garages, the sidelights of a car pierced the darkness. Theresa's car, probably, or that fellow Crane's. She would be making for that. Of all the ... He thought many bitter things as, aided by his lamp, he hurtled through half melted snow up to his ankles. The sound of the engine being started reached his ears as he drew nearer, and then the headlights were switched on. He made a last jump forward, tripped over something lying in the snow, and sprawled face downwards. Picking himself up, he wheeled round, the light held high above his head, and discovered the body of a man. He brought the light lower, and saw that the upturned face was that of Ashley. He let out a shout capable of carrying far and wide, and reached the car as Theresa was pressing an experimental foot upon the accelerator. She turned to him impatiently and asked:

'What is it now?'

'Maybe I'm theatrical,' he said, one foot upon the running-board, 'but Ashley is lying unconscious a few yards away. You wouldn't know anything about that, I suppose?'

He could not tell from her expression whether she did or not, and at that moment the unmistakable figure of Vauxhall slouched into view from out of the surrounding darkness. He said:

'The lady doesn't know anything, and neither do I.'

'How long have you been out here?' Inigo asked.

'Longer than I care to think about. I got the car out, like she asked me to, and that's all I know.'

'You didn't see Mr Ashley there when you came out?'

'I didn't see anything.'

Inigo's shout had now brought to the scene Charlie Best, stumbling from the direction of the house, and Bob Snell and

Ridley, who might have come from anywhere, each carrying an electric torch.

'Over there,' Inigo said, and indicated the spot where Ashley lay. 'We'd better get him into the house, before he passes out with cold.' He added to Theresa, 'You'll come along too.'

'It in no way concerns me,' she said. 'I'm going to Cudge. So will you please take your big foot . . . '

But she was to learn that being small had its disadvantages. Without any apparent effort, Inigo opened the door, leaned over and whisked her out of the car and set her on the ground beside him.

'Not before I've talked to you,' he said.

She stood there, speechless and shaking, but whether from cold or fear or anger it would have been difficult to say. Bob Snell came ploughing his way across the intervening space to them.

'Someone's slugged 'im,' he said hoarsely. 'There's somethin' ruddy funny goin' on around 'ere, and I'm goin' to get the police.'

Saying which he pushed past Inigo and Theresa and climbed into the car. She said coldly:

'Not in *my* car, Mr Snell. I'm driving to Cudge, and I'll call in at the police station on my way, but I'm going alone.'

'Sorry, lady,' he said, but there was no real apology in the phrase. 'You can drive if you like, it don't make no difference to me. But there's somethin' barmy goin' on, and I ain't standin' for it.'

'I think we'll talk this over before we get in the police . . . ' Inigo was beginning when they heard Ridley's voice yelling:

'God Almighty, Look what I've found.'

Mechanically and with some speed, Inigo moved in that direction, a few yards from where Best was trying unaided to lift Ashley's inert body. Ridley was shining his torch upon the snow, where a patch of blood was clearly visible. Vauxhall, kneeling beside him, said:

'It's blood, all right.'

'Suppose it is?' Inigo retorted. 'You've seen blood before, haven't you? No need to yell like a maniac.' He turned on the instant, but was too late. Theresa had already slipped beneath the driving wheel of the car, and it shot forward as if entered for a race. Frustrated and angry, he stood looking after the rear-light as the vehicle slid past the house and took the corner into the driveway. He swore. Best came up and said:

'Before we *all* go nuts, d'you think we might get Ashley into the house? He's had a conk on the head that isn't doing him any good.'

He was right, Inigo thought. It was not much good giving chase to Theresa, with a start like she had and a car such as the one she was driving. She would be coming back, anyway, and when she did ... Meanwhile, Ashley might be dying, for all he knew. He turned and caught the arm of Vauxhall, who seemed about to fade into the blackness.

'Here, you and Ridley get him up to the house,' Inigo said. He would feel better with these two safely in a lighted room, instead of playing ducks and drakes with them in the darkness of the grounds. Vauxhall began, 'I don't see—'

'Carry him in, blast you!' Inigo roared, and without further protest they stooped and lifted Ashley between them and went towards the house, with Inigo and Best following. The latter said in an undertone, 'What do you make of it?'

'I wish I knew,' Inigo said. 'If we can bring Ashley round, perhaps he'll be able to tell us something.'

In the drawing-room, they laid the unconscious man upon the couch. Mr Carpenter, who had been sitting before the cosy fire, rose shakily, a glass of whisky in one hand, and peering across at

Ashley out of bloodshot eyes, muttered, 'What's this? Another little murder?'

'You shut up,' Vauxhall said, and as Best and Inigo looked round for some means of revival, he moved adroitly to the communicating door and stood with his back to it. In his hand had appeared a useful size in revolvers. Ridley, who had observed this manoeuvre with interest, leaned upon the back of the couch and waited expectantly. Vauxhall went on, 'That's all for tonight, gents. You can stop worrying who did it, because I did it. He was all fixed to monkey with the car again, so I slugged him. Unsolicited confession. He's a split. I frisked him, so I know.'

'Well, I'll be damned!' Charlie Best exclaimed. His tone was inappropriately mild. 'Is that thing you're holding loaded?'

'You'll find out if you try anything funny. Ridley! Lock all the bloody doors and take the keys and hop out and get the bloody car started.'

'Which bloody car?' Ridley asked, moving quickly to obey the first part of his instructions.

'The one in the front, you fool. The other's not going.'

A shout of indignation came from Inigo, who had been listening as if stunned. But this suggested act of open piracy broke the spell put upon him by the theatrical-looking weapon in Vauxhall's hand. He really was the most versatile of butlers. Inigo could have kicked himself for overlooking Dylis's advice to be wary. He said:

'Not *my* car. If you want to get anywhere in a hurry, try running.'

Vauxhall was amused, in a sour kind of way.

'I can do that, too,' he said. 'But meantime I'll take the car.'

'After we worked on it like slaves all day? Not likely. I don't want it messed up again.' Inigo, genuinely annoyed about the

215

car, was also wondering whether he could make a dive round the couch and tackle Vauxhall by the legs. He decided he could, if he acted quickly.

'I didn't mess it up, *he* did,' Vauxhall said, with a wave of his free hand in the direction of Ashley. Then seeing the look on Inigo's face, he added, 'Stay where you are, or it'll be the worse for you. Carpenter! Come on, you drunken old swine. We've got to get out of here.'

He moved a little to one side to allow Ridley to pass through into the dining-room. They heard the latter lock the door in there leading on to the passage, and go out through the french windows. Mr Carpenter, who was leaning against the mantelpiece for support, finished his whisky at one swallow, blinked several times, and said:

'I'm not coming.'

'Don't be a blasted fool. Going to stay here and get jugged?'

'To hell with you!' Carpenter said, reached for the whisky bottle and proceeded to pour himself another drink. The neck of the bottle rattled against the glass despite his efforts to keep it steady.

'Let me give you a hand with that, old boy,' Best said. 'Could do with a drop myself.'

'*Stay where you are!*' Vauxhall warned him, his voice deadly quiet. 'Are you coming, Carpenter? I'm not leaving you behind.'

'Go and blister in hell,' the latter said. 'I'm sick of the lot of you. I'm going to have a drink.'

'For the last time, come on, or I'll drill you.'

The glass in one hand and the bottle in the other, Carpenter looked at the man with the gun and there was a wealth of contempt in his bleary eyes. Then with a jerking movement of his arm, he flung the bottle across the intervening space and ducked down into his chair. His aim may not have been accurate, but it was telling, for the gun was knocked clean out of Vauxhall's hand, and neither Inigo not Best, who had been watching the interplay with close attention, was slow to grasp the opportunity. As Vauxhall sprang after his weapon, Best kicked it to one side, and Inigo brought up his fist and delivered a blow that sent the man to the ground and into the mists of oblivion.

'Vauxhall meets his Waterloo,' Best chuckled, and Inigo, looking down at his fallen adversary, said in a bemused way:

'I never thought I'd have the nerve to hit a butler.'

Mr Carpenter, observing that the situation was well under control, sat back and contentedly sipped his whisky.

'And now for Ridley,' Best said, picking up the revolver and inspecting it with interest.

'But it's my car ... ' Inigo was protesting, when his comrade-in-arms cut him short by pointing to the still inanimate Ashley.

'Look, that man needs attention. You're the expert, mountaineering, rescue parties and that sort of thing. And you don't have to have *all* the fun, do you? This is going to make a lovely story. "*How I captured a desperado single-handed.*" I've no idea what this is all about, but I'm enjoying it. See you presently.' He went out.

Somewhat disconsolate, with two unconscious bodies on his hands and another, in the shape of Mr Carpenter, well on the way, Inigo set about restoring one of them. He found an unopened bottle of brandy in the dining-room, uncorked it, poured a generous measure into a glass and held it to Ashley's lips. Brandy, he reflected, was in great demand in this house. No wonder Theresa kept an ample supply. He would do a little restoring on himself just as soon as Ashley came round. But the blow that unfortunate man had received had obviously been delivered by a master hand. Resentfully Inigo looked down upon the fallen Vauxhall, sprawled across the carpet, and hoped, with some vindictiveness, that he would stay like that for a long time. He continued to force the life-giving liquid down Ashley's throat, and was gratified to observe signs of revival. But Ashley's eyes had a curiously blank expression when they opened, and he asked in a muffled voice:

'Did we get him?'

'He got you,' Inigo said. And as Ashley slowly turned his head and looked about the room, he added, indicating Vauxhall, 'but we got *him*.'

'Not that ugly mug,' Ashley muttered. 'Although we want him, too. It's Crane I'm talking about.'

Then his head fell back and he was again unconscious.

# Chapter XVII

There came a frenzied banging on the drawing-room door, and Dylis's voice called:

'What's going on in there?'

'Nothing,' Inigo shouted back. 'Except that everyone's passing out and I'm on the way. The door's locked, and I haven't got the key.'

'Who has got it, then?'

'Ridley, but he's not here. Can't you please go upstairs and stay there for a bit like a good girl? Just until we've got this all worked out?'

'No.' She kicked at the door. 'How can I get in? Can't you force the lock?'

'Go round by the french windows,' Mr Carpenter bellowed suddenly from the depths of his chair. 'And shut up, some of you. I'm getting a headache with all this noise.'

'You'll have a worse one before the night's out,' Inigo said exasperated. 'Don't take any notice of him, Dyl. Go upstairs, there's a dear. The grounds aren't safe, and neither is anywhere else, but upstairs is better than the grounds.' Ashley was showing no sign of revival. Inigo poured two glasses of brandy this time, and added, 'Charlie's out there, chasing around with a gun. I don't think he can shoot, but he might try. That's why it's dangerous.'

'Is he one of them, then?' Dylis shrieked through the keyhole.

'No, he's one of us.'

'Then why has he got a gun?'

Inigo was silent, watching Ashley in some anxiety. After a moment or two, Dylis went away. But it was not very long before she appeared through the dining-room, having, on Mr Carpenter's advice, made her way out by the back of the house and in by the french windows. She was looking calm and self-possessed, but very weary.

'I didn't see anyone in the grounds,' she said. 'What's been happening?'

'Nothing to what's going to happen when I find that fellow Crane.' Inigo rose from the side of the couch, and she saw Ashley lying there with blood on his forehead, his eyes closed. 'Vauxhall outed Ashley and then got belligerent with a gun, so we had to out him. Theresa has driven off in her car, or Crane's car, which-ever it is, and Ridley was proposing to go off in mine, so Charlie's gone after him with Vauxhall's gun. I only hope he doesn't shoot himself in the process. Why didn't you take my advice and stay upstairs? But I might just as well argue with myself. Trust you to be in at the death.'

Dylis stepped over Vauxhall's recumbent body and knelt beside Ashley. She inspected his injuries with care.

'I'll get some water and bandages,' she said. 'Inigo, why don't you ask Mr Carpenter about Crane? He ought to know.'

But Mr Carpenter had drifted into profound slumber, his heavy breathing filling the quiet room.

'He's too tight to care,' Inigo said. 'But according to Vauxhall, Ashley's something to do with the police.'

'That's quite possible.' Dylis frowned, watching his ministrations to the unconscious man. 'It would certainly account for a lot.'

'And although I reckon Vauxhall as a prize liar, he'd hardly have bashed Ashley if he'd been one of them.'

'No . . . ' Suddenly she clutched his arm. 'Inigo! Why didn't we think of it before? Charlie Best . . . *he's* Crane!'

'Charlie?' Carefully Inigo put down the brandy bottle upon the table and stared at her. 'But it's incredible. He's such a decent sort of bloke . . . '

'I know . . . I know. You like him, so he must be all right. But don't you see how it fits? That friendly manner of his, it could deceive anyone. And he's quite attractive enough for a woman like Theresa to fall for him. I've seen them exchange some very soft looks from time to time. I expect old Howe and Raddle are in it, too, and have skipped off already, since it seems to be every man for himself now.'

'And Best was pretty quick to rush out with that gun,' Inigo agreed thoughtfully. 'A neat job that, if he's Crane. He can catch up with Ridley, and the two of them beat it together.'

'Unless we stop them,' Dylis said, buttoning her coat.

'I'm going alone,' Inigo answered with decision, and snatched up his lamp. 'I can't let them get away with this, but I don't want you mixed up in any scrapping, Dyl. You stay here and do what you can for Ashley. He might pass out altogether if he's left alone. The doors are locked, so no one can get in, and you'd better lock the french windows after me, I'll call out when I get back.'

Saying which he went swiftly out through the dining-room before she could make any protest. The night was still very dark and the grounds devoid of sound or movement, save for the rustling of snow-clad branches in a rising wind. Ploughing his way along to the drive, Inigo could clearly see in the light from his lamp the tyre marks of the cars that had preceded him. One of them had skidded badly. Beyond the drive, he turned right, along the road that led to the main highway, and quickened his footsteps at sight of the headlights of a car drawn up at the side of the road a few hundred yards ahead.

There came the sound of men's voices raised in altercation, and as he drew nearer, he saw a group of six indistinguishable figures, and another car, without lights, stationed on the other side of the road. He crossed to that side, and hiding the light of his lamp, approached cautiously. It was his car, and the other looked as if it might belong to the police. His theory was confirmed as one of the figures moved farther into the reflected light and showed himself to be in uniform.

Treading silently over the intervening space, Inigo said, 'Pardon my butting in . . . '

They all spun round, and he could see them more clearly. Ridley, with a policeman holding one arm and Charlie Best holding the other, a uniformed man on either side of them and a man in a trilby hat and heavy overcoat, who asked sharply, 'Who's there?'

'My name's Brown,' Inigo said, and could hardly repress a slight grin at the conventionality of the phrase. But his expression changed as Ridley, taking advantage of the interruption, wrenched himself free, and ducking beneath the constable's arm, was off up the road within a split second. Emitting a shout, Charlie Best followed, with two of the constables also in hot pursuit. Inigo was about to dash after, but felt his arm gripped by the man in the trilby hat, who said, 'Just a moment. I'd like to have a few more details, if it's all the same to you.'

'But they're getting away.' Inigo was suddenly annoyed,

excited, and full of the will to action. 'Ridley, and that fellow Crane. They're both wanted by the police, or if they're not, they ought to be.'

'Did you say Crane?' the other asked, almost gently. 'William Henry Crane?'

'I don't know him as well as all that. He calls himself Best, a journalist . . . '

'That's what he told us,' the man said. 'But we don't take any chances. They won't get far, either of them. Now, who did you say you are? I'm Detective Sergeant Grabham, C.I.D., and this is Sergeant Forbes from Cudge.'

Inigo drew a deep breath, restraining his impatience with an effort. He began to explain, but such was the tenseness of his manner that his story did not sound nearly as convincing as the truth should, until Sergeant Forbes, who had been listening intently, broke in to affirm, with a slight Yorkshire accent, that he knew Mr Warner Brown well, that he recognised the old man's nephew from the family likeness and a recent photograph, and was going on to describe his many visits to Wintry Wold during the course of his duties at Cudge in the good old days.

But at that moment a car came forcing its way along the road in the direction of Wintry Wold, its headlights penetrating the darkness ahead with a blinding glare, thrown back by the glistening snow. Of necessity, it was travelling at much less than its normal speed, but even so it had passed before any of them could make a movement.

'That's Crane's car,' Inigo shouted, glimpsing the number plate. 'My uncle's wife got away in it earlier, but I can't think what she's doing, turning back.'

'On the run,' Detective Sergeant Grabham said laconically, as there approached another car, identical with his own. It went by with a vaguely groaning sound, as if the obstacles it had so far encountered were beginning to tell.

'We'd better get after them,' Inigo suggested. 'The road gets worse farther on.'

'No need, sir. That'll be Inspector Morden, and he'll have everything under control.'

'Look,' Inigo said, exasperated by this apparent complacency. 'My uncle's dead, and I think he was murdered, and his wife had something to do with it. She won't just drive home and sit there waiting for you. She'll be taking the road that goes through Deathleap Pass. But there's another road that cuts across the lower slope of the Scar and links up with the Pass on the other side. You could cut her off that way, and be sure of getting her. It's a short road, but dangerous.'

'I haven't seen one round here that isn't,' Grabham said. 'How d'you get to it?'

'I'll show you if you like. That's my car over there.'

It seemed an eternity before the Detective Sergeant made up his mind, held a murmured conversation with the man from Cudge, who nodded his understanding and approval.

'Right,' Grabham said, and with sudden and extraordinary swiftness, for he was a big man, plunged across the road and into the stationary vehicle. Inigo followed, put out his lamp and stowed it away. Then taking the driving seat, he overcame a slight difficulty in starting the car, put her into reverse, backed into a convenient space, turned, and began the drive along the road past Wintry Wold and up towards the winding, climbing way that led to Deathleap.

Their headlights picked out the road, rutty, snowbound, improbable. To right and left they could see nothing, which was as well, Inigo thought grimly. For the heights dropped away so unexpectedly in places that by daylight such a stretch was apt to be disconcerting. Once they glimpsed the tail-light of the police car, which appeared to be in difficulties. Then they found themselves in difficulties, and by the time they were clear, there was no sign of other traffic on the lonely road.

A few minutes later, they had turned off upon the short cut, and it required all Inigo's driving skill to keep the car climbing. They took the sharp bend at the top, where the cut joined the Pass, with an unpleasant swivelling movement, and Inigo pulled up, blocking the narrow road.

'Is this it?' Grabham asked, peering through the windscreen.

'This is it,' Inigo rejoined, and gritted his teeth as there came into their line of vision from the winding way to the right the headlights of two cars, one some fifty yards behind the other. It might be just a routine job to Mr Grabham, but to him it was a personal matter. He opened the car door and stepped out into the teeth of the wind.

# Chapter XVIII

Dylis sat by the fire, consuming hot coffee and sandwiches, and trying not to picture Inigo, shot through the heart and lying somewhere in the snow. It had been as much as she could do to restrain herself from rushing out after him, but common-sense had prevailed, and instead she had turned her attention to bringing some kind of law and order back to the drawing-room.

She had been obliged to force the lock of the door leading on to the passage, to procure first aid materials for Ashley, who with his head bathed and bandaged, now lay on the sofa in a state of semi-consciousness which, if not entirely satisfactory, was at least encouraging.

Vauxhall was still in a world of his own, but she had taken the precaution of binding his hands and legs with curtain cords. Mr Carpenter, on the other hand, had come to life sufficiently to note her activities with a certain dour amusement.

'Not taking any chances, eh?' he said, when she finally relaxed in a chair opposite. Then he lapsed into his accustomed silence, viewing with blank ingratitude the coffee, black and strong, that she had placed on the table beside him, until he hit upon the happy idea of adding to it a measure of whisky, whereupon he drank it down with every evidence of satisfaction.

'Damned fools!' he burst out suddenly. 'Trying to get away with murder. If I'd known in time . . . ' His voice trailed away, and he stared broodingly into the fire.

'You liked Mr Brown?' Dylis asked.

'Liked him? I detested him. Sanctimonious old bore.'

'Then why didn't you go when Vauxhall wanted you to?'

'Murder. Don't like it. Never have. Don't like Vauxhall, either. I wasn't going to be bullied by that outsize thug. And what difference does it make? May as well die in jail as anywhere else. One hospital's the same as another. Damned fools! . . . They never appreciated the work I did for 'em.'

He leaned back, muttering to himself, and afraid that he was about to fall asleep again, she prompted, 'What work was that?'

'Pornography!' He almost shouted the word. 'And damned good pornography, at that. I ought to know, I printed it.' He reached for the whisky bottle, helped himself, and stared into his glass in sullen reflection. 'But all they ever thought about was money. That's all old Brown thought about, too, that and his wife, which is as good as saying the same thing. I'd have been sorry for him, if he hadn't been such an old bore. Didn't smoke, didn't drink. He only had us here under protest. But she told him she had to have money, and it didn't take her long to show him the easiest way to get it. Served him right, though. Marrying a smart piece like that. Couldn't ever think what he saw in her. She made me sick, with her "Mr Carpenter, will you do this?" And, "Mr Carpenter, will you do that? *Please*, Mr Carpenter."'

He produced a fair imitation of Theresa's voice and emitted a thin cackle of laughter.

'It had its funny side, after you lot turned up. To hear her trying to get Vauxhall to act the butler was enough to make a cat die laughing. She kept on at him, but she might just as well have saved her breath. Nothing'll ever turn him into anything but what he is, except a rope round his neck. But she's like that, all milk and honey until crossed, and then look out for the fireworks.'

Dylis raised her head, at a sound from the sofa. Ashley had opened his eyes, and was struggling to a sitting position. She went across to him. 'Feeling any better?' she asked.

'A little, thanks.' His eyes smiled, though his mouth was grimly set as he put a hand to his bandaged head. Glancing at the still huddled figure of Vauxhall, he asked, 'Where are the rest of them?'

She was about to reply, when there came a loud hammering upon the french windows in the dining-room. 'That'll be Inigo, I expect,' she said, and ran through to fling open the windows and discover a tall man in police uniform who demanded, 'Detective Inspector Ashley, Miss? I was told he's here.'

'So he is,' she said. 'But only just.' She led the way and he followed, to stand in the communicating entrance, his eyes, in a flushed and healthy face, taking in the occupants of the room and focusing upon Ashley. The latter said, 'Come in, Sergeant . . . you're a very welcome sight. What's the news?'

The sergeant moved quickly forward. 'This is a bad business, sir,' he said. 'We met Mr Brown, and he said you'd been hurt. No bones broken, I hope?'

'Only my head,' Ashley assured him. 'And that feels as if it had been split in two. I'd almost given you up for lost. Isn't Inspector Morden with you?'

'He's still on the chase, sir. We did the first part of the job, but were held up. But we picked up one of the vans earlier this evening, driven by a man named Jackson. Couldn't get much sense out of him, but we got the impression he was on the run. Then a bit later we got into difficulties, and along came a car driven by Ridley. We apprehended him . . . '

'What about Crane?' Ashley interrupted impatiently.

'We got him, too, sir,' the sergeant announced with quiet pride. 'He came along about the same time, on foot, and questioned, said he was chasing Ridley. He was armed, and became violent when we doubted his story . . . The two of them tried to make a dash for it, and led us a bit of a dance, but I've got them outside in the car now safe enough, with two of my men . . . '

He spun round, and Ashley got laboriously to his feet, as there came the sound of footsteps again outside the french windows. The sergeant said, gripping Ashley's arm, 'Steady, sir. You're not out of the wood yet, you know. That's the rest of our lot, I reckon. They were all after that young woman, Mrs Brown. She passed us in Crane's car . . . '

The worst of Dylis's fears were relieved when Inigo walked into the room, smiled vaguely and flopped down into the nearest chair. He looked awful, his hair all over the place, his dark eyes staring straight ahead of him. He was followed by Sergeant Grabham, and a strange man in a tweed overcoat with a soft felt hat jammed over his eyes. The latter removed the hat as he entered, and Ashley greeted him, shaking him warmly by the hand.

'Hallo, Morden. I've never been so pleased to see anyone in my life. You're looking a bit done up, though. Take a seat and tell us all about it.'

Morden glanced quickly round. He looked younger than Ashley, with a rather long face, a jutting jaw, and heavy eyebrows.

He nodded to Dylis, stared for a moment at the dozing figure of Mr Carpenter, and the unconscious Vauxhall, before seating himself. Dylis mechanically handed round cigarettes, put one between Inigo's lips and lighted it for him. He thanked her with a smile and went on staring into space. Ashley said, 'Well, come on, man. What happened?'

'We were on our way up here,' Morden explained, 'when we almost ran into Crane's car. We couldn't see who was driving, but I sent the others on to report to you, and gave chase. We went right past here, climbing all the time, and then we came to a stretch where there's a lovely drop on one side and something that looks like a mountain on the other . . . '

'That's the beginning of the Pass,' Inigo said. 'Sergeant Grabham and I were coming up from the other way. There's a bend at the top and just as we turned and pulled up, we saw Mrs Brown. She saw us about the same time, I should think. I'd blocked the road. I suppose she thought her only chance was to reverse and make a dash for it past the Inspector, who was still some way behind where the road is wider.'

'Fat chance she'd have had,' Morden said.

'She tried it, anyway. She put the car into reverse, and must have misjudged . . . It went over the edge of Deathleap.'

'Killed?' Ashley queried, as Inigo paused, running a hand through his hair.

'It's a drop of about five hundred feet,' Inigo said, and Morden added, 'The car burst into flames. Lit up the country for miles, and I don't mind saying it shook me to see the road we were using. When I'm driving over that sort of place I prefer not to see it too clearly.'

A silence enfolded the room. Dylis, feeling ill, dropped down on to the nearest seat, which happened to be the pouffe, recalled that it was Theresa's favourite, and stood up again. Ashley leaned against the mantelpiece and thoughtfully blew smoke rings into the still air.

'Suppose we get this straight,' he said at last. 'You say Theresa Brown went off alone in Crane's car . . . '

'Not alone,' Inigo said. 'Snell was with her, poor devil. She was supposed to be giving him a lift, but I don't know . . . '

'Snell?' Ashley repeated. 'Are you sure?'

'Of course I'm sure. I saw them go, just after you got knocked out, but I was too late to stop them.'

'Was he still with her when the car went over?' Ashley glanced at Grabham, who nodded, and said, 'He was sitting right beside her. We saw him as she put it into reverse. He was one of the vanmen, Mr Brown said, but . . . '

'He was Crane,' Ashley said wearily, and turned to Sergeant Forbes. 'I don't know who you've got outside in your car, but you've certainly got the wrong man.'

'He's got Best,' Inigo supplied, leaping to his feet. 'This is awful! We made sure he was Crane . . . '

'But not sure enough.' Ashley smiled a little. 'Bob Snell was Crane, all right. He could lay that accent on with a trowel, when he felt like it. But normally he had a classy way of talking, and dressing, believe me. Morden, be a good chap and go out and release Mr Best before he starts a press campaign against the inefficiency of the police force. I was wondering what had happened to him.'

'Who is he?' Morden asked, rising. 'Anyone important?'

'Said he was a journalist, sir,' Sergeant Forbes submitted, preparing to follow. 'Sorry, sir, but his story sounded thin to me . . . '

'He is a journalist,' Ashley assured him. 'I know him by sight. But he's a good sort, and he'll forgive and forget, I daresay. You'd better send in your men to collect this one . . . ' With his foot he indicated Vauxhall. The sergeant nodded, and he and Grabham and Morden left together.

'I think we'd all better have a drink,' Inigo said. He went into the dining-room and returned with glasses and a further bottle of brandy, which he proceeded to distribute. Pouring an extra glass, he said, 'For Charlie. Something tells me he's going to need a lot of smoothing down.'

'For once your faith was justified,' Dylis said. 'I'm afraid that mistake was my fault, Mr Ashley. I started the rumour about Charlie.'

He met her troubled gaze with a smile. 'We all make mistakes,' he observed. 'But don't ever be tempted to join the police force, Miss Hughes. It's the devil of a life. My God!' He took a few steps from his place by the mantel, staggered a little, and clutched a hand to his head. 'I'd almost forgotten that man I picked up earlier . . . '

'Mr Brown's valet?' Dylis queried, as Inigo caught Ashley by the arm and aided him to the nearest chair. 'He's all right. I've been looking after him. I gave him some hot soup and he's sleeping.'

'Good girl.' Ashley rested his head between his hands. 'I guessed who he was, but I wasn't certain. I want to talk to him when we can both think clearly. I want to talk to you, too.'

They were interrupted by Morden, returning with Charlie Best, a very dishevelled Charlie, his eyes reproachful.

'A nice couple of friends you are,' he said, looking from Dylis to Inigo. 'Trying to get me pinched for murder.'

'Have a drink,' Inigo said hastily, pushing the glass into his hand.

'And a cigarette,' Dylis suggested, lighting one for him.

Charlie grinned, accepting both, and sat down opposite Mr Carpenter. 'Don't fret yourselves,' he said. 'I've never been known to rat on a pal, and I won't hold this story against you. But I'd like to hear the rest of it, out of professional interest.'

He glanced up curiously as the two constables entered. With complete indifference, they lifted the insensible Vauxhall and carried him out. He might have been a load of hay, so far as they were concerned.

'They're taking him and Ridley back to Cudge,' Morden said, coming in a few seconds later, and accepted, with murmured thanks, the drink that Inigo offered. 'I'm going on presently.' He glanced significantly at Mr Carpenter.

'Good idea.' Ashley lighted another cigarette and turned to Dylis. 'What has Ledgrove said to you, Miss Hughes, if anything?'

She told him briefly, also the gist of her own recent adventures adding, 'He didn't tell me about the van, though. And when he broke out of the barn he was too far gone to care what had been going on. But he said there was a lot of machinery in there.'

'I've no doubt there was,' Ashley said. 'But there isn't now. They loaded it on to the van which Jackson drove away, along with all their other stuff. We've been after them for some time in connection with this game, the printing and distribution of all kinds of junk that comes under the heading of illicit publications. They've had their headquarters at various places throughout the country, but up till now whenever we've tracked them down they've cleared everything and just got away in time. They'd lie low for a while and then start up again.

'It was after one of these lulls, I believe, that they took over this place and Warner Brown's other house in Cumberland. The vans, of course, were used for distribution to their depots up and down the country, although for delivery to the various

233

places which stock that kind of thing, they used something less conspicuous. We confiscated a lot of it from time to time, but it was very difficult to trace.

'Then we had a bit of luck when one of our men picked up one of theirs whom he knew by sight, and tailed him from the Great North Road as far as Yorkshire. That narrowed down the search, and it wasn't long before we'd got Crane taped, and we discovered that his lady friend, Theresa Cressidy, had married Warner Brown. We finally got it worked out so that Morden and his men were to raid the house in Cumberland, while I picked up Crane in London, and followed him to wherever he was going, which I was pretty sure would be here. We kept in touch by phone and we were to meet at Cudge three days ago, but I was held up and so was everyone else.

'It was impossible then for me to contact my colleagues by phone, to let them know how things were this end, so I just had to let them ride. I could have tried walking into Cudge and waiting for them there, but having got so far I thought I might just as well look this place over. I knew they'd come on here, anyway, although I wasn't at all sure when. But until I knew who was working with Crane and who wasn't, I didn't want anyone to leave this house.

'First thing I did, that night, after everyone was tucked up, or supposed to be, was to open up the garages. I'd got a key that fitted; those padlocks aren't very difficult. One garage was empty, but in the others was a car which I took to be Theresa's Brown's, or her husband's, and another which I knew to be Crane's. And in the back of his was a dark blue suit which had a sort of perfumed smell about it. I looked it over carefully, and found it was saturated in some kind of oil with a strong smell. I didn't think so much about it then. It might have been hair oil for all I knew.

So I finished the job I'd started, locked up the garages again, fixed the van and the other car parked outside, and came in.

'I went up and took a look at Mr Warner Brown, and found a bottle of your oil, Miss Hughes, that had been upset beside him on the table. And I hadn't much doubt but that it was the same oil as that on Crane's suit, if it was his suit, and that seemed pretty obvious. But to make sure, I took the bottle with me.

'I went down to the garage again to check up with the suit. It was only the slenderest bit of evidence, but it suggested that Crane had been up there in Mr Brown's room, and the bottle being turned over might have indicated a struggle. And I had an idea that Mrs Brown's story about Ledgrove's going for the doctor was so much eyewash. I thought it possible they had him hidden away somewhere. So keeping that suit in mind . . . '

'It was a dark blue one, you say?' Dylis cut in. 'I saw something of the kind lying in Mrs Brown's wardrobe. Do you think it might have been the same?'

'Quite likely. Crane may have used her room to change his clothes, and taken it down to the car afterwards, or got Vauxhall to do it. He certainly changed them somewhere, because he was all got up nicely as the vanman when I caught him up in the drive.'

'But he said then he'd stayed at a farmhouse or something, didn't he?' Best asked.

'All my eye. There's only one farmhouse within walking distance of this place, and I stayed there. So even if I hadn't known Crane by sight, I'd have known he was lying. What I think he did was to spend the rest of the night here, and slipped out in the morning in time to come up the drive. Who started that story about another vanman, anyway?'

'Mrs Brown,' Dylis said. 'I believe she just said the first thing that occurred to her to explain away the van.'

'Probably. I'd never met Crane, either as himself or Snell, but I'd seen plenty of photographs of him. I lost him several times on the way up here, and I thought I'd lost him again, when my car finally stuck. I wasn't sure just where this house was, and I didn't aim to freeze to death in the car all night. So I went over to the farm, and they were very decent about it, and directed me in the morning, I recognised the tyre marks of Crane's car in the drive, and then I saw him just ahead. Fortunately, he didn't know me, and he spilled his story first about staying at the farm. The only thing I could say then was that I'd slept in my car.'

There came stirrings and mutterings from the direction of the armchair, and Mr Carpenter rose, to stand swaying on the hearthrug, confronting them, blinking his eyes.

'Damned bad luck Crane got here at all,' he said. 'If he'd broken his blasted neck on the road there wouldn't have been any murder.' After which he slumped back into his chair and stared glassily into the fire.

'So you've finally come to life,' Ashley said. 'What was that supposed to be? An official statement?'

'Can't take a statement from a man in my condition,' Mr Carpenter said. 'Call yourself a split? You ought to know that.'

'It's a problem,' Ashley admitted, but he did not sound very worried about it. 'You're not often sober, are you?'

'Haven't been sober for five years.'

'As long as that? Well, we'll sober you up presently. So you're the printer of this establishment. I thought I recognised the work of Cock-eyed Carpenter, the man who got drunk once too often.'

'Damned silly. Can't get drunk too often. Can't get drunk *enough*, that's the trouble.'

'A pity,' Ashley said, and added, 'They tell me you were top of the trade until you took to drink.'

'You're wrong,' Carpenter contradicted. 'Anything I did before was mere tippling. I never did any serious drinking till I got in with this bunch of amateurs.'

'Have it your own way, but it's all over now. There won't be any drink where you're going.'

'I shan't last long enough to care, with all the things I've got wrong with me. I feel like hell.'

'When did you first know about the murder plot?' Ashley asked.

'This evening. They kept it dark between the four of them, until then. They never did get any change out of me, so I wasn't what you'd call popular. They couldn't do without me, and there I had 'em. But they never let me on the inside of anything. If they had've done, things wouldn't have turned out so bad. Take that first evening, when the van turned up according to plan. I was all for loading it up and sending it off, same as usual. But not she. Crane was coming up from London. He'd told her to hold everything until he got here, and what he said was law. He had some idea about changing the routes, she said, and she'd got to wait. I told her that was daft, with the weather getting worse all the time, but she wouldn't listen to me.

'Then up rolls the old man's nephew, and that puts the tin hat on it. She didn't tell me, then, just what a hole she was in, but she said I'd got to act like a friend of her husband's. I told her, straight, I was a printer, not a ruddy actor, and I just shut up and didn't say anything much. Then along came all these other misfits, and I packed up altogether and went to bed. Next day I heard that old Brown had died, but it didn't bother me.

'I knew they were in a jam about the van, because the weather had got too bad to drive it away, like I knew it would. But since she hadn't seen fit to take my advice, I didn't see myself helping to clear a lot of ruddy snow. The van was already loaded, Vauxhall and his pal Ridley used to see to that, and Crane reckoned if they could get the drive clear, Jackson could take a chance on getting it off before anyone was up this morning, and he'd follow in his car, and show him the route.

'That all went very nicely, but what they didn't reckon with was you mucking up all the cars last night while they were getting a nap. Crane blew up this morning when he found out. He wasn't sure if it was a practical joke, or something worse, but what he did decide to do was to get the machinery out of the barn, quick as he could, and load it on to the van, which wasn't full. He reckoned that it was too risky to leave anything about, and if he could get the van working again by the evening, he and Jackson would get away under cover of dark.

'But loading the machinery was a bit of a problem, with all these misfits about. So they worked on the van all day, and after dark he fixed it with his piece to start a screaming scene, so as to get everyone inside and keep them inside for a bit, except himself and Jackson, and Vauxhall and Ridley. It wasn't until afterwards that I got on to what happened. She started screaming all right, and with the things she'd got on her mind it must have been easy.'

'I thought that fit of hysteria was exaggerated,' Ashley said. 'She may have been startled when she glimpsed me sliding out of the room, but not nearly as startled as I was when she started to yell like that.'

'It was you she saw, was it? I thought it was just another bit of play-acting. I'll give her this much, when she did a thing, she did it well. She had you all mucking about in here, while the others were working outside. For once it looked as if things were going all right, until Crane came in, to let her know that Ledgrove had skipped.

'When you'd all shied off, and he and she were alone here, except for me, they got talking. They'd got plenty to talk about, and not much time. Our classy butler and his mate had gone out to get the car for her, and to take another look round for Ledgrove. Remember the way she said to them, *"And look out for anyone you may see around"*? That's what she meant. I only got that afterwards, when they let out that Ledgrove had been in the barn, but wasn't any more, and if they didn't find him he'd be a prize witness that old Brown hadn't died naturally.

'I got mad then, and told them what a pair of so-and-so's they were. But they were too far gone to care. All they were thinking about was saving their skins while there was anything left to save. Vauxhall and Ridley had got the machinery on to the van, while Crane was looking for Ledgrove. Then while their backs were turned, off went Jackson with the van. I daresay it was the first he'd heard about any murder, and he wasn't standing for it, any more than I was. Crane said they'd got to get after Jackson, before he did something crazy, but they'd only got one car working, his car, and that was supposed to be hers.

'She said she'd put it out she was going to Cudge for the doctor, and Crane could go along as if she was giving him a lift. I said that was daft, she'd plugged that doctor story too often, and what did she think the rest of us were going to do? She got all high and mighty then, said there was only one thing left to do, and that was for us all to skip as soon as we could. After they'd gone, she said Vauxhall and Ridley and me would have to get away in young Brown's car. It was up to us, she said, to use our wits.

'Well, I wasn't going to use my wits in any wild cat schemes. But I let 'em get on with it. I reckoned they'd slip up somewhere, and sure enough they did. Vauxhall's always been too handy at knocking out anyone in his way. Out goes Crane to have another look round for Ledgrove, just in case, and to tell the boys his plans, though I don't expect they liked the sound of 'em any more than I did. And she turns to me, and she says, "Mr Carpenter, you will *please* come with me and make a thorough search of the house to see if Ledgrove is hiding anywhere inside."

'"And what," I said, "do you think we're going to do, if he is? Another little murder?"

'"You'll see," she said, and what she expected to do I don't know, a pocket size like she was, but I knew what *I* was going to do if we came across him. I never liked him much, but I never liked murder, either. We didn't find him, but we did run into young Brown. I turned it in then. I thought they could damned well all get on with it, and I came in here for a drink. The next thing I knew was our butler and his pal carrying you in between them, and a nice mess they'd made of everything, all told. To crown it, Vauxhall brings out his pet gun and tries to make a grand exit, with me tagging along beside him like a stray dog. I'd see him in hell first.'

'You very likely will,' Ashley said, 'if you can pull yourself together sufficiently to attend a court of law.'

'I'll be glad to. I'll be glad to shop 'em.'

'Good.' Ashley rose, stretching himself. 'I think I'll take a look at Ledgrove.'

Morden also rose, and announced that so far as he was concerned, the day's work was over, apart from a few minor details.

'Why not stay the night?' Inigo suggested. 'We've plenty of space, as Mr Ashley will tell you.'

Morden smiled. 'Thanks just the same, but I've got to get back to Cudge.' And he added, to Mr Carpenter, 'You'd better get your things, because I shall require you to accompany me, and it's a long drive.'

240

'It'll be a pleasure,' the latter said. 'I've been wondering how much longer you windbags were going to be. And with all due respect to the new owner, whoever that might be, this house is like a blasted cemetery.'

Ashley said, 'I'll stay, if you don't mind, Mr Brown. I've got to get a statement from Ledgrove, and he may not be in any condition to give it yet. Sergeant Grabham had better remain here with me, when he gets back.'

Inigo looked worried. 'I'll have to go over to Cudge in the morning. There's still the matter of my uncle, and the garage. Miss Hughes has her car stuck on a precipice.'

'And Mr Howe's needs attention,' Charlie Best put in.

Morden said easily, 'I'll notify the garage that you want assistance. And we'll be over with the police surgeon tomorrow, Mr Brown. We've got a full day's work ahead of us. There'll have to be an inquest, of course.'

Inigo nodded, and was about to say something, when the door to the passage opened, and Mr Raddle stood in the aperture. He looked anxious and bewildered, as he said, 'Mr, Howe wishes to know the reason for the recent disturbances. He is not a man normally to complain, but . . . '

Ashley stopped him with a look. 'You can tell Mr Howe from me,' he said, 'that we've just been taking a little exercise in the fresh air.'

'Oh.' Mr Raddle gazed all round at their expressionless faces, and added, 'With Mrs Brown's permission, I should like to prepare supper for Mr Howe. He has not eaten for many hours.'

'Mrs Brown isn't available at the moment,' Ashley said quickly. 'But I'm sure Mr Brown won't mind if you carry on as usual.'

'You go ahead,' Inigo agreed, and when Mr Raddle had bowed

241

himself out, he added, 'It's not such a bad idea, either. Would the rest of you like something?'

'Not for me, thanks,' Morden said. 'But who is this Mr Howe?'

Ashley laughed. 'A gentleman who believes in taking all the pleasure out of life and leaving only the hardships. The joke is, he's lectured everyone on the benefits of fresh air and exercise, and now he's sick himself . . . ' He stopped short, but there was a twinkle in his eyes as Dylis seized upon the statement.

'Did you say sick, Mr Ashley?' she asked. 'Since when?'

'Er . . . last night, I believe. I went along to see him today, just to check up on his identity. He asked me not to say anything about it.'

'Oh, he did? Thank you, Mr Ashley. Inigo, Charlie, we're going to see Mr Howe right away.'

'We can't do that . . . ' Inigo began, but she cut him short. Morden said, as they were about to leave, 'Well, goodnight. I'll see you in the morning.'

They said goodnight, and Mr Carpenter rose suddenly, looking much more lively than usual, and even attempting a smile as he extended a cold hand to Dylis.

'May as well say cheerio,' he remarked. 'You're the only one who hasn't given me the gripe.'

Dylis, hardly knowing whether to be flattered, or sympathetic, or just to go off into hearty peals of hysterical laughter, shook hands and murmured something which she hoped was appropriate.

'Well, that beats all,' Charlie said, as they went out, and mounted the stairs, aided by a lamp which Dylis snatched up from the hall table. She did not bother to reply. Outside Mr Howe's room, she paused and knocked, and when the familiar voice answered, she pushed Inigo forward.

'You go in first,' she said. 'He might be drifting about in a state of nature. But I don't think so.'

She swung open the door, and reluctantly Inigo entered. He began, 'Excuse me, Mr Howe, but . . . '

'What is the meaning of this outrage?' Mr Howe burst out. 'First I hear voices raised in altercation, cars racing to and fro . . . '

'You can come in, Dyl,' Inigo said. 'Mr Howe is wearing a dressing-gown.'

'*The* dressing-gown,' she said, bouncing round the door, to discover Mr Howe seated in an easy chair before the fire, a small table at his side covered in sheets of manuscript paper. His dressing-gown was of some dark brown material, rather like sack-cloth. His face was a study of anger and dismay. He leaped to his feet when he saw her, then clutched a hand to his back and emitted a hollow groan.

'There! You see?' she continued in triumph. 'He's the man who made that horrible noise outside my room last night. You were coming along the corridor, Mr Howe, and you dropped your torch. When you bent down to pick it up, you were taken suddenly with lumbago, and let out a yell, just like someone being stabbed in the back. I came dashing out just in time to see you, all bent up, hobbling round the corner. That's the dressing-gown you were wearing, and this is the torch. Recognise it?' She brought it out of her coat pocket and waved it in front of him.

He attempted dignity, righteous indignation, nonchalance. It was no use. She swooped across to the mantelpiece, slammed down the torch and picked up a small, empty bottle. It was labelled, *Quickease . . . the three-day cure for lumbago*.

'This is one of the bottles that disappeared from my room,' she said. 'After all your magnificent lectures, Mr Howe, you couldn't admit that you were suffering from rheumatism. So although you didn't believe in cures, you sent your secretary along to get that stuff from my room, in case there might be something in it. And there is, or you wouldn't be able to stand up straight, even though it's still painful. But you'll be quite normal by the day after tomorrow, as no doubt you realise. I seem to remember that your secretary said you would be ready to leave by then.'

Mr Howe sat down. Charlie Best, grinning, went across to warm himself by the fire, and Inigo, now ranged firmly on Dylis's side, asked, 'Well, what have you got to say?'

'Nothing,' Mr Howe said. 'The facts, as presented by this impertinent young woman, are substantially correct. I may say, however, that an affliction of this nature has never before fallen to my lot, and I attribute it entirely to the unhealthy conditions prevailing in this house.'

'You can say what you like,' Charlie Best interrupted. 'But personally I think you ought to be ashamed. And I'm not sure that Miss Hughes couldn't prosecute you for libel, slander, plagiarism, infringement of copyright and unlawful entry.'

'Come, come,' Mr Howe said. 'This has gone far enough. I am perfectly willing to pay Miss Hughes for the use of her so-called cure.'

'I'm not asking you to pay for it,' Dylis said. 'I'd have given it to you if you'd had the courage to ask for it. There's only one price you're going to pay, Mr Howe, and that is, you've got to stop running down patent medicines, cures of any kind. You're writing a new book, aren't you? Well, you cut out any hints you may have put in regarding our products and those of any other firm in the business, and you can add a line or two to the effect that if, after all this fresh air and exercise, a person gets sick, then there's no harm in paying a visit to the local chemist. And in return we'll promise not to let this little episode get about. Won't we?'

Her supporters nodded, and their three pairs of eyes regarded

Mr Howe in a solid front. He moved uneasily, cleared his throat once or twice, and said at last, 'Very well. I agree to your . . . er . . . terms, Miss Hughes. And now will you be so kind as to remove your presence from this room? Mr Best, in the circumstances . . . '

'You can cut out the presidential address,' Charlie said. 'I've already decided not to visit your hideout. I've seen enough of the coming Ice Age to last me for some time. We're getting the garage people along in the morning, and they'll fix your car for you. But of course if you still prefer to walk through the snow there's plenty of it about. I'm going back to the lights of London, bless 'em. How about giving me a lift, Inigo?'

'Surely,' Inigo said. 'We'll collect Dylis's old truck, if it hasn't blown over, and all go back together as soon as we can. This girl drives one of the most miserable monsters I've ever seen . . . '

'I should be glad,' Mr Howe cut in, 'if you would conduct your mechanical discussion elsewhere. My sole wish is to take a light repast and retire to bed.'

For once, Dylis felt friendly towards him. She had seen in the eyes of Inigo and Charlie that light peculiar to men who are about to plunge into a debate on cars and their characteristics. With a perfunctory good night, she led them resolutely away.

In the corridor they encountered Mr Raddle, carrying a tray laden with a plate of cereal, three slices of dry toast and a jug of cold water. But in his free hand he held a large and succulent meat sandwich, the consumption of which appeared to be affording him immense satisfaction. He bowed to them in passing.

'So he's broken out at last,' Charlie observed. 'I thought he would. Poor old Howe, with revolution in the camp, and lumbago in the back.'

But his grin lacked its usual spontaneity, and in silence they went downstairs.

# Chapter XIX

'Maybe it's not such a bad old car,' Inigo said, when he and Dylis, in her much-despised vehicle, were on their way to spend Christmas with her people in Worcester. The cold spell still held, and although the roads in that part of the country were not so bad as those in Yorkshire, he had taken upon himself the responsibility of driving.

Transport still being extremely precarious, there had not been much in the way of an alternative. They had returned to London, after experiencing sundry minor mishaps on the way, to be greeted with stories of trains delayed and passengers having to make the best of a bad job, car owners having to help themselves and each other out of their difficulties, and London itself suffering from frozen pipes and their attendant discomfort. Inigo had returned to its obliging owner the car he had borrowed, but no other owners of cars seemed to be in an obliging mood. In any case, he would not have felt inclined to risk a borrowed or hired car upon the roads again, until such time as conditions improved.

Dylis's car was different. It was not the risk to that, but to their joint lives that he thought about, as it battled nobly along the snow-clad highway. He had tried chaining the back wheels, but its independent nature did not take kindly to chains, and the idea had to be abandoned.

'It's a rattling good car,' Dylis said, proud of its propensity for taking on all obstacles.

'You're right, there. Rattling is the operative word.'

'What other car would stand up to being left on the edge of a precipice out in the cold, and then being bounced about by garage people without any sensitivity or decent feeling?'

Inigo laughed. 'I think they had half a mind to push it over the edge and be blowed to it, if you hadn't been keeping a stern eye on them.'

He took a sharp bend in the road, and the car moaned to itself and slackened speed. Ahead of them was a long and gradual incline. They had climbed, without haste, for a couple of hundred yards when the car stopped, the sound of the engine died away on the evening air, and they began to slip backwards, slowly, and then with increasing speed.

'The brake!' Dylis screamed, as Inigo switched off the engine altogether. 'Why don't you use the brake?'

'I've got my foot jammed on it,' he shouted back, 'but it's not making any difference.'

He seized the handbrake, but it was of no avail. They careered wildly down the remainder of the hill, skidded on the slippery surface, shot across the road, and stopped halfway up a tree-lined bank. They sat and looked at each other in silence for a moment or two. Inigo passed a hand over his forehead. He said:

'I thought those people at Cudge were supposed to overhaul it?'

'So did I. They charged me enough. Compton and Webber nearly swooned in each other's arms when they saw the bill. What are we going to do now?'

'Get out and tie it together with string, I suppose.'

247

'We passed a house up the road. Perhaps we could get help there?'

'No more help,' Inigo said. 'I'll do this myself, if it kills me, and it probably will. You'd better sell this car, if you can get anyone to give you half-a-crown for it.'

'But what would I do for getting about the country?'

'I've got a remedy for that, too.' He rested his arms on the steering wheel and regarded her thoughtfully. 'I've written to my father, telling him roughly the details of the Wintry Wold affair. I'll have to stay over here until it's all settled, and the estate wound up. Then I shall be going home . . . '

'But what's all this to do with me?'

'I was coming to that. I suggest you tell Compton and Webber to start looking for a new partner.'

'But *why*?'

'Because Compton, Webber and Mrs Brown sounds damned silly to me,' Inigo said.

After which they forgot, for the time being, the precariousness of their position.